CAL

THE ORCS WERE crossing the river, coming in their direction. Fortunately, they had not yet spotted the group of men standing on the vantage above them.

Looking down through the cover of the trees, Dieter saw massed ranks of goblins hauling siege engines, orcs riding boars and chariots, goblin wolf riders; he even thought he caught a glimpse of a troll. He swallowed hard, finding his mouth was suddenly dry.

This was no mob of raiders or scouting party. It was an entire greenskin army, he suspected larger in size than anything the general had expected.

To make matters worse, the orcs were headed straight for the Hochlanders' camp.

A WARHAMMER NOVEL

CALL TO ARMS

MITCHEL SCANLON

For Jon Carr, mensch.

A BLACK LIBRARY PUBLICATION

First published in Great Britain in 2010 by
BL Publishing,
Games Workshop Ltd.,
Willow Road, Nottingham,
NG7 2WS, UK

10 9 8 7 6 5 4 3 2 1

Cover illustration by Clint Langley.

Map by Nuala Kinrade.

UK ISBN: 978 1 84416 812 5
US ISBN: 978 1 84416 813 2

See the Black Library on the Internet at
www.blacklibrary.com

Find out more about Games Workshop
and the world of Warhammer at
www.games-workshop.com

Printed and bound in the UK.

THIS IS A dark age, a bloody age, an age of daemons
and of sorcery. It is an age of battle and death, and of the
world's ending. Amidst all of the fire, flame and fury
it is a time, too, of mighty heroes, of bold deeds
and great courage.

AT THE HEART of the Old World sprawls the Empire, the
largest and most powerful of the human realms. Known
for its engineers, sorcerers, traders and soldiers, it is
a land of great mountains, mighty rivers, dark forests
and vast cities. And from his throne in Altdorf reigns
the Emperor Karl Franz, sacred descendant of the
founder of these lands, Sigmar, and wielder
of his magical warhammer.

BUT THESE ARE far from civilised times. Across the
length and breadth of the Old World, from the knightly
palaces of Bretonnia to ice-bound Kislev in the far north,
come rumblings of war. In the towering Worlds Edge
Mountains, the orc tribes are gathering for another assault.
Bandits and renegades harry the wild southern lands of
the Border Princes. There are rumours of rat-things, the
skaven, emerging from the sewers and swamps across the
land. And from the northern wildernesses there is the
ever-present threat of Chaos, of daemons and beastmen
corrupted by the foul powers of the Dark Gods.
As the time of battle draws ever nearer,
the Empire needs heroes
like never before.

In times of defeat, all men are cowards.
In victory, they are all heroes.

From *The Testimony of
General Ludwig von Grahl*
(unexpurgated text)

PROLOGUE
SEASONS OF WAR

It was a hot day.

Deep in the forests of northern Hochland, the sun's rays lanced through the gaps in the woodland canopy overhead. To the men of the scouting patrol, currently following a trail that skirted the province's ill-defined border with the Middle Mountains, it felt like they were riding through an oven. The air was stifling. Their helmets and armour increased their discomfort, the burden weighing heavily on their necks and shoulders.

Despite this, they were watchful. As Sergeant Johann Gessler halted his mount and reached down to take a drinking flask from his saddle bag, he was pleased to see his men had kept their discipline despite the heat.

He had sent two men ahead as a vanguard to scout the trail but it was important the main body of the patrol maintained a state of readiness, warily watching the forest around them for signs of ambush.

Counting the vanguard, and the sergeant himself, the patrol numbered ten soldiers in total. With such sparse numbers, it was vital that everyone stayed sharp. Their mission here was routine, but the proximity of the mountains meant they could not relax their guard for an instant. His troops were lightly armoured, and armed only with swords and shields. If they encountered any serious opposition, their job was to run and warn others – not to fight.

Gessler and his men were competent riders, but they were swordsmen by profession – infantrymen rather than horse soldiers. In the field, the armies of the Empire made use of pistoliers and outriders in the role of light cavalry. But such illustrious troops were in short supply, especially when it came to serving garrison duty at a dismal outpost in the hinterlands. It was not uncommon in such postings for foot soldiers such as Gessler and his men to be given horses and then find themselves deployed in a scouting role as mounted infantrymen. It was not an ideal solution, but his time as a soldier had taught Johann Gessler to be thankful for small mercies. Whatever other hardships might lie ahead, at least they wouldn't have to walk.

Even as Gessler removed the stopper from the flask and took a long drink, he was careful to keep one eye on the forest. The region had a dark reputation – one he knew was entirely deserved.

'You ask me, this is a fool's errand,' his second-in-command Kurt Walden said, pulling his own horse in beside the sergeant's. 'I don't care what those wood-cutters told Captain Ziegler. We won't find anything along this trail. It's the wrong time of year for beast-men.'

'There is a season for beastmen, then?' Gessler asked with gentle sarcasm. 'Like quail, you mean? Or wood pigeon?'

Smiling, he offered Walden the flask. Despite the banter, he valued the other man's company. Walden was ten years Gessler's senior. He was an old hand in the northern forests, while Gessler was a new arrival, posted from Hergig only two months ago. As an experienced campaigner himself, Gessler knew his life depended on the quality of the men around him. He and Walden had quickly become fast friends.

'You can laugh, but everything has its season,' Walden scowled in reply. 'Men, animals, beastmen – we all have our cycles. It's the way of things.'

Taking the flask, Walden drank deeply, before making a face as though he had been poisoned.

'Water. I had hoped for schnapps, brandy, even watered beer. Something to cut a man's thirst.'

'If you want a real drink, you'll have to wait until we get back to the fort,' Gessler chided him, half in jest. Twisting in his saddle, he gazed at the woods about them and the smile disappeared. 'Beastmen have been sighted in the area. That makes it a serious business, even if you don't believe the reports.'

'A wild goose chase, that's what it is,' Walden grimaced as he handed the flask back to the sergeant. 'I wasn't joking when I said it was the wrong time of year for beastmen. And I wasn't talking about us

13

hunting them like they were quail or pigeon. Usually it's the other way around – we are the prey and the beastmen are the ones doing the hunting. Like any hunter, they know there are seasons for the different kinds of game. There's a season for deer, and wild bull, and boar. And, if you're a beastman, there's a season for war; a season for hunting men.'

'And this isn't that season?' Gessler asked.

'It's the wrong part of the year,' Walden shook his head. 'You wouldn't know it from this damn heat, but the summer is nearly over. Beastmen don't live by the harvest like we do. They cluster around fixed points, like the forests here and the mountains, but they change their hunting grounds depending on the season. The same seasons determine when they go to war.'

Walden removed his helmet, revealing a set of features weathered to the appearance of old leather by years spent guarding the province's northern frontier. Pulling a cloth from inside his tunic, he used it to wipe away the beads of sweat glistening on his face.

'Granted, it can be difficult to second-guess them,' Walden said, adjusting the chin strap before he put the helmet back on. 'But usually, if beastmen go to war, it will be in early spring or late autumn. If it's spring, it's because the young gors are eager to prove themselves by killing enemies and taking trophies. It's worse, though, when they attack in the shank of autumn. If that happens it means there's a hard winter ahead and the weather has forced them to move down from the uplands into human territory.'

'You seem to know them well.'

'I should do. I've had twenty years fighting them in these damned forests. You learn some things in that time.'

It was a familiar theme. In the brief period they had served together, Gessler reckoned he had heard Walden expound at least a dozen times on his pet theories regarding Hochland's enemies. Already, he felt he could recite them by heart.

The ratmen were a myth, no doubt made up by the dwarfs to keep people away from their mines. Elves and Bretonnians might as well be a myth, since they were seen so infrequently in Hochland. Orcs were dangerous, but they lacked cunning. Beastmen only attacked at certain times. Goblins were cowards and they had no discipline – they were hardly worth bothering about.

According to Walden, the greatest threat to Hochland came from the neighbouring province of Ostland. 'Never let an Ostlander into your home,' he was fond of saying. 'He'll cut your sister's throat and have unnatural congress with your livestock. And that's only if he's in a *good* mood.'

It wasn't that Gessler completely rejected such notions. Certainly, Walden's opinions on the ratmen made sense, and they shared a common prejudice against Ostlanders. For the main part, however, he tended to regard most of Walden's claims as little more than country wisdoms; entertaining in their way perhaps, but likely to prove spurious if they were ever put to the test.

Still, he could see no reason to tell that to Walden. In the two months he had known him, Gessler had come to be impressed by the other's abilities as a soldier. The older man was a good second-in-command. He could be relied upon in a crisis. With that in mind, it did no harm to humour him.

'Well, I hope you're right,' Gessler said. 'If it turns out the sightings of beastmen hereabouts are just so much hot air, then I'll be happy.'

Putting the flask back in his saddle bag, he glanced up along the trail. While he and Walden had been talking, the rest of the patrol had gotten ahead of them.

'But, in the meantime, they have to be investigated. We'd better get moving before we lag any further behind and the others think we've decided to make camp. I'll tell you what, though, Kurt. If it turns out you're right and there are no beastmen out here, the drinks are on me when we finally get back to the fort.'

'You're on,' Walden told him.

They spurred their horses. Together, they rode down the trail.

THE CAUSE OF Gessler's downfall had been a woman, a beautiful girl with laughing eyes and hair like spun gold.

Her name was Sylvia. They had met on a cool spring evening. At first glance, seeing a young woman standing alone and unattended outside the barracks gates in Hergig, he had taken her for a streetwalker. Closer inspection of her clothes and manner had proved him wrong. She had the look of a girl of good family; not one of noble blood perhaps, but only a rank or two below it.

Playing the gallant soldier, he had introduced himself and offered to walk her home. She had taken him to a large house just off the Konradin Platz and asked him inside. There, one thing had led to another.

'A general's daughter?' his commanding officer had spluttered in outrage the next day. 'How could you?'

'I didn't know.'

'Didn't know? Every soldier in Hergig has heard of Sylvia von Bork! They scratch their privates whenever she passes.'

'I didn't think she could be the same girl. She was so beautiful. And it wasn't as though she told me her last name…'

'I bet she didn't. Well, whatever happens now, you've done it to yourself, Gessler. Bad enough the old man came home to find you storming his daughter's ramparts. The fact you decided to salute him without pulling your britches up first only added insult to injury. I wouldn't be surprised if he calls you out. Where will you be then? A sergeant, fighting a duel with a general…'

It had not come to that. When it was a matter of removing a stain against his daughter's honour, General Joachim von Bork was inclined to more subtle tactics. Within three days of the incident, Gessler had received orders that he was being transferred to a new regiment. Henceforth, his military career would be spent at an isolated fort on the northern frontier, guarding Hochland's border with the Middle Mountains.

Initially, he had been surprised at the relative mildness of the punishment. It seemed strange the general had not used his influence to have him stripped of his rank. The reason became clear once he arrived at the fort to take up his duties. As one of only two sergeants stationed at the garrison, Gessler found he was expected to lead scouting patrols into the forests on an almost daily basis.

The borderlands were a dangerous place. Chaos warriors, beastmen, greenskins – all of them made their home in the Middle Mountains. Already, in two months at the fort, Gessler had seen more action than he might have faced in an entire year in some less hazardous posting.

It was not difficult to see it was all part of von Bork's plan. The general had no need to get his hands dirty killing the man who had 'dishonoured' his daughter. Not when he could send him to the northern frontier and hope some obliging orc or beastman would do the job for him. The fact that Sylvia had already been willingly dishonoured on several past occasions was neither here nor there.

Possibly, the general did not believe the gossip about his daughter. If such was the case, Gessler supposed any father had a right to his illusions.

It seemed harsh, however, that he was expected to bear the burden of them at the potential cost of his life.

'SERGEANT! WE HAVE seen smoke!'

They travelled for another hour before they finally saw sign of the enemy. Duhr, one of the men from the vanguard, came riding back down the trail as though he had a daemon after him.

18

'Sergeant!' Duhr brought his horse to a halt in front of Gessler and saluted. 'Sergeant, we saw smoke. It was a little further down the trail. A big cloud of black smoke, rising above the treetops.'

'Which direction?' Walden asked, coming to join them.

'That way,' Duhr turned in the saddle and pointed east. 'Edelmann said he thought it might be coming from Kerndorf.'

'That's a village, about three leagues east of here,' Walden said, smoothly filling in the gaps in his new sergeant's knowledge. 'Maybe a dozen families live there.'

'This close to the mountains?' Gessler raised an eyebrow. 'It seems a perilous place to build a home.'

'They're here for the engelwurz,' Walden told him. Reading Gessler's look of confusion, he elaborated. 'It's a plant. The locals eat it like a vegetable, but its real value is as a medicinal herb. The variety that grows near the mountains is particularly potent. The doctors from Hergig pay a lot of money for the seeds and leaves.'

He shrugged.

'You're right, though. It's dangerous. But times are hard, so people risk it.'

'Is the village defended?' Gessler asked him.

'There'll be a palisade wall and a defensive ditch,' Walden answered. 'The villagers around here are not shy when it comes to protecting themselves. Most of the men will be experienced archers. Even the women and children will know how to use spears.'

'All right, then,' Gessler said. 'We'll head for Kerndorf and see if they need help.'

He turned to Duhr.

'Ride back to Edelmann and tell him we're on our way. If you see any enemies, you're to turn back and warn us. Otherwise, I want you to hold your position until the rest of the patrol gets there.'

'Understood, sergeant.'

Saluting once more, Duhr spurred his horse and raced back up the trail.

'What about the fort?' Walden said. The rest of the patrol had gathered around them, awaiting orders. 'Should we send a messenger back to warn them?'

'No, not yet,' Gessler shook his head. 'I want to know what's going on before we raise an alarm. For all we know, Kerndorf might have already fought off any raiders. We don't even know what caused the fire. It could have a less dramatic explanation. Maybe someone got careless. In weather like this, a thatched roof can be dry as tinder.'

He looked at the faces of the men. It was only natural he saw some nervousness, but there was nothing that suggested overt fear or panic. Again, Gessler found he was pleased. They were good soldiers. They would do their duty.

'We will travel in single file,' he told them. 'No matter what happens, you will not dismount unless ordered to do so. I want you to be ready to withdraw at all times. If we run into anything that's more than we can handle, we will pull back immediately. If Kerndorf is in trouble, we will help if we can. But our first duty is to the fort. We are scouts, not a war party. Is that understood?'

The men nodded their assent, almost as one.

'Good.'

Easing his horse further along the trail as the riders arranged themselves in single file, Gessler took up position at the head of the column. He raised his hand.

'Move out.'

BY THE TIME they reached Kerndorf, the worst of the fire had died down. The smell of smoke was thick in the air, along with the odour of burned flesh. Approaching cautiously on horseback, Gessler saw the gates of the palisade wall that surrounded the village hung open. They yawned on wooden hinges, a section of the thick timber bolt that had once held the gates shut lying shattered on the ground between them.

Nothing moved inside the village when he looked through the gates.

'Moeller! Schultz!' he ordered two of his men forward. 'Scout inside. If you run into trouble, I want you to raise the alarm and get out fast.'

'It looks like hell hit this place,' Walden said as the two scouts disappeared into the village. 'Maybe I was wrong about the beastmen.'

'We'll see,' Gessler replied. He cast a wary eye at the forest surrounding them and turned to another of his men, a broad-faced farmer's son with pock marked features.

'Schimmel, you're on lookout duty. When we enter the village, you're to stay here and stand guard. I especially want you to keep a watch on the forest. If anything starts moving out there, I'm to hear about it from you first. Understood?'

After a few minutes, Moeller rode back into view. Framed either side by the gates, he waved his shield, giving the sign that everything was clear.

Taking the lead, Gessler led the rest of the patrol into the village. Once past the walls of the palisade, it was as though they had entered a slaughterhouse. He felt his horse give a nervous shiver beneath him, disturbed by the smell of death.

Bodies, both human and animal, were strewn all about them. The people of Kerndorf had been killed alongside their livestock, murdered in the enemy's mad rampage. Gessler saw that chunks of flesh had been cut from some of the corpses, though whether for use as food or as trophies he could not be sure.

He felt his gorge rise. He had been a soldier for ten years and he had seen other massacres, but the carnage at Kerndorf ranked with the worst. Everywhere he looked he saw sundered bodies. Images impressed themselves on his mind in no particular order. Most of the huts were burned out, but a few were surprisingly intact. He saw a child's doll, made of straw. It was lying amid a pile of corpses. He couldn't see the owner, but somehow the presence of the doll made it all seem more real.

'Whoever they were, it didn't take them long to get past the gate,' Walden said, his eyes casting expertly about as he tried to read the course of the battle from the evidence of its aftermath. 'Otherwise, you'd expect to see more men killed at the palisade. As it is, it looks as though the enemy broke in and slaughtered the villagers as they made a last stand here, in the centre of the village. Poor bastards. They didn't have a chance.'

He turned to the sergeant.

'It looks like I was right after all. This wasn't done by beastmen.'

'How can you tell?'

'If beastmen had attacked this village, I would expect to see more damage,' Walden replied. 'They would have utterly laid waste to the place: smashing the huts, trampling crops, poisoning the well – destroying everything that had any smell of civilisation about it. The walls would be covered in beastmen symbols daubed in blood, while the whole place would stink of beast piss and dung.'

'I see,' Gessler nodded. He considered the matter. 'Who, then? Chaos warriors? Greenskins?'

'Greenskins would be my guess,' the other man answered. 'I haven't seen any tracks, and they seem to have taken the bodies of their dead with them, but the greenskins destroyed this village. I'm sure of it.'

'I don't think they were alone, Kurt,' Gessler said, gazing past him. He had noticed something while Walden was talking. 'Look at this.'

A corpse lay slumped in a sitting position against the wall of a nearby hut. Together, Gessler and Walden moved closer to inspect it. The body belonged to a well-muscled man in his early forties, from his clothes and leather apron perhaps the village blacksmith. It took no great understanding of medicine to see how he had died. On the lower right half of his body the flesh had been scoured from his bones as though it had been dissolved, leaving a foul-smelling puddle of liquid staining the earth around him.

There was a corroded lump of metal lying by the man's skeletal hand. Gessler could not be sure, but he suspected it was all that was left of the blacksmith's hammer.

'Merciful gods, the stench!' Pulling a cloth from his tunic, Walden clapped it over his mouth. 'It smells like sour milk and rotting fish, but a thousand times worse. What do you think happened to him?'

'I don't know. Some kind of acid, maybe? Here, there's something else.'

Gesturing to the ground, Gessler pointed to the outline of a footprint by the body. Elsewhere, the ground had been baked too hard by the sun to show any tracks, but the puddle by the blacksmith's body had softened the earth enough for the killer to have left an imprint by his victim.

The footprint was three or four times the size of a man's. The foot that made it had been unshod. It was shaped unusually, with a broad flat span at the ball of the foot, narrowing to a sharp, almost talon-like heel. Whatever it was, the creature possessed four claws in place of toes.

'Sigmar protect us,' Walden said quietly, crossing his hand from shoulder to shoulder as he made the sign of the hammer. 'It is the mark of a daemon.'

'I don't think so.' Gessler shook his head. 'I've never seen one before, but I think it could be the footprint of a–'

His words were cut off by the sound of a shouted alarm coming from outside the village. Recognising the voice of Schimmel, the lookout, Gessler turned and spurred his horse toward the palisade gates. Walden and the rest of the patrol were right behind him.

Shouting an incoherent warning, Schimmel came riding toward them. Suddenly, dozens of unseen archers unleashed a volley of arrows from the trees. Most of them missed their mark, but enough struck home that Schimmel and his mount were transformed into pin cushions. The horse screamed, tumbling its rider to the earth as it collapsed and died.

'Schimmel!'

Moved by a vague notion of rescuing the wounded man, Gessler galloped through the gate. It was too late. As he drew nearer, he saw that Schimmel was dead. One of the arrows had hit under the browline of his helmet, the shaft sprouting from the ruin of Schimmel's eye like the stalk of some pitiless fruit.

'It's no good, sergeant!' Walden had kept pace with him all the way. 'You can't save him! Quickly, we have to retreat! Sweet Sigmar! Look! They're in the trees! They're coming!'

Alerted by Walden's warning, Gessler spotted dozens of stunted figures emerge from the forest on either side of them. He saw a succession of inhuman faces as they poured from the forest in ever greater numbers.

Goblins!

Sizing up the situation, he realised he and his men were already surrounded. They were outnumbered. Ready for the kill, the goblins charged forward.

'Patrol, form a line!' Gessler shouted at the top of his voice, straining to be heard above the strange whoops and cries of the approaching enemy. 'Form up on me! Get into position!'

Manoeuvring his horse to face the charging mass of goblins, Gessler drew his sword as his men urged their horses forward to take up position on either side of him. The goblins were close now, close enough that he could see their red eyes, close enough he could almost feel their eagerness. Granted courage by numbers, they were sure of their victory, certain there was no way Gessler and the patrol could escape.

Weighing his options, Gessler had immediately realised the patrol had only two choices. One, they could retreat to the village, taking cover behind a palisade wall which had already proven incapable of keeping out the enemy.

Preferring to risk danger against certain death, Gessler decided on the *second* option.

'Patrol!' He shouted, pointing his sword in the direction of the onrushing horde. 'For Hochland! For your lives! Charge!'

They were infantrymen on horseback, rather than true cavalrymen, but at that moment the distinction seemed irrelevant. Taking steel from their sergeant's example, the patrol charged forward. Crossing the short distance before the goblin archers had time to loose another volley of arrows, they ploughed into the enemy ranks.

Caught by surprise, the greenskin attack faltered as the goblins at the front turned and tried to get out of the way of the onrushing horsemen.

Gessler felt a shock run up his arm as he brought his sword down on the head of a goblin. He struck out again, and again, his sword rising and falling in a bloody arc of destruction as he cut a swathe through the enemy.

He heard goblins screaming, squealing, and shrieking as they were cut down by flashing blades or trampled beneath iron-rimmed hooves. In the madness of melee it was almost impossible to judge the rest of the patrol's progress, but he caught glimpses of Walden and Duhr either side of him, following his lead as they carved their way relentlessly through the enemy ranks.

The sergeant and his men were still outnumbered ten to one, but the change in their fortunes was readily apparent. The goblins had attacked expecting an easy kill, but the patrol's charge and the casualties they had taken had given them second thoughts. Even as Gessler slashed his way deeper into the enemy's massed ranks, it was clear they were on the brink of collapse. The goblins' confidence was visibly draining away, leaving them on the verge of panic.

It was what Gessler had hoped for. The goblins might not fully rout; they might only retreat a little way before their leaders could rally them, but for Gessler's purposes it made no difference. All he needed was for the enemy to falter long enough for him and his men to get away.

A shiver passed through the goblin ranks. Striking his sword down with even greater ferocity into the enemy morass, Gessler redoubled his efforts. The moment he had tried to create was close now. The goblins were wavering. Another second and they would break and run.

Abruptly, he heard a terrifying roar and his plans were left in tatters.

Bellowing in bestial fury, an enormous shape came lumbering from the forest. It took a moment for Gessler to see it clearly, but as the creature emerged from the shadows he realised his earlier guess as to the identity of the blacksmith's killer had been right.

It was a troll. Gessler had never seen one before, but there was no mistaking it. The monster easily stood more than twice as tall as a man. It was bluish grey in colour, covered in thick warty lumps that gave its skin a rocky texture almost as though the creature was made of stone. It carried a roughly-hewn wooden club, but one glance at its claws and fangs suggested it had no real need of the weapon.

He heard a cheer from among the goblins. They seemed to draw strength from the troll's appearance, redoubling their efforts. Hearing a human scream, Gessler turned to see Duhr being dragged from his horse, too far away to be helped.

He heard other, more guttural cries as hundreds of orcs began to emerge from the forest to support the goblins.

In an instant, the complexion of the battle was changed entirely. The orcs were made of sterner stuff than their lesser brethren; it would take more than the best efforts of a few men on horseback to put them to flight. With their arrival, any hope of causing a panic in the enemy ranks was lost.

Meanwhile, the Hochlanders' own charge had lost its momentum. Pushed forward by the orcs behind them, the goblins were pressing in more fiercely, making the weight of numbers tell.

Hemmed in, it was only a matter of time before Gessler and his remaining men were killed. Worse, the swelling enemy ranks cast the greenskin presence in a different light. There were too many of them for this to be a raiding party. Horrified, Gessler realised it was more than likely he was looking at the beginnings of a full-scale invasion.

Spurring his horse, he committed himself to a last, desperate gamble. Fighting his way through the goblins standing in his path, he yelled a battle cry and charged his horse toward the troll.

The monster seemed to recognise his challenge. It turned to face him, mouth widening in a hungry smile.

Gessler knew it was suicide. If he had been armed with a lance, he might have stood a chance of impaling the creature, spitting it like a piece of meat before it could reach him. As it was, he had a sword. He was as good as dead, but the concerns of the moment banished thoughts of fear. If he could distract the troll long enough, he might buy enough time for one of his men to get away and warn the fort of the enemy presence.

Reacting before the man could get close enough to strike it, the troll lashed out with its club. Gessler felt a searing pain in his thigh. He was thrown from his saddle, the world spinning crazily for a second before he landed jarringly on the hard sun-baked ground.

Dazed, he tried to stand, only to find he seemed strangely unable to support himself. Looking down, Gessler saw his left leg had been reduced to a pulped mess by the troll's blow.

He heard his horse whinnying in terror. Glancing behind him, he saw the poor animal lying on its side. Its back was broken, the splintered bones of the spine sticking out from underneath the saddle. He was moved to try to help it, to end its suffering, but it was a forlorn thought. Unable to walk, he could hardly help himself, never mind administer a mercy stroke to the dying animal.

A shadow fell across him. Looking up, Gessler found he was face-to-face with the troll. The monster was standing over him. Grinning, it leaned forward to inspect its prize, saliva drooling from its mouth and leaving discoloured patches in the grass as it dripped to the ground.

Time seemed to slow. As he faced the last moments until his death, Gessler found the world grew distant. He could hear the sounds of battle, the roar of orcs and the screams of men, but they felt far away, drowned out by the noise of the troll's breathing.

Gessler's final thoughts were of a beautiful girl with laughing eyes and hair like spun gold. He did not blame her for his misfortunes. He had known her only a few hours, but he supposed he loved her. In another world, perhaps they could have been happy.

The troll opened its mouth. The last thing Gessler saw was its teeth. Then, darkness swallowed him.

PART ONE
RED HARVEST

(Geheimnistag – Nachgeheim – Early Erntezeit)

From
The Testimony of General Ludwig von Grahl
(unexpurgated text):

It began in late summer. As the month of Vorgeheim drew to a close, a vast army of orcs and goblins emerged from the Middle Mountains. Sweeping past the network of forts and watchposts that guarded the frontier, the greenskins pushed deep into northern Hochland.

At their head was a new leader. Through a mixture of brutality and cunning, an orc chieftain called Morgoth Ironfang had managed to combine the fractious orc and goblin tribes of the Middle Mountains into an effective army. In time, it would become clear Ironfang was a far more able opponent than most of his human adversaries were inclined to credit, but for the moment that revelation still lay in the future.

In the meantime, Ironfang's forces cut a destructive swathe through northern Hochland, destroying every settlement in their path.

In Hergig, the first news of the invasion reached the Elector Count's court on the night of Geheimnistag, the so-called 'Day of Mystery' – one of the most ominous dates in the Imperial calendar. None dared say it aloud, but many at court wondered whether it was a sinister omen.

Whatever the case, Count Aldebrand Ludenhof of Hochland was not a man to be swayed by omens. Ordering that an army should be immediately dispatched to repel the invasion, Count Aldebrand made known his wish that the orc chieftain's head be delivered to him so he could mount it on a pikestaff.

Of course, it takes time to raise an army – regiments need to be mustered, supplies have to be organised, and so on. Accordingly, several weeks passed before the Count's army took to the field, allowing the greenskins time to push even deeper into Hochland. Soon, the roads from the north were crammed with refugees, while the sky was black with the smoke from burning villages.

As for my own situation, at this moment of darkest crisis for my homeland, I found myself stalking the corridors of my summer house on the Talabec, condemned to the premature retirement that had been forced on me by my enemies at the Elector's court. I have never been a political animal; too much the old soldier to speak gladly to fools or play the dirty business of politics. Perhaps I was foolish in this. Certainly, at that moment, finding I was forced to endure long days of enforced inactivity while the land I loved was in peril, I had reason to regret some of my past actions. But wishes are the same as the dedications on tombstones: heartfelt they may be, but they can do little to change what has already been done.

Naturally, I did my best to reverse my exile. From the instant I heard of the orc invasion, I fired off letters sent by messenger to the Count and his staff, offering my service in whatever capacity was deemed necessary. The response was always the same. My pleas were returned with felicitations as to the state of my health, alongside assurances my services were no longer needed.

I should enjoy my leisure, the messages said. Let other men take up the strain of battle; I had earned my retirement through years of hard campaigning. It was time to let younger men put their shoulders to the stone.

I recognised the sardonic handiwork of some of my rivals in these messages, in the way they said one thing while they meant another.

Don't bother us, von Grahl, was the real message hidden between the lines. Your time is over, old man. Good riddance, we no longer need you.

And so, while war raged through northern Hochland, while her people were slaughtered, I found there was nothing I could do.

Of course, I followed the progress of the war as well as I could. Old habits die hard. In my study there was a full set of maps of Hochland and the surrounding provinces, left over from my campaigning days. As news, rumours and reports came from the front, I made marks and notations on my maps, trying to keep some sense of how the war was going.

I was helped in this regard by the fact I still main-tained some friends at court. There were a few old warhorses like myself, still in positions of command, who had not as yet been put out to pasture. By drawing on these friendships, I was even able to wheedle out the occasional piece of privileged information. I might be unable to have any effect on the campaign, but I was better informed than most.

Not that it helped my mood, not any of it. In particular, I found myself concerned when I heard Count Aldebrand had decided to appoint General Erich von Nieder to command the campaign against the greenskins.

I knew von Nieder of old. The two of us had clashed many times over the years on matters of tactics, strategy, protocol, even coming close to fighting a duel once, many years ago. I had always regarded the man with disdain. To my mind, he was cast from the same mould as many of the unctuous toadies who spent their lives trying to gain influence at the Elector's court. I viewed him as an arrogant blowhard who had risen to his office on the back of political manoeuvrings rather than through any real skill as a general.

Unfortunately, no one was interested in my opinions on such matters. Forced to follow the progress of the war from afar, I could only hope von Nieder proved me wrong. With the future of Hochland at stake, I had to trust von Nieder's abilities and hope he could deal with the crisis.

Otherwise, I feared the worst…

CHAPTER ONE
DANGERS OF THE ROAD

'MAKE YOURSELF COMFORTABLE,' the cart driver had told him once the money changed hands. 'We've a long journey northwards and you might as well make the best of it.'

Three weeks later, as the cart jolted through the latest in a long series of potholes, Dieter Lanz remembered the words with a certain ill-humour. Within a few hours of the journey beginning, Dieter had learned an important lesson of travel: there is no comfortable place in the back of a goods cart. Much less in one piled high with supplies being transported to provision the army currently at camp in the northern forests.

Granted, like the other carts in the caravan, there was a canvas covering over the back that shaded it from the elements, but it hardly outweighed its remaining defects. The roads the caravan had been following for the last three weeks were little more than a series of trails winding a roundabout path through the northern reaches of the Great Forest. The trails were not made for ease of travel, but weeks of heavy traffic had transformed them into a rutted, wheel-scarred obstacle course.

The cart hit another pothole, forcing Dieter to catch a heavy salted ham to stop it falling on him. Placing the ham carefully to one side, he cast an exasperated glance at the uniformed soldier lying in the back of the wagon with him. Seemingly oblivious to the hardships of their journey, Holst was asleep, snoring loudly as he pillowed his head against a crate.

'Sigmar's beard, but your friend can sleep,' the cart driver Otto called down to him from the front of the wagon. 'I've never seen the like. We've been on the road three weeks, and I swear he's been snoring for most of it.'

Dieter had no doubt of that. Having shared the back of the cart with Holst ever since Hergig, he had become unhappily accustomed to the other man's habits. Asleep, Holst provided a one-man symphony of noises: snores, groans, snorts, mutterings in his sleep, not to mention regular flatulent cannon bursts. So far, Holst had spent all but a few hours of each day sleeping, emerging from his bear-like state of hibernation only when food was in the offing.

'Still, it's a useful talent to have in the army,' Otto continued, ignoring the trail ahead as he craned his neck around to look in the back of the wagon. 'You spend a lot of time on the road. Better to sleep through it than be bored, I suppose.'

Sensing the driver was in a mood for conversation, and having had enough of Holst's snoring to last him a lifetime, Dieter climbed over the partition separating the back of the cart from the front and sat down next to Otto. The driver may have made him pay twelve shillings for the dubious luxury of riding in the back of the cart rather than walking, but Dieter held no particular grudge. The man was good company, and without his camaraderie Dieter would have been condemned to spend the journey listening to Holst snore, wheeze and fart his way toward their destination.

'Of course, it's better to sleep than to fight,' Otto said, turning his eyes back to the road now Dieter was by the side of him. 'No offence, my young friend, but I think you're mad. Imagine wanting to be a soldier. Never mind being so set on it you're willing to travel from Hergig into these damned forests, chasing some pretty boy regiment of sword-wavers in the hope they'll recruit you. Mad, that's what it is.'

'But you're making the same journey,' Dieter protested in good humour. In the last three weeks, he and Otto had argued the point several times. 'If I'm mad, what does that make you?'

'Ah, but I'm in it for profit,' Otto said. Feeling in the back of the wagon, he brought up a half-empty bottle of wine and pulled out the stopper. 'It makes all the difference. You can keep all your talk of glory, honour and the rest of that arse-water. I'm a greedy man and I don't mind who knows it. There's only one thing that would bring me this far north along these Sigmar-forsaken trails. Silver.'

Gesturing with the bottle, Otto pointed to the long line of carts ahead of them.

'It's the same with all these others. Some are professional victuallers, like me. Others are first-time men. Amateurs. The war brings 'em out. It gets so anyone with a cart thinks they only have to fill it with provisions and take it north to be rolling in coin like a pig in fresh manure.'

'I wouldn't have thought there'd be that much money in supplying soldiers,' Dieter said to him.

'No? Well, you'd be wrong there. The army quartermasters will pay a fine penny for every scrap of food they can get their hands on. Never mind what the troops themselves will pay for drink, black snuff, and any other luxuries a man can manage to transport north.'

Otto took a long draught from the wine bottle, before continuing.

'You see, this is the best time to be victualling – early in the campaign, when the supply lines are still not properly sorted. I hear the Count called up twenty thousand men. That's a lot of hungry mouths. And the generals and quartermasters know if they don't see to feeding 'em, the men will desert. There's lots of armies end their days that way. Not killed by the enemy, or even by disease. They just melt away through lack of supplies.'

'But, if that's true, there's more at stake here than just money,' Dieter said, appalled. 'The rumours say there's a horde of orcs ready to come sweeping down through Hochland from the mountains. Surely it's your duty to help the army, not try to make a profit from them?'

'Duty?' Otto spat out a mouthful of phlegm, tinged pink from wine. 'That's another one of those arse-water words like glory and honour. I have a wife and family. Duty won't put bread on their table, nor replace me if I get killed by the orcs in the woods. Silver, Dieter. And gold. They're the only things with real value in life. Everything else is pig shit.'

'But what about Hochland? If the rumours are true, the entire province could be in danger.'

'Pfah.' Snorting in contempt, Otto took another pull from the bottle. 'You're young, my friend – that's the problem. When you get older, you'll realise these things are not uncommon occurrences. The orcs are *always* invading. Or, if it is not them, it's the Ostlanders, or the undead, or the followers of the Ruinous Powers.'

Still gripping the bottle tightly in his hand, Otto made the sign of the hammer.

'Someone is always trying to kill us here in the Empire. We are surrounded by enemies. War is the natural order of things. After a while you realise it's better not to think of it. If you dwell on these things too much, you'd never get a good night's sleep. Not like your friend there. Now there's a man who knows how to avoid his cares.'

Jerking a thumb behind him Otto indicated Holst, still asleep in the back of the cart. A sack of flour perched on a stack of crates beside him had developed a small tear at the corner, dribbling white dust into Holst's face. Even that was not enough to wake him. Sniffing in unconscious irritation, Holst blew out from under his lips and turned on his side.

Not for the first time since they had met, Dieter found himself staring at Holst intently. The soldier was a large man, with a bearish build and a broad tanned face distinguished by an impressively bushy moustache. When he wasn't snoring like a sleeping milch cow, Dieter had found him to be a boisterous, personable fellow, much given to loud opinions and expansive gestures.

They had met in Hergig, at the barracks of the 3rd Hochland Swordsmen. The 3rd was a famous regiment. Nicknamed the 'Grey-and-Scarlets', or simply 'the Scarlets' for short, the men of the 3rd wore a distinctive uniform that set them apart from the other Hochland regiments.

Holst was wearing the uniform now: a grey doublet, scarlet undershirt, hose that were grey on one leg and red on the other. There were slashes in the fabric of the doublet, running along both arms and down either side of the torso, which allowed the colours of the undershirt to peek through, creating an effect eerily reminiscent of bloody wounds as though the wearer had suffered injury in battle. As well as the uniform, Holst wore a steel breastplate and an open helmet topped with a feather dyed red and green, the state colours of Hochland.

Taken together, the effect should have been impressive. Certainly, it set Holst apart from the other soldiers they had met on the road, most of whose uniforms followed drab variations on the more typical Hochland colour scheme of red and green.

Holst had told Dieter his story soon after the pair had met. He was a member of the Scarlets, but he had been wounded in a tavern skirmish some weeks back with the soldiers of a rival regiment. Although his injuries were now healed, they had caused him to arrive too late to join the muster when the regiment had been sent north. Since Holst was eager to rejoin his comrades, he and Dieter had agreed to travel north together. It had been Holst's idea to bribe one of the victuallers to take them in his wagon, rather than walking. Although, in a development that Dieter now recognised as part of a pattern, Holst had persuaded him to pay the entire bribe himself, citing his recent 'medical expenses' as the reason for his lack of coin.

Dieter had dreamed of joining the Scarlets almost since he was a child, but he was finding it hard to marry his inner ideal of the regiment with the representative example currently taking up valuable space in the back of the wagon. Holst was not what he had expected. Dieter supposed he had come to regard the Scarlets as heroes. There seemed little that could be called heroic, however, in a sleeping, farting oaf with a face covered in flour.

'Soldiering is not all it's cracked up to be,' Otto said, as though divining Dieter's thoughts. 'Nor are soldiers, for that matter. Don't get me wrong. It's a useful skill, knowing how to kill. Valuable, even. But, then, that's the problem with soldiers. They sell their skills for a few pennies, when any sensible man would realise there's better ways to make money from your sword arm.'

The forest was surprisingly quiet. Dieter had grown up in the country, in an old mill on the outskirts of a small village. He was accustomed to the sounds of the wilderness: the call of birds, wild animal cries, and the howl of wolves. This far into the woods, he would have expected more noise, a forest cacophony. Thinking about it, he realised the creatures of the deep woods were unused to the presence of human beings, much less a caravan of rattling, noisy carts.

For all that, the forest seemed quieter than was normal. Abruptly, Dieter realised the woods were all but silent. There were no sounds from among the trees, not even the distant murmur of birds. It was unsettling. He could only hear the noises of the caravan and the gentle whisper of the wind through the leaves of the trees.

'You understand what I'm getting at?' Otto said, offering him the wine bottle. 'I've seen you practising your fencing with the caravan guards. You're good, Dieter. Too good to be wasting your talents on soldiering. You'd make a damn sight more money by joining my operation. Victualling's a hard trade; there's always some bastard looking to steal your gold or pilfer goods from the cart. Then there's the dangers of the road to contend with: bandits, highwaymen, deserters, beastmen and the like. A man can be a lot surer of his profits if he's got someone with a good sword arm standing beside him. I can pay you a shilling a day and cut you in for one tenth of the profits, minus expenses of course. Added to which, naturally, I'll teach you the trade. Well? What do you say?'

They were his last words. Suddenly, a massive spear flew from the forest and embedded itself in Otto's chest, pinning him to the cart like a butterfly stuck to its mount. The wine bottle fell from Otto's dead hand and smashed to the ground.

Unsheathing the sword at his side, Dieter turned as a chorus of bestial roars came from either side of the trail. He saw horned, goat-legged creatures appear from among the trees to attack the line of carts. Recognising them as beastmen, he grabbed his shield from the back of the wagon, casting an eye at Holst under the canvas. The swordsman had begun to stir, his slumber rudely interrupted by the tumult of screams and shouts as the caravan came under attack. The air was suddenly filled with the sounds of battle: the yells and alarms of the guards, beastmen battle-cries and the shrieks of panicking animals.

'Holst!' Dieter yelled at the sleeping soldier. 'Get up, dammit! We're being attacked!'

He kicked a small cask toward the man, hoping the impact would rouse him. Unperturbed, Holst grumbled in his sleep and turned over onto his side.

Glancing back outside, Dieter saw dark figures moving toward their cart. The time when he could afford to waste precious seconds trying to wake Holst was past. Jumping down from the cart, Dieter hefted his shield and made ready to meet the beastmen's attack.

There were three of them. Each one stood at a little less than Dieter's height. They were armed with spears. In place of horns, their heads were crowned with stubby nubs, like the seed-horns of an imma- ture stag. Dieter recognised them as the lesser breed of beastmen, reportedly less dangerous than their bigger, horned brethren. Still, lesser breed or not, they had him outnumbered.

The first one charged him, a little ahead of the others. Dieter met its spear-thrust with his shield, deflecting the blow downward and to the left as he had been taught. At the same time, he slashed out with his sword, catching the creature at the side of the temple with a blow that split its head open. With a scream, the beastman fell.

The other two were more cautious. Instead of charging him headlong, they kept their distance. Making use of the superior reach of their spears over his sword, they jabbed at Dieter, one trying to hold his attention while its brother-beast tried to get behind him.

Wise to the trick, Dieter took the offensive. Charging the nearest beastman, he met its spear jab with his shield and pushed into it, forcing the creature to stumble backwards as it tried to prevent the spear being jarred out of its grip. The beastman slipped. Taking advantage of his enemy's momentary confusion, Dieter stabbed low with his sword, catching the beast in the side as it fell.

In the meantime, the third beastman had charged towards him. Whirling away from its fallen brother, Dieter parried a spear thrust with his sword, relying on his attacker's momentum to bring them into close quarters. For a moment, as the beastman struggled to unlock the haft of its spear from the crossguard of Dieter's sword, they were face to face.

Up close, the monster was repugnant. It leered at him in bloodlust, eyes staring at him in hatred. There was a sickening smell about it: the musk of a herd animal mixed with the charnel stench of blood. With his free hand Dieter smashed his shield into its face. Snout bloodied, the beastman lost its grip on its spear, allowing Dieter to hook his blade underneath and stab upwards, burying a good length of Empire-forged steel into the thing's heart.

He had no time to celebrate his victory. Whichever way he looked, Dieter saw men and beastmen locked in life-or-death confrontation as the caravan guards and drivers did their best to hold their own against the beastmen raiders. Ahead, he could see some of the carts had been dragged to the edge of the trail and overturned onto their sides – though he could not be sure whether these were the work of the caravan's defenders or accidents caused by draught animals that had panicked at the beastmen's attack. Similarly, from Dieter's vantage, it was impossible to tell which side was winning. It was clear the outcome of the battle could still swing either way.

Intending to add his own efforts to the caravan's defence, Dieter looked about him in search of any defender nearby who might need his help. Before he could make his decision, however, he heard a deafening, bleating roar behind him. It held a definite note of challenge.

Turning, he saw an enormous beastman moving toward him. It was a gor, the larger of the beastman breeds. This one stood nearly one-and-a-half times as tall as Dieter, not counting its horns which spread wide from its head and curled back on themselves like the horns of a goat.

In the eighteen years of his life to date, Dieter had experienced the misfortune of meeting with beast-men on several occasions. Given the size of the creature currently bearing down on him, he judged it must be a leader among its kind – not a chieftain perhaps, but certainly some form of champion or favoured warrior. It reminded him of the bloodthirsty beast spoken of in the tale of Tomas Wanderer, the 'gallanting Knacht' whose death was commemorated in a nursery rhyme told to the Empire's children.

The monster was covered in scars, some evidently gained in battle, others self-inflicted and shaped in the manner of sigils, as though the beast had carved and branded some prayer to its heathen gods into its living flesh. Dozens of trophies dangled on leather cords from its body: teeth, claws, fingers, bones, even severed heads, taken from a variety of prey, including humans.

The beastman roared again. It lowered its axe and shield, leaving its chest unguarded as though daring Dieter to strike it. Dieter could not be sure, but he thought the beast was smiling.

'Gharrr-Kar,' the creature rasped, its voice sounding frighteningly human for something so clearly not. 'Gharrr-Kar! Kharnn Gor!'

Dieter could not be sure whether it was the creature's name, a challenge ritual, or even some form of beastman oath. He was not entirely certain whether the noises the monster was making were even words.

'Gharrr-Kar… Gharrr-Kar! Kharnn Gor!'

Raising its axe, the monster stormed towards him with surprising swiftness. Dieter barely had time to prepare his shield before the blow was struck. He did not meet it directly, instead slanting the shield sideways at an angle to deflect the blow and channel its force away from him. Even so, his shield was split in two. Dieter felt the axe blade whisper past his skin as it cut through the arm straps and dragged the broken pieces of the shield away. An inch or two closer and it would have cut through the flesh of his arm like a butcher's cleaver.

The beastman attacked once more, swinging its axe on the backstroke as it came at him remorselessly. Dieter jumped backward just in time to avoid the blow. Dodging to one side as the creature swung the axe again, he tried to stop himself being pushed back against the cart.

It was hopeless. The monster was relentless. It was all Dieter could do to stay clear of the blade – the axe strokes came too quickly to allow him to escape. He had managed to steer away from the cart itself, but instead his retreat had pushed him toward the dray team hitched in front of it.

From the corner of his eye he could see the horses fidgeting, frightened by the violence going on around them. So far, only the narrowness of the trail and the fact there was another cart parked directly in front of them had stopped them from bolting. If the beastman forced him back any closer to them, the animals would panic. Squeezed between them and the advancing beastman, it was a question of whether Dieter would have his head whipped from his shoulders by an axe or have his skull split by a kicking hoof. As matters stood, he had precious few other choices.

'Holst!' Dieter called out, hoping to at last rouse the sleeping man in the cart. 'Help me! I need you, dammit!'

His words brought no response. Risking a quick glance to see if there was anyone else nearby who might help him, Dieter was disappointed to find there was no one close enough for him to call to. All along the trail, dozens of men were engaged in their own individual battles, each too busy trying to survive to help or even notice him. To Dieter, it felt like he might as well have been the last man in the world. In the middle of battle, surrounded by bloodshed, he had never felt so alone.

Desperately, Dieter took a gamble. Trying to read the rhythm of the beastman's attacks, he timed it to the gap between axe strokes and leapt forward, thrusting his sword out with all his strength. Making a target of the creature's throat he thrust diagonally upward, praying the unexpectedness of the attack would give him an opening.

It worked. The beastman tried to defend itself with its shield, but before it could close the gap Dieter's sword struck home. The blade stabbed through the bottom of the monster's chin, spearing up through the tongue and palate into the brain. Briefly, the beastman stood transfixed, a look less of pain than of surprise on its face. The eyes went blank. Like a puppet cut free of its strings, the monster collapsed, pulling Dieter's sword after it.

Feeling naked without his blade, Dieter bent forward and tried to remove his sword from the dead beastman. It was wedged fast. Afraid the blade might snap if he tugged too violently, Dieter wriggled it from side to side, trying to work the weapon free.

Suddenly, he heard another roar, close at hand. Looking up, he saw a second gor emerge from the forest and start to stride purposefully down the trail toward him. It was even more monstrous than the first, its mutated body bearing a third arm jutting freakishly from the top of its shoulder as a sign of some dark god's favour. Two of the creature's hands held axes, the third held a spear. As it moved closer, it opened its mouth, uncoiling a length of barbed, leprous tongue dripping poison like the tail of some hellish insect.

Despairing of freeing his sword in time, Dieter pulled a knife from his belt and backed away. Compared to the beastman's arsenal, it seemed a pitiful weapon: a single-edged blade with a cloth-bound handle, made more for skinning rabbits and cutting twine than killing enemies. It was all he had.

'Holst!' Dieter called out again, more in hope than expectation. 'Where are you? I need help!'

Careful to keep one eye on the approaching monster, Dieter cast about for a better weapon. His gaze alighted on the axe belonging to the gor he had just killed. It was a massive thing with a broad, heavy blade – a two-handed weapon by human standards, although the beastman had wielded it in one. Dieter had never wielded an axe against anything more dangerous than a tree trunk, but it had to give him a better chance than the knife.

The beastman came closer. Making a show of its dexterity, it simultaneously tossed its two axes from one hand to the other so they crossed past each other in flight. The monster seemed to be taunting him, daring him to make a dive for the weapon of its comrade. The fallen axe was barely a few feet away, agonisingly close. Calculating the odds, Dieter decided his only chance was to leave it to the last possible instant, dive for the axe and hope for the best.

The beastman extended its tongue further. Glistening with venom, the appendage whipped and snapped in the air as though it had a mind of its own. Dieter felt like a rabbit watching the dance of a snake, waiting for the strike.

Abruptly, the tongue stiffened. It shot back into the beastman's mouth as the creature opened its jaws wide and screamed in pain. To Dieter's surprise, the monster's weapons dropped from nerveless hands. It fell to its knees, eyes wondering how it could have been brought so low. It pitched forward, face down into the dirt.

'Well? Are you going to get your sword? There's plenty more beasts where that one came from.'

It was Holst. He was standing behind the fallen beastman, its blood fresh on the blade of his sword. With the layer of white flour dusted over Holst's face, he looked faintly ridiculous – although, at that moment, Dieter was overjoyed to see him no matter what he looked like.

Scrambling to follow Holst's advice, Dieter hurried to get his sword. Having retrieved it, he found Holst following close behind him.

'We'll make a stand here,' Holst said. 'Some of the guards seem to be making a good fist of fighting off the beastmen near the head of the caravan, but we're too far away from them to get there. They'd run us down before we took a dozen steps.'

As Holst talked, Dieter became uncomfortably aware of movement in the trees nearby. Something was watching them.

'You see them?' Holst asked, spotting the direction of his gaze. 'A beast herd. They held back to let their champions have a go at you. I take it those three dead ungors are yours as well? That piece of work is probably what attracted the champions' attention. Anyway, now they're dead, the rest of the herd won't mess about. There'll be no more single combat. They'll rush us in one mass, try to take us through weight of numbers.'

The movement intensified. Dieter saw a number of beastmen emerge from among the trees. They were of the smaller kind, the ones Holst called 'ungors'. Watching the enemy gather, Dieter was struck by how much he and Holst were outnumbered.

'We fight back to back,' Holst told him. 'That way, we cover each other. I've seen your sword-work, lad, and it's fine. But this isn't the time for fancy moves. This is war, not fencing. A beast comes at you, you kill it. You keep things hard, fast and simple. You don't worry about the next beast, or the one after that. They'll come at you in their own good time, and you'll get them then. You understand me?'

'I understand,' Dieter answered.

'Right then, let's get to business.' Turning his back so he and Dieter faced in opposite directions, Holst called out in a loud voice to the beastmen. 'What are you waiting for, you bastards? We killed your champions. Come get what they got.'

The enemy hardly seemed to need the encouragement. Having gathered their forces in sufficient quantity to counteract the nervousness they felt at facing the men who had defeated their champions, the beastmen charged toward Dieter and Holst. In the long seconds as they waited for the ungors to reach them, Dieter felt a queasy feeling in the pit of his stomach. He counted more than a dozen of the enemy, even as yet more ungors emerged from the forest to join the attack. Looking from face to face of the creatures charging towards him, Dieter saw a succession of features all set in the same general lines of savagery, rage and hate. He wondered how he and Holst could ever hope to hold them back.

Then, the enemy was upon them and the time for misgivings was past.

As before, one beastman ran ahead of its fellows, more eager for the kill. Dieter met it with cold steel, deflecting its spear thrust with his open hand as he jabbed the point of his blade deep into its chest. The next beastman followed hot on the heels of the first. Dieter parried its attack with his sword, responding with a swift riposte that left his enemy clutching a wound in its throat. The third one Dieter unbalanced with a skilful feint, before disembowelling it with a flash of his blade. He snatched the dying beastman's shield as it fell, experimentally testing its weight as he prepared to face his next opponent.

'Don't get cocky,' Holst growled from behind him. 'Keep it simple.'

In battle, Holst was a revelation. For weeks, Dieter had only known him as his snoring companion on the dull journey northward. Now, in his element, Holst was like a tiger. Where Dieter was a fencer, Holst was a street fighter. He made war a matter of brutal practicality. He fought with sword, shield, elbow and knees: Dieter didn't doubt the other man would be willing to use his teeth if that was what it took to kill an enemy.

From the corner of his vision, he saw Holst head butt an ungor, striking with the brow of his helmet to smash the creature between the eyes. As that beast-man fell, he lashed out at another, striking with his shield rim at its throat before finishing it with a quick stab of his sword. In his own way, he was as relentless and purposeful as any back-alley brawler. He made sure when he hit someone, they did not get up.

Despite the two men's best efforts, the position was hopeless. Even as he dispatched another beastman with a thrust of his sword, Dieter realised they were only delaying the inevitable. There were too many beastmen. For every one they killed, another moved forward to take its place. Already, he and Holst were being hemmed in, forced to fight in the ever-decreasing space afforded by the press of beastmen around them. Soon, they would be overwhelmed.

Relief when it came was sudden and unexpected. Dieter heard a voice cry out.

'Forward! Forward the 3rd! Forward for Hochland!'

A trumpet sounded nearby, signalling a charge. Other voices joined it. Almost before Dieter could work out what was happening, the mass of beastmen around them dissipated as the creatures fled. He saw a group of swordsmen come charging from the forest, clad in the same grey and red uniforms as Holst.

Dieter's heart caught in his mouth as he realised their identity. They were the Scarlets. Seeing them in the flesh brought to mind the childish dreams of his younger years, when he had idled his days at the mill looking forward to the time when he would come of age and could become a soldier.

The Scarlets attacked with controlled ferocity, cutting through the beastmen like a scythe. As they swept the enemy before them, Dieter heard the same battle cry repeated, taken up by the chorus of dozens of voices.

'Forward the 3rd! Forward for Hochland!'

Before he knew what he was doing, he had taken up the cry himself. With Holst beside him, Dieter joined the Scarlets in pursuing the fleeing beastmen. The finesse he had used earlier in fighting the enemy was gone. Caught up in the moment, he lashed out at the beastmen as they ran. With the battle turned in the caravan's favour, he was eager for vengeance. He fought without thought of strategy or tactics. His sword rose and fell, lost in a haze of blood.

Too soon, there were no more enemies left to fight. As the last of the beastmen fled from the trail into the forest, Dieter made to follow them.

Holst stopped him. The big man stepped in front of Dieter, sword sheathed and his hand held out in a warding gesture.

'Leave them. We'd be fools to chase them through the forest and the beastmen know it. The woods are theirs. Anyway, they've been put to flight. It's over, lad. Cool your fires.'

Coming back to his senses, Dieter realised he was breathing heavily. Sheathing his own sword, he glanced down at the thick wooden shield he had taken from one of the dead beastmen. In the aftermath of battle, it seemed an unclean thing, carved with strange and sickening runes. He threw it away.

Wiping at the sweat staining his face, he turned to inspect the men and carts of the caravan. It was difficult to judge from where he was standing, but he gathered more had survived than he would have expected. He supposed the victuallers and their guards were hardy men, accustomed to the threat of ambush on lonely roads.

He looked toward the cart he and Holst had been riding in. Otto was still in the same place, pinned to his seat, the haft of the beastman spear jutting from his chest.

'Aye, it's a shame,' Holst said, following the direction of Dieter's gaze. 'He seemed an all right sort. But, that's war for you. You never know when you'll get it. All you can hope is that your comrades give you a good send-off. With that in mind…'

Having apparently decided a suitable period of mourning had passed, Holst began to move toward the cart.

'You have to be sharp about these things,' he called over his shoulder. 'If we wait too long, the other victuallers will have picked the cart clean. Otto had some good wine and food. And, besides, I'm sure it's what he would have wanted.'

Vaguely appalled by other man's behaviour, even though he could recognise its practical bent, Dieter watched as Holst jumped into the back of the cart and disappeared under the canvas as he started tossing out items. Soon, a heap of provisions lay on the ground.

'You there!' a voice called out from behind Dieter. 'Don't you know that looting is a crime?'

'Personally, I'd say it's only a crime if you get caught,' Holst replied, smiling as his face peeked out, still covered in flour, from under the canvas. 'And that's hardly likely with useless bastards like you serving as sentries.'

'Is that right?' the voice asked. 'Well, in that case, I have an observation. You, sir, are a damnable, pox-ridden cur. Your mother, assuming any woman would admit to that offence, was a harlot with carnal knowledge of every dung-seller, ratcatcher and body snatcher in the Greater Hergig area. Also, your face appears to be covered with a light dusting of flour, making you appear even more of an idiot than you already are. I call you out. As does my colleague.'

Turning, Dieter saw two soldiers approaching in the uniform of the Scarlets. The first, evidently the one who had spoken, was a dark-haired man of medium height, with a hawkish nose and quick, grey eyes. His blond-haired comrade was taller and thinner, with an ascetic, intense air about him that seemed to sit uneasily with his profession. If it were not for his uniform, Dieter might have taken the second man for a scribe or a priest.

'Call me out, you say?' Holst jumped out of the wagon, landing beside his pile of stolen goods. 'The two of you? I accept the challenge. Do you want me to fight you one after the other, or both at once? Frankly, given the fact you look like a pair of pus-dribbling simpletons, I can't imagine it'd make any difference.'

His grin widening, Holst advanced and embraced the men, first one, and then the other.

'Gerhardt! Rieger! It's good to see you. So, the orcs haven't killed you? What news of the war?'

'Slow going,' the dark man shrugged. 'We haven't seen any greenskins yet, though if you listen to rumours they've been laying waste to settlements all across the frontier. So far, the only action we've seen is against beastmen like the ones that attacked your caravan. Naturally, of course, that's all because of the orcs.'

'How could that be?' Dieter asked him. 'Beastmen and orcs don't work together.'

He regretted speaking almost immediately. Until then, the two new arrivals had ignored him, but now they turned to regard him with dispassionate eyes. Although he did his best to maintain his composure, Dieter felt distinctly uneasy under their scrutiny.

'Who's this?' the dark one asked Holst. 'It's not like you to pick up waifs and strays on the road, Holst.'

'Not unless they're female,' the blond man offered, speaking for the first time.

'Indeed,' the dark man nodded. His eyes narrowed as he stared at Dieter. 'What about it, boy? You've got the bright-eyed, eager look of a would-be recruit

59

about you. Have you come to make war on Hochland's enemies? Or are you just lost in the woods, like the rest of us?'

'My name is Dieter Lanz,' Dieter said, refusing to be intimidated. 'I have come to join the Scarlets.'

'Really?' The dark man turned away to look at Holst. 'Where'd you find him? Is he some illegitimate son that you fathered on a doxy, come to track you down? Or a creditor, perhaps? There's a few of them who'd be willing to follow you all the way to the Chaos Wastes if they thought it'd make you pay what you owe. Certainly, he can't be a soldier.'

'Ah, leave the lad alone, Gerhardt,' Holst said. 'He did all right. Granted, he asks stupid questions, but he pretty much does what you tell him. And he's a dab hand with a sword.'

'In that case, he'd better come with us.' The dark-haired one, Gerhardt, turned toward Dieter. 'To answer your question, the orc advance has forced some of the beastmen tribes to flee their territory like animals running from a forest fire. That's why these beastmen here attacked your caravan – the orcs have driven them away from their usual hunting ground, so they're hungry. Any more questions?'

'Uh… no…' Dieter found himself almost squirming at the intensity of the other man's gaze. At the same time, he wondered at the ferocity of the orcs that they could send terrifying monsters like the beastmen scurrying before them like frightened rats.

'Good.' Gerhardt turned away. 'Well, come on then. We haven't got all day. We will escort this caravan back to our encampment, then you can see

Captain Harkner, our regimental commander. If you want to be a Scarlet, boy, he's the man you need to impress.'

CHAPTER TWO
NIGHT IN CAMP

Dusk was falling by the time they reached the Empire encampment. Having left behind a detachment of men to build pyres to burn the beastmen's bodies, the Scarlets had transferred the human dead to the back of one of the carts and escorted the caravan back to the camp without delay. Despite the poor quality of the roadway, they made good time and the journey passed without further incident.

By then, Holst had introduced Dieter to several of his comrades. The blond, thin one was named Rieger, Dieter learned, while the dark-haired one called Gerhardt turned out to be the de facto leader of the group of soldiers who had saved the caravan. The Scarlets had been posted to patrol the camp's outer perimeter, hence their timely rescue. The forest landscape was misleading, but it turned out the caravan had actually been much closer to the camp when the beastmen attacked than Dieter expected.

The army was camped in a wide clearing by the side of a babbling forest stream. Dieter caught his first sight of the encampment as the descending sun turned red as it reached the horizon. Given the company Dieter was keeping, it gave the scene an appropriately scarlet cast.

'Red sun is falling, old Morr is calling,' Holst said, indicating the sunset. 'I remember I heard that once, from a farmer or shepherd – I don't recall which. I suppose it's what you'd call a country wisdom. Farmers and shepherds are full of such sayings. It's always beware ye this, or beware ye that. And who knows what any of their nonsense means? Granted, you hear these things and they stick with you. But most of these sayings are meaningless.'

'And yet you decided to share one with us anyway?' Rieger asked, his voice friendly but gently mocking. 'I suppose your mind is so full of wisdom, it should come as no surprise that something occasionally spills out.'

'Kiss my arse, Rieger,' Holst grunted back. 'I didn't say it was important. I was just trying to make conversation. I take it you'd prefer it if we trudged along in silence?'

Holst had become somewhat crotchety since they had resumed their journey. With the arrival of his regiment, he now walked by the side of one of the carts, guarding its flank as it trundled slowly toward camp. Holst had been compelled to give up his comfortable position in one of the carts by the fact he had now returned to duty, but Dieter had given his own place up willingly to allow a wounded man to ride in his stead. Beside which, now the Scarlets were there, he wanted to be in their company.

They were not quite as he anticipated. Dieter had not given much thought to it on his way from Hergig, but he supposed he had expected something more in line with his childish imaginings. He had thought the members of the 3rd would be well groomed, their uniforms immaculate, their armour and weapons polished to a gleaming shine.

The reality was less impressive. The sword was a weapon that required more skill to use effectively than a spear or halberd, and, as swordsmen, the Scarlets were counted as an elite among the infantry. They walked with a natural swagger as befitted their status, but their uniforms were hardworn, even threadbare in places. Their breastplates and the blades of their swords were blackened, daubed with mud he supposed so they would not reflect the sun in situations when stealth was needed.

Dieter understood the realities of campaigning. He knew war was a harsh, dirty business that bore little resemblance to the fine tales of the storytellers and the balladeers. Still, he had idolised the idea of the Scarlets since childhood. The realisation they were simply soldiers, no different from fighting men anywhere else in the Empire, seemed almost disappointing.

'Holst says you are the son of Helmut Schau?' Gerhardt said to him.

'Not his son. But he raised me. My mother died when I was an infant. Helmut and his wife Marta took me in. They brought me up alongside their own children.'

'A good man,' Holst said. 'Did you know I saved his life?'

'Don't listen to him,' Rieger interrupted. 'Holst didn't serve with your foster father, any more than the rest of us did. Helmut Schau was retired by the time we joined the regiment. We only know of him because his name lingered on in the tales of some of the old-timers.'

'You are mistaken, Rieger,' Holst shot back. 'I remember the event clearly. It was at the Battle of Tannesfeld–'

'Again, another lie,' Rieger shook his head. 'I have heard Holst tell the same story of the Battle of Tannesfeld more than two dozen times. Depending on who's listening, he claims to have saved the life of Helmut Schau, Captain Harkner, Ludwig Schwarzhelm, the poet Felix Jaeger, or even the Emperor Karl Franz himself. The story is usually followed immediately by an attempt to borrow money from the victim.'

'You know, you talk too much, Rieger,' Holst frowned petulantly. 'How's a man to keep himself in the style he's accustomed to when you keep scaring people off? "Oh, don't lend money to Holst," you say. "He'll only go and spend it." It's got so there's no one left I can turn to when I'm a bit short.'

'Have you considered I might be trying to save you from yourself?' Rieger replied sardonically. 'You borrow money easily enough, but it's the repayment of the loans that always gets you in trouble. What about that last tavern brawl in Hergig? The one that left you invalided out of the regiment for a month? Wasn't that about money?'

'Only peripherally,' Holst sniffed. 'Those bastard halberdiers had the effrontery to suggest I'd been cheating at cards. Of course, after that, I had to fight them. The honour of the regiment was at stake. Anyway, who appointed you as my conscience? If I wanted a priest to be my confessor, I'd go find one.'

'You needn't worry,' Rieger smiled. 'I'm not trying to save your soul, Holst. Nor dissuade you from further sin. That is a task beyond even our Lord Sigmar himself.'

The lead elements of the caravan had reached the perimeter of the camp. While Gerhardt went forward to consult with the sentries guarding the camp's approaches, Dieter cast his eyes over the camp itself.

The magnitude of the camp was the first thing that struck him. He had heard the Count of Hochland had called up twenty thousand men, a sizeable complement. Only now, confronted by the scale of their encampment, did he believe it.

The camp was on a low rise, allowing him to take in much of its breadth in one vision. At its outskirts the camp was protected by a ring of pickets, sharpened wooden stakes set close enough together to deter the attack of enemy cavalry, guarded by a mixed sentry force of handgunners, halberdiers and spearmen.

Reinforcing their efforts, Dieter saw that several cannons had been situated at regular intervals in protected positions behind the pickets. All around the perimeter, a wide corridor of the forest had been cleared, creating open territory designed to offer no cover from the camp's artillery. Dieter did not doubt that any enemy assaulting the camp would be made to regret it.

Ahead, at the point where the trail they had been following crossed the camp's perimeter, Dieter saw Gerhardt was in deep conversation with the captain of a unit of handgunners on sentry duty. A temporary wooden barricade had been laid across the trail, blocking progress to the camp. With a gesture from the handgunners' captain, the barricade was lifted from its position and moved aside to allow entrance.

The caravan resumed its journey. As they passed by the men guarding the barricade, the Scarlets traded insults with the handgunners. It all seemed in good humour, but Dieter heard comments bantered back and forth that he was sure would make the most boorish man in his village back home blush. In particular, the two groups of soldiers seemed to delight in insulting each others' prowess, whether in military matters or more private areas.

Having passed into the camp proper, the caravan moved toward a broad, flat area set aside for carts. Finally ensconced in the safety of the camp, the victuallers began to draw their wagons to rest, removing the dray teams from harness and seeing to the men wounded in the beastman ambush. Surgeons were summoned, and stable masters, to see to human and equine needs.

Having consulted at length with the captain at the barricade, Gerhardt had returned. The Scarlets gathered around him expectantly, Dieter with them.

'All right,' Gerhardt said. 'You've got an hour to yourselves. Clean up, then go to the kitchen tents and see if you can scrounge some food.'

He turned to Dieter as the other men dispersed.

'Not you. You're coming with me to see Captain Harkner.'

'So, you know Helmut Schau? What did he tell you to say to me?'

Ten minutes later, Dieter found himself in the tent of the regimental commander, Captain Harkner. The captain was a burly man in his late forties, his blond hair and full beard starting to grey with age. He stared at Dieter intently, clearly trying to size him up.

'Well? Orc got your tongue, boy?' The captain's eyes narrowed. 'I asked you a question. Obviously, the bastard Schau would have told you to say something to me when we first met. What is it?'

'I…' Dieter had rehearsed the moment in his head a hundred times on the road, but now it was upon him his mouth felt dry. 'He told me to say you are a son of a whore and you cheat at dice.'

For a moment, there was silence in the tent. Then, much to Dieter's relief, the captain laughed.

'I see nothing has changed with the old scoundrel, then? Still moaning over his gambling losses, is he? He was so piss-poor when it came to games of chance, it always surprised me he ever managed to build enough of a stake to retire from the army and go into business. What profession did he choose in the end? Tavern keeper?'

'Miller. He bought the watermill in a village named Bromstadt. It's a good ways south of here, in the country east of Hergig.'

'A miller?' Harkner raised an eyebrow. 'I never thought I'd hear Helmut Schau had chosen a life grinding flour. Still, I suppose it's a living.'

The captain shrugged.

'So, you said you had a letter for me? Let's see it.'

His hand going into his shirt, Dieter pulled out a cowskin wallet. Opening it, he carefully removed a folded piece of parchment and handed it to Harkner. The captain took it without a word. Adjusting his position to stand underneath an oil lantern hanging from one of the tent poles, he unfolded the letter and began to read.

Time seemed to move with glacial slowness. Nervously, Dieter took in his surroundings. Gerhardt stood beside him. Having led him to the command tent, Gerhardt had reported the beastman attack on the caravan to Captain Harkner before introducing Dieter to him. In front of them, spread out over a table with folding legs, a roughly proportioned map of the area had been drawn in charcoal on the smooth side of a large sheepskin.

A sergeant called Bohlen stood on the other side of the table, his hand raised to his mouth to stifle a yawn as they waited for the captain to finish reading. Dieter gathered Bohlen would normally have been commanding the patrol that had saved the caravan from the beastmen's ambush, but he had been called away to a briefing with Harkner, leaving Gerhardt to lead the patrol in his place.

Harkner continued to examine the letter at no great speed. Trying not to stare, Dieter noticed the captain's lips moving almost imperceptibly, his mouth shaping the words as he read. Finally, the captain finished.

'Schau didn't write this letter,' he stated flatly. 'The man I knew couldn't read. Even if someone taught him his letters in the years since, he wouldn't write so elegantly. This was written by an educated man.'

'The village priest wrote it on his behalf. But it was Helmut who asked him to do it. And he had Father Gottlieb read it back to him when he was finished, so he'd know the priest had written the things he wanted.'

'Hmm, if this letter is to be believed, you have the makings of a fine soldier,' the captain said, his eyes burning into Dieter's face as though looking for a reason to doubt it. 'Of course, Schau and the priest know you. They could be gilding the lily, making you sound better than you are.'

Folding the letter, he handed it back to Dieter.

'What about before you got here? You can't have come straight from your village to this encampment. You must have gone to the barracks in Hergig first. Did you meet our recruiter, Sergeant Rippner?'

'I did.'

'He wouldn't have let you go without testing your swordsmanship. He made you fight with wasters, yes – wooden broadswords? Usually, he makes the young bloods fight two or three bouts with him, making sure he gives them a good few bruises. Well? What did he say to you afterwards?'

'I…' Dieter paused momentarily in discomfort. 'He said I was a waste of spit and whichever father sired me had no doubt long ago learned to regret it. He said, at best, my swordmanship was passable.'

'Passable, eh? Coming from "the Ripper" that's high praise. Most would-be recruits are lucky if he gives them anything more than a kick in the jewels for their trouble. You must know one end of a sword from another, then?'

'Holst said he gave a good account of himself when the beastmen attacked,' Gerhardt offered. 'A bit cocky and flash, perhaps. But nothing that can't be drilled out of him.'

'I see,' the captain nodded. He glanced over his shoulder. 'What about you, Bohlen? What do you say?'

'We are short-handed anyway,' the sergeant shrugged. 'If he turns out to be no good, we can always put him at the head of the line, let the orcs solve the problem for us.'

'A vote of confidence all round, then?'

Turning away, Harkner walked over to a large travelling chest and opened it. Fishing inside, he brought out a parchment, a quill and a bottle of ink and took them over to the table.

'All right, do you know how to write or should I make your letters for you?' he said, setting the items down.

'I know how to make my name,' Dieter told him. 'Father Gottlieb taught me.'

'Good.' The captain spread out the parchment, dipping the quill in the ink. 'Sign your name here. The rest of it is already made out.'

Dieter recognised the crest of the Count of Hochland at the head of the paper, but the rest of the parchment was a mystery to him. He scratched his name at the place where the captain's finger pointed, the quill quivering in his hand as he performed the unfamiliar task.

'Good enough,' Harkner said, inspecting Dieter's handiwork. Putting the parchment carefully to one side to avoid smudging the wet ink, he pulled a draw-string purse from inside his tunic and took out a shilling.

'Do you accept the discipline of the Count and his subordinates, including myself and my sergeants?' the captain said, the words evidently learned by rote and oft-repeated. 'Do you give yourself to the defence of his lands and his vassals, such defence to be made at any cost, up to and including the loss of your life? Do you accept the strictures of military service, said service to last a period of not less than twenty-five years? To agree, you only have to say yes.'

'Yes.' Dieter had thought forward to this day often. Now it was here, he felt the hairs rise at the back of his neck.

Harkner held up the coin. It was old and worn, but even in the dim light of the tent Dieter could see the Count of Hochland's profile embossed on its surface.

'There is a protocol to these things, boy. Even now, even though you signed the paper, you can still back out. But from the second you accept this coin, that's it. You'll be in the Count's army. Understand me, you seem a good lad, but there's no room for kindly feeling in the army. If you fail the regiment, I'll come down on you hard. If you desert, or show cowardice, you'll be executed. Other infractions can see you fined, beaten, flogged, or even branded with a hot iron. It's a hard life. Oh, there's glory in it for some. But, usually, only after they're dead.'

'I understand,' Dieter said. 'But I know what's expected. I won't fail.'

'Brave words.' Captain Harkner stretched out his hand and offered him the coin. 'All right, we'll finish it. Do you accept this shilling, knowing that you are now a soldier? Do you swear, in the name of Sigmar and all the gods of the Empire, to do your duty?'

'I accept it,' Dieter said, taking the coin. 'I swear I will do my duty.'

'And what of you?' Harkner turned to Gerhardt and Bohlen. 'Do you see this act? Is it witnessed?'

'We see it,' they said in unison. 'It is witnessed.'

'Very well. It's done.'

Smiling, the captain turned back and held out his hand for Dieter to shake it.

'Welcome to the 3rd, lad. Welcome to the Scarlets.'

AFTERWARDS, AS THEY made their way back to the others, Gerhardt tried to explain something of the words the Captain had spoken.

'It's an old thing, the wording of it,' he said, as they walked through the camp. 'They say it dates back to the founding of the regiment, when the 3rd were granted their regimental charter by Count Mikael Ludenhof. Supposedly they were the words Count

Mikael used when he recruited a group of survivors from the Siege of Hergig to form the Scarlets. But Helmut Schau must have told you all this?'

'He did,' Dieter agreed.

By then, he was wearing a new helmet and breastplate, and carrying a shield emblazoned in the regimental colours. Gerhardt had taken him to visit the regiment's quartermaster in the wake of signing his papers in the captain's tent.

The quartermaster, an acerbic old soldier named Stens, had also offered Dieter a new sword, but he would not have given up the sword he was already carrying for the world. It was a gift from his foster father, Helmut. A piece of good, long Empire steel, forged by a swordsmith from Reikland called Huber, allegedly a disciple of the master swordsmith Magnin. It was perfectly balanced, razor-edged, and Dieter was well used to it. It was the weapon Helmut had presented him with on his fifteenth birthday, when he judged him fully grown and sword-trained enough to put the half-weight weapons and wooden wasters of his childhood behind.

Helmut had started training Dieter in swordsmanship almost as soon as he could walk. In those early days Dieter had harboured no ambition to be a soldier, but Helmut Schau took the opinion it was part of a father's task to teach his children to defend themselves. For the better part of sixteen years, he had taught Dieter everything he knew. They had started fencing with willow switches when Dieter was just a toddler, progressing on to thicker lengths of stick over time. From there, they moved on to wooden wasters, then blunt half-weight training swords, and finally the real thing.

As the years passed, Helmut had taught Dieter the use of sword and shield, the sword alone, sword and dagger, dagger only, and grappling. He had even taught him the basics of long-hafted weapons, to guard against the day he might find himself in a position where he was forced to pick up a fallen spear or halberd to defend himself.

Increasingly, as their lessons progressed, Dieter had realised he wanted nothing more than to become a soldier, to emulate the man who had raised him with such care. Inevitably, when he considered a military career, there was only one regiment that attracted him – the same regiment the man he considered his father had once served in.

Today, Dieter had achieved his ambition. If he was left with one regret from his meeting with the quartermaster, it was that he still did not have a uniform. With scowling ill grace, Stens had explained they did not take a supply of uniforms on campaign with them. There was already too much for the Scarlets' baggage train to carry, what with provisions, camping equipment, cooking utensils, replacement weapons, armour, and so on. Nor did they have any suitable cloth to give to the seamstresses to make a new uniform for him from scratch. For the time being Dieter would have to do with a feather to wear on his helmet, dyed red and green in the colours of Hochland, and a grey and scarlet ribbon to tie around his bicep, indicating his regiment.

'Anyway, there's every chance it'd be a waste of time givin' you a uniform,' Stens had commented archly. 'Seamstresses charge an arm and a leg for 'em. And, for all we know you'll get killed in your first engagement.'

Grudgingly, Stens had agreed to see if he could procure enough coloured cloth to have a uniform made for Dieter. In the meantime, the new recruit would have to do without.

It was a small matter, but to Dieter it was important. He would not truly feel like a member of the 3rd until he had a grey-and-scarlet uniform like the others.

'No doubt you are eager for action?' Gerhardt asked, intruding on his thoughts. Evidently, he had misread the reason for Dieter's silence. 'I wouldn't worry. It could be we'll see some tomorrow.'

'Tomorrow? Have more beastmen been spotted near the camp? Or orcs?'

'Not as such.' Gerhardt shook his head.

Around them, night was falling. They made their way through the sea of tents, guided by the torches set at regular intervals throughout the camp. It was Dieter's first time with an army out on campaign, and he was struck by the plethora of sights, sounds and smells all around him.

He heard the hubbub of conversation, the harsh screech of whetstone on metal as blades were sharpened and armoured plates were scraped free of rust. He smelt the mouth-watering aromas of meat roasting on a spit over an open fire. He saw men of dozens of different types and regiments rubbing shoulders.

He saw spearmen, halberdiers, artillerists, handgunners, and archers. He saw learned engineers, haughty knights, cocksure pistoliers, grizzled outriders, swaggering free company adventurers and mercenary crossbowmen. He saw the entire panoply of a provincial army and its militia auxiliary, ready to go to war. He saw it all, and he felt a spark of pride to be part of it.

It was said the orcs worshipped gods in their own bestial image. Let their gods help them, for the men of the Empire would not.

'General von Nieder has ordered the entire army is to break camp tomorrow morning,' Gerhardt said. 'We are to head further northwards. It seems like no one knows for sure, but the rumour is the orcs are about twenty leagues north of here.'

'So we are going north to find them, then?' Dieter's voice was expectant. 'We are going to bring them to battle?'

'That's the plan,' Gerhardt nodded. 'But first we have to break camp. It's a thing that most people don't realise, but an army is never more vulnerable than when they are about to leave a fortified position. Take this camp here, for example. It may only be a temporary encampment, but it has its own defences. If an enemy attacked now, they'd have to negotiate the outer pickets, not to mention facing an artillery barrage as they crossed the open ground to get to us. For the moment, we're as snug as a tick nesting on a cow. But, come tomorrow, it'll all be different. You see what I'm driving at?'

'You mean when we break camp we have to dismantle our defences?' Dieter said. He was not sure whether Gerhardt was trying to test him or teach him something.

'Exactly. And that makes us vulnerable. Imagine an enemy army is sitting somewhere nearby, watching this camp. The second they see us packing up the camp's defences, they'd know that was the time to strike. With the whole army squeezed together in one place like this, we'd be an easy mark if it wasn't for the pickets and artillery. So, that being the case, what would you do about it? It's important you should learn this, because what's true for an army also holds true for smaller groups of men. Well, young blood? What say you?'

'I'd say it's important to send out scouts before the army breaks camp,' Dieter replied after he had considered the matter. 'They'd comb the immediate area, making sure there aren't any enemy forces nearby. That way, the army would know they could break camp in safety.'

'Good,' Gerhardt smiled. 'In this case, the Scarlets have been given that duty. Some of the huntsmen that the army uses as scouts have reported seeing sign of goblin tracks in the woods to the west of here. From all accounts, General von Nieder doesn't put much store in the huntsmen's reports. But, to be on the safe side, we've been ordered to sweep the woods first thing in the morning, before the army breaks camp.'

Gerhardt paused, letting his words sink in before he continued.

'You'd better get an early night, young blood. We enter the woods at dawn. If you wanted action, that's when you'll find it.'

CHAPTER THREE
SOLDIER IN THE MISTS

THE NEXT MORNING was cold. In the uneasy half-light before dawn, Dieter found himself standing with the other men of the regiment, lined up facing the woods to the west of the camp.

A damp blanket of early morning mist hugged the earth, obscuring the outlines of the trees ahead. Once the sun rose and the day began in earnest the mist might well burn off, but in the meantime it was hard to see more than ten paces in any direction. Shivering, Dieter realised he had taken the heat of the last few weeks for granted. The weather had changed; summer had given way to autumn.

'I always used think this was the worst of it,' Gerhardt said quietly, from beside him. 'These times when you find yourself standing, fidgeting at your sword, waiting for the command to get under way. You get used to it, though. Believe me, after fifteen years in the army you realise you can get used to anything.'

Given the bad light and the oppressive nature of the fog, it was hard to see too much of the soldiers around him. Idly, Dieter wondered how many of them felt the same sense of nervous apprehension.

Gerhardt was right: he did find this was the worst of it. Yesterday, when he faced the beastmen, it had been comparatively easy. There had been the threat of death, the exertion of a life-or-death struggle, but his actions had come to him automatically, ingrained by years of training with Helmut Schau and spurred on by the natural instinct to survive. Today, in the uncertain pre-dawn light, there was more time to think.

He had been introduced to many of his new comrades last night, before they bedded down. It was difficult to tell much after such a short acquaintance, but for the most part they had seemed welcoming enough. There was a natural reticence against being too friendly or too forthcoming; Helmut had warned him about that.

'Remember, you will be the new man,' Helmut had told him. 'Don't expect too much in the way of friendship when you first join the barracks. They will wait to get the measure of you first. One day, their lives may depend on you and your character. They'll want to know what kind of man you are before they welcome you.'

In common with many other regiments in the army of Hochland, the 3rd was divided into a series of ten-man sub-units called files. Dieter had been assigned to the file commanded by Sergeant Bohlen, alongside

Gerhardt, Rieger and Holst. He had learned the names of the other men of the file were Kuranski, Breitmeyer, Rosen, Krug and Febel. It was hard to tell too much about them after such brief acquaintance, but Dieter supposed he would get to know each of them in time.

Behind them, lost in the mists, the rest of the camp was waking up. Dieter heard sounds drift towards him, muffled by the fog. There was the clatter of pans as the cooks saw to breakfast, the noise of voices as the sentries changed watch and orders were shouted back-and-forth.

Somewhere, Dieter heard a woman's voice singing. A camp follower no doubt, giving voice to a sarcastic song as she taunted one or more of her lovers.

Oh sailors they get all the money,
Soldiers they get none but brass.
I do love a jolly sailor,
Soldiers they can kiss my arse.

The song raised a smile from Dieter, easing the mood of nervousness that had settled upon him. He realised it was a trick which might stand him in good stead in years to come. It was better to laugh and think thoughts of good humour, rather than dwell on his anxieties. Blinded by the fog, it was easy to fall prey to unreasoning fear.

Abruptly, he heard a rolling series of drumbeats. Captain Harkner had told the regimental drummer to give the signal to advance. Keeping pace with the other men around him, Dieter moved forward as the Scarlets entered the forest.

* * *

'KEEP CLOSE,' GERHARDT had told him as they prepared for the expedition. 'It's your first time out and you haven't drilled with us, so stay within sight of me, Holst and Rieger. Follow what we do. As long as you've got one of us in view you'll be all right.'

It was good advice, but Dieter quickly found it was easier said than done. From the moment they entered the forest, the mist seemed to swallow them.

Within a few paces, it was so thick the men around him were reduced to little more than amorphous silhouettes. He could no longer tell one from another, much less follow any particular shape and know it was Gerhardt, Holst or Rieger. Instead, the most he could do was to stick close to one of the silhouettes and hope for the best.

The Scarlets had not entered the woods alone. A group of local huntsmen had been assigned to them as guides.

They reminded Dieter of the professional huntsmen he had known in his home village of Bromstadt: hard-faced, gimlet-eyed men in black cloaks, armed with bows. Such men could spend weeks at a time living in the deep forests, foraging to survive as they tracked their prey – whether that prey was wolves, bears, orcs or beastmen. Sometimes, if he possessed a particularly mercenary disposition, a huntsman might even hire on to track his fellow man – hunting fugitive criminals and bandits in return for a bounty.

There were four huntsmen in total with the Scarlets. Two of them had disappeared into the forest, scouting ahead of the expedition, while the other two accompanied the Scarlets to make sure they didn't get lost.

Dieter only hoped the huntsmen knew the forest as well as they claimed. Otherwise, in the current conditions, far from scouting the area he had no doubt they could be wandering around it for days without ever finding anything.

It was hard to judge time surrounded by the mists, but by Dieter's estimation several minutes passed before he noticed an unsettling development. From the first, the forest had been quiet. The Scarlets were under orders to move through the woods as stealthily as possible, but even so it had been possible to catch the break of twigs and crunch of leaves underfoot as the soldiers passed through the woodlands. Without any warning, Dieter suddenly realised he could no longer hear those sounds.

In its place, the forest was eerily quiet. Turning to the man silhouetted by the side of him, Dieter realised to his horror he was looking at a tree, its shape disguised enough by the mist that he had mistaken it for one of his comrades. Appalled, he scanned his surroundings and saw that none of the silhouettes around him were moving. With a sinking heart, it occurred to him that he was alone.

His first impulse was to cry out, but he remembered his orders were to maintain stealth. Stifling his cry, he considered his options.

He was no great huntsman, but he had lived his whole life in the country, giving him a wealth of skills to draw on. Cautiously, he moved to the nearest tree and rubbed his hand over the bark. Determining which side of the tree had moss on it allowed him to roughly estimate the compass direction. Coupled with the fact he knew the Scarlets were supposed to be moving north-west, he headed off in the same direction, reasoning he would likely cross their path sooner or later.

At the same time, the temptation to shout out in the hope of attracting his comrades' attention was almost overwhelming. Resisting the impulse, Dieter reminded himself they had been sent into the woods to scout for greenskins. If any of the enemy were nearby, his call for help would draw them like crows to a carcass. Besides which, he was proud. It was his first duty with his new regiment, and he did not want it to be remembered as the time he got lost and endangered their mission. It was not in his character to accept such humiliation lightly.

Telling himself he would give it another quarter-league before he stopped and took stock of his situation, Dieter continued on. Wary of the fact he was on his own, he had drawn his sword. He moved carefully forward, his senses alert, listening intently for any sound which might give him warning either of the Scarlets' presence or an enemy's.

Spotting a bulky shape further ahead in the mists, Dieter altered his course to move closer toward it. Intrigued, he wondered as to its nature, until the mists suddenly parted for a split second revealing its identity.

It was a small hut, of the kind used by woodsmen, charcoal burners and others who made their living in the forest. A light was burning beneath the window shutters. Advancing to within hailing distance, Dieter briefly considered calling out to its inhabitants. Thinking better of it, he crept over to the front door.

Transferring his sword to his shield hand in a blade downward position, Dieter made ready to push the door open. It was another of the tricks his foster father Helmut had taught him. Rather than sheath his sword or discard his shield to open the door, he relied on his forearm to control the shield while his left hand held the sword, giving him a free hand to ease the door open quietly instead of kicking it down and alerting whoever was inside to his arrival. If trouble occurred, he could quickly swap the sword back to his right hand and take up the proper grip on his shield, ready for action.

Gently lifting the latch, he opened the door. Inside, he saw two men in the uniform of the Scarlets, standing with their backs to him. They were both hunched over a shape in the middle of the hut floor.

'You wouldn't think her bones would be so strong,' one of them said, straining at something. 'Wait a minute… I think I've got it…'

There was an audible *crack*, the sound nearly as loud as a gunshot in the cramped confines of the hut. Horrified, Dieter realised the two men were stooping over the body of an old woman, lying dead on the floor between them. Finishing his task, the one who had spoken started to straighten his knees. As his hands came up, Dieter saw he was holding a ring.

'There,' the man said, inspecting his prize. 'The metal's only pewter, but I'm pretty sure the stone is a garnet. Morr only knows how some old peasant woman ended up with a gem like that.'

He looked up and saw Dieter.

'Look sharp, Febel!' He stood suddenly. 'We have company. Hmm, it's the new young blood. What is his name?'

'Lanz,' the other man said, displaying a mouthful of blackened teeth in what Dieter could only guess was an attempt at a smile.

'Lanz. That's it. Stupid name for a swordsman. With a name like that, you'd think he'd have joined a spear regiment.'

Having recovered from his initial shock, Dieter realised he recognised the two men. Their names were Krug and Febel. They were members of the same file as him, commanded by Sergeant Bohlen. Krug was the larger of the two: a gaunt man with a shaved head whose pock-marked face did little to make him look more appealing. Febel seemed inclined to stay in his shadow. A born follower and toady, his face had a rattish cast to it.

'Well, what's the matter, young blood?' Krug said, taking a cautious step forward. 'You don't say much, do you? Cat got yours?'

'The old woman,' Dieter said. 'What have you done to her?'

'Done?' Krug looked back at the body and shrugged. 'We did nothing. The old bitch was dead when we got here. If you don't believe me, you can see for yourself. Touch her cheek. You'll see that she's stone cold.'

'She probably dropped dead when she heard the orcs were coming,' Febel elaborated. 'That's what we thought, anyway. Either way, the place was picked pretty clean by the time we got here. You ask me, her family probably decided they couldn't waste time burying her. They wouldn't want to be around when the orcs get here. So they packed up, scarpered, and it was too bad for dear old granny–'

'Shut up, Febel,' Krug cut him off. 'You're talking too much. Before we stand here telling each other stories, I want to hear what the young blood thinks of things. I don't like the look in his eye.'

The hut had been ransacked. Initially, Dieter had been distracted by the discovery of the corpse, but as he took in his surroundings, it became clear to him that Krug and Febel had been busy. The hut's meagre furnishings were in disarray. The bedsteads had been overturned and the bedding pulled open. In places, they had even ripped up the floorboards.

'You have destroyed this place,' he said. 'You have smashed these people's belongings. You defiled the old woman's body. And for what?'

'About twenty pennies worth,' Febel said. Sensing Dieter's anger, he had started to nervously back away. 'Least, that's what Krug reckons it comes to. It's not too bad, but it could've been better. Sometimes, these peasants have real treasures hidden away. You'd be surprised what you find. I remember one time…'

'Shut up, Febel,' Krug growled. 'He's not looking for an inventory. Are you, young blood? You got that high and mighty look, like you're about to take exception.'

'You are soldiers,' Dieter felt a rising fury grow inside him. 'More than that, you are Scarlets. You are members of the 3rd. Yet, you stole from this poor woman. You destroyed her home. You acted like thieves or graverobbers!'

'Graverobbing's a business same as any other,' Krug said. His expression darkened. 'You're awful full of yourself for someone who joined the army yesterday. You ain't a captain, boy. Or a sergeant. You're just a snot-nosed shit-dribbler with ideas above himself.'

Krug took a step forward. He stared at Dieter menacingly.

'If you know what's good for you, you'll stand off – right now. I was in the army when you were still sucking greedy at your bitch-mother's teat. You don't want to make me an enemy, boy.'

'I killed at least six beastmen yesterday,' Dieter told him. 'Not one of them was as ugly as you are. They smelled better, too.'

Without realising it, he had swapped his sword over to his right hand. Now, he saw Krug unsheath his own sword.

'I warned you, boy,' Krug said. 'Looks like I'll have to teach you a lesson.'

Seeing Krug take up a fighting stance, Dieter went into his own stance. Some small part of him said he had let things spiral out of control. He had been a Scarlet for barely a day, yet he was about to fight one of his fellow soldiers. Part of his mind told him he should withdraw, report the matter to Sergeant Bohlen and let military justice deal with Krug and Febel for their looting. Still, pride would not let him back down.

Febel had retreated to the side of the hut, but Dieter knew he should keep an eye on him. He didn't trust Febel not to stab him in the back while he was dealing with Krug.

Krug took another step forward. Already, matters had gone too far for a peaceful solution. There would be blood.

Suddenly, Dieter heard a low, mournful sound from out in the forest. He recognised it at once.

It was clear Krug and Febel had recognised it as well. Embarrassed, Krug lowered his sword. For a moment they stood in silence, listening to the sound, trying to work out its direction.

It was the sound of a hunting horn – the one Captain Harkner carried with him. It was a pre-arranged signal, a call to arms.

Somewhere, out in the mists, the Scarlets had met the enemy.

CHAPTER FOUR

RISING SUN

'The horn,' Febel said as the last notes of it died. 'The others are in trouble.'

Their conflict abruptly put aside, the three men rushed to the door of the hut and pushed outside.

'Don't think I've forgiven you, Lanz,' Krug said as they stood in front of the hut and attempted to find their bearings. 'We will settle things later, you and I.'

'You can count on it,' Dieter replied. 'Now, shut up. I'm trying to listen.'

The horn sounded again. Its tone seemed eerie in the haze. Listening to its elongated, keening cry, Dieter was reminded of one of the tales Helmut Schau had told him as a child. It was said the daemons of the Ruinous Powers sometimes hunted in the forests, driving a pack of monstrous hounds before them. Dieter was not sure whether he believed the tale, but he suspected the horn used by the huntmaster of the

damned when he summoned his hounds sounded
something like the noise they could hear in the mists.
He suppressed a shiver.

'It's coming from over there,' Febel said, pointing in
an approximate direction.

Hurrying as fast as was possible given the conditions, the three men raced off in the direction of the
sound. As he ran with the others, Dieter was careful to
keep his senses sharp. The fog was so thick, it would
be all too easy to blunder directly into the enemy.

For a second, Dieter wondered whether the mist
was entirely natural in character. He had heard the
shamans and sorcerers of the Empire's enemies were
capable of every manner of trick: spells that could
conjure storms, plagues of insects, pestilences and
other miseries. Surely an impenetrable wall of fog, to
better be able to ambush their human opponents,
would not be beyond them?

As swiftly as the idea occurred to Dieter, he rejected
it. He told himself the haze around them was simply
a natural phenomenon, typical of the season. It was
an early morning mist, nothing more.

Suddenly, three brutish shapes reared up out of the
mists. Catching sight of them just in time, Krug and
Febel raised their shields and made ready to meet
their new opponents. Falling in beside them, Dieter
raised his shield as well. Wary of the fact that he had
not yet drilled with the Scarlets, he was careful to
leave some space between himself and the others –
standing close enough so he could cover their flank,
but not so close he might get in their way and endan-
ger them all.

The monsters were orcs. Dieter had never seen them in the flesh before, but one look at the creatures' jutting jaws and slab-browed, bestial features was enough for him to identify them from the descriptions of Helmut Schau.

Each of the orcs was armed with a shield and a heavy sword with a huge, cleaver-like blade. Where their human opponents were quick to adopt battle formation, the orcs fought without regard for any such tactical subtlety. Bellowing with rage, they charged forward, red eyes shining at the lure of bloodshed.

One of them made for Dieter. Stepping forward to meet its charge, Dieter reminded himself of the lessons learned fighting beastmen the day before. When the orc lashed out at him with its sword, Dieter was careful not to meet the blade directly with his shield for fear the orc's attack would smash right through it. Instead, he feinted with the shield as though he was going to parry with it, before sidestepping the attack at the last moment.

As the orc's blade slashed through empty air, Dieter thrust his sword at the gap created in the creature's guard. The blade struck home, stabbing deep through the monster's hide and into its chest. Pulling the sword free as the orc grunted in pain, Dieter resumed a high guard position, confident his enemy was about to fall.

He was wrong. Turning to face him once more, the orc spat out a mouthful of dark blood and showed its teeth in a snarl.

Dieter was sure he had stabbed the creature in the heart, but incredibly the orc seemed hardly fazed by the wound. Redoubling its efforts to kill him, the orc charged forward once more, swinging its sword as it uttered a roaring cry of defiance.

Trying a variation on his previous tactic, Dieter dodged the blow and tried to slash at the back of its legs, aiming to hamstring the orc for an easy kill.

This time, the orc was ready for him. Catching him with the edge of its shield, it swatted Dieter like a fly, hitting him with a force that sent him reeling. Barely managing to keep his feet, Dieter took a more open stance as the orc turned to face him again, hoping to tempt his enemy into making another charge.

He did not have to wait long. With a roar, the orc lumbered forward. Making another feint, Dieter jinked as though he was going right, before he suddenly rushed to the left. The movement exposed the orc's right side as it lifted its sword to strike. Dieter thrust his own sword forward with all his might, the blade stabbing between the monster's ribs and digging deep. Pulling the weapon free with a twist, Dieter stabbed at his target a second time before the orc could react. Disengaging swiftly, he took a step backward, moving to a safe position beyond the orc's reach.

Again, the orc snarled in defiance. But, this time, the damage done was more than it could shrug off. It moved a step forward. Then, another step, its sword falling from a dying hand even as it tried to shuffle onward to revenge itself on its enemy. Before Dieter's eyes, the orc collapsed to its knees and slumped forward as its lifeless body fell to the ground.

Breathing an uneasy sigh of relief, Dieter looked about him, checking on his companions. Krug and Febel had defeated their opponents, but Dieter felt a brief sliver of pride as he noticed the orc he had killed was larger than either of theirs.

In the course of the fight, with his mind focused on his duel with the orc, he had been only dimly aware of the sounds around him. Now, Dieter realised he could hear the noises of a nearby battle.

Without a word between them, he pushed on into the mists with Krug and Febel beside him, seeking its source.

After another few minutes' progress, the origin of the sounds became plain. As ever, it was difficult to see clearly through the film of the mists, but it was quickly apparent they had come upon the main centre of the conflict.

All around them, Scarlets skirmished with orcs and goblins. Throwing himself headlong into the struggle, Dieter caught two goblins unaware as they made ready to shoot arrows into the backs of the soldiers with their bows. Smashing one to the ground with his shield, Dieter split the other goblin's head in two with a blow from his sword.

Spotting one of the Scarlets was in trouble, Dieter raced over to support him. The man was facing two orcs armed with spears. Hemmed in on either side, the man had lost his shield. He had been forced back against a tree as the orcs closed in on him scenting victory.

Charging to the man's aid, Dieter attacked one of the orcs. Taking advantage of the element of surprise, he stabbed his sword into the thick mass of muscle where the orc's head met its shoulders. It was like cutting through bundled layers of cowhide, but by putting all his strength and momentum behind it Dieter killed the creature with a single blow.

Becoming aware of Dieter's presence, the second orc turned to meet him – only to be spitted like a piece of meat as Dieter and the trapped Scarlet thrust their swords in tandem, running the monster through.

'My thanks, young blood,' the man said. 'You're like an answer to my prayers. I thought I was done for there.'

It was Rieger. Before, in the mists and the confusion of battle, Dieter hadn't recognised him. Looking about him, Dieter realised he had lost sight of Krug and Febel when he leapt into the fray.

'Where are the others?' Dieter asked as he and Rieger paused for a few seconds to catch their breaths.

'The rest of the file, you mean?' Rieger gestured with his sword at the tumult around them. 'Somewhere in this disorder. True to form, we blundered into the greenskins in the mists. I'd almost think they were waiting for us, but they seemed as surprised at the turn of events as we were. After that, it was all blood and madness. A typical battle in other words.'

Hefting his sword, Rieger picked up his fallen shield and strode on to rejoin the skirmish.

'Come on, Lanz. We've rested long enough. Stay close to me and let's show these greenskins what war really means.'

Letting Rieger take the lead, Dieter followed him into combat. At first, he was unsure whether the older man was not just charging blindly back into the fight. It quickly became clear, however, that Rieger had a specific aim in mind.

Ahead, an embattled group of Scarlets were desperately trying to hold off a much larger force of orcs and goblins. Yelling at the top of his voice, Rieger charged at the nearest orc, his sword swinging in a deadly arc.

'Forward the 3rd!' Rieger shouted. 'Forward for Hochland! Forward the Scarlets!'

Around the battlefield, the battle cry was repeated as other men took up the chant. Standing close to Rieger, matching him stroke for stroke as they cut relentlessly into the greenskins before them, Dieter joined in the cry. Rising above the cacophony of battle, the sound reached a stirring crescendo.

'Forward the 3rd! Forward for Hochland! Forward the Scarlets!'

The cry did its work. It seemed to spur the Scarlets on to greater efforts. With renewed ferocity, they laid into the greenskins. Goblins and orcs died in ever greater numbers, lessening the disparity between human and greenskin forces.

Almost imperceptibly at first, a change came over the enemy. Whether it was the result of his and Rieger's unexpected attack from behind them, the Scarlets' renewed efforts, or the battle cry booming across the field of slaughter, Dieter could not be sure.

It started as the goblins broke and ran, leaving their larger cousins to fight on without them. No longer possessing superior numbers, the orcs were left at a sudden disadvantage. Making their own numbers tell, the Scarlets redoubled their assault. Outnumbered two to one in places, the remaining orcs were swiftly dispatched.

The fighting ended with unexpected abruptness. Finishing a fallen orc with a stroke from his sword, Dieter looked about him to find another enemy and saw there were none left standing. In their place, the surviving Scarlets stood on the battlefield, surveying the scene. The sense of relief was all but palpable. For an instant, blessed silence reigned.

It was only a brief respite. Within seconds of the fall of the last enemy, a new tumult replaced the receding storm of war. Men wounded in the battle called out for aid, their comrades rushed to them, sergeants yelled orders. Other men, glad to be alive, clapped their hands, shouted oaths, exulted to the heavens.

'You survived then?'

Turning at the sound of a voice behind him, Dieter saw Gerhardt approach him, followed by Holst. Their weapons and armour were splattered with orc gore. Glancing down at himself, Dieter realised he was in the same condition.

'Well?' Gerhardt asked. 'What did you think of your first time in the field with the Scarlets? I take it you did your duty?'

'He did fine, Gerhardt,' Rieger said. 'A credit to his teacher. I never met Helmut Schau, but he must be a lion to raise such a fierce cub.'

Dieter had briefly lost sight of him in the scrum of battle, but the blond man appeared at his side once more, polishing blood from his sword.

'I did my best,' Dieter said. Ordinarily, it was his habit to project a shield of bravado, but in the aftermath of so much bloodshed he felt strangely humble.

'Don't get cocky,' Gerhardt warned him. 'I won't belabour the point now, but I told you to stay close. We thought we'd lost you in the mists. You were lucky you didn't run into the orcs on your own. If that had happened, your head would be adorning some chieftain's trophy-pole right about now.'

The mists were starting to clear. In the east, the sun had become visible above the treetops, a baleful eye staring down at the carnage. Looking up at it, Dieter realised it felt good to be alive.

He did not have the chance to savour the emotion for long. As he stood talking with Gerhardt and the others, a warning cry attracted their attention. Spotting a soldier standing a little distance away, waving frantically to beckon them towards him, they went over to see the source of his unease.

The soldier was standing at a place where the ground unexpectedly dipped. The early morning mist having lifted, burned off by the rising sun, it was possible to see their surroundings properly for the first time.

As Dieter walked forward, he took advantage of the improved visibility to scan the area. With the clearing of the mists, it had become obvious they were standing on the lip of a river valley. Looking downward, he saw a gentle slope falling down to a snaking river which had carved its way over thousands of years through the surrounding woodlands. Dieter did not know what the river was called, but based on their location he judged it to be one of the tributaries of the Talabec, carrying cold melt waters from the Middle Mountains down to join the Talabec south of the Howling Hills.

Whatever the soldier had seen had caused no little consternation. At first, as Dieter joined the small group of men standing at the lip of the valley, he could see no sign of anything untoward. Then, glancing in the direction of the soldier's pointing finger, he saw something that turned his blood to ice.

There were greenskins in the valley. There were tens of thousands, more of them than he could count. Comparing their numbers to the relatively limited force of orcs they had fought in the mists would have been like comparing a raindrop to the wide expanse of the ocean.

The orcs were crossing the river, coming in their direction. Fortunately, they had not yet spotted the group of men standing on the vantage above them.

Looking down through the cover of the trees, Dieter saw massed ranks of goblins hauling siege engines, orcs riding boars and chariots, goblin wolf riders; he even thought he caught a glimpse of a troll. He swallowed hard, finding his mouth was suddenly dry.

This was no mob of raiders or scouting party. It was an entire greenskin army, he suspected larger in size than anything General von Nieder had expected.

To make matters worse, the orcs were headed straight for the Hochlanders' camp.

CHAPTER FIVE
A STRANGE THUNDER

'I HAVE SPOKEN to Captain Harkner,' Sergeant Bohlen said. 'The good news is that the regiment is retreating. The bad news is that we are the rearguard.'

Several minutes had passed since the presence of the orc army had been discovered. In that time, decisions had been made.

A runner had been sent to find Captain Harkner. Arriving at the scene to see things for himself, the captain had immediately ordered the men to pull back from the lip of the valley. So far, the greenskins had been too busy squabbling amongst themselves as they crossed the river to notice they were being watched, but Harkner was wary the enemy might have sent scouts on ahead of them. Accordingly, he pulled his troops back into cover, leaving only a few men as lookouts to monitor the greenskins' progress.

After that, the captain had summoned the senior men from each file to a terse conference.

To Dieter, they seemed the longest moments he had ever known. Excluded from the deliberations, ordered to wait with the other men of his file while Sergeant Bohlen consulted with the captain, he was painfully aware of the orcs' proximity.

In reality, he supposed the greenskins were at least half a league away as yet, all of it uphill and across heavily forested terrain. As long as the enemy cavalry remained unaware of their presence, it might take them as long as half an hour to reach the Scarlets' position. They might even bypass them entirely, missing them in the cover of the woodland. Still, Dieter did not relish the prospect of betting his life on those odds.

By the time Bohlen returned, it was clear the other members of the file held similar views to Dieter. They gathered around the sergeant eagerly, hoping for good news.

They were quickly disappointed.

'Ours is the most dangerous job,' Bohlen told them. 'But someone has to do it. When the captain asked me if I thought we were up to it, I had no hesitation in telling him we were.'

'Lucky for us,' Krug muttered under his breath, his words attracting hostile stares from those close enough to hear them.

'Do you have a problem, Krug?' Bohlen glowered at him.

'No, sergeant.'

In the aftermath of the skirmish, it had become plain Krug and Febel had survived intact. As yet neither of them had said anything to Dieter about the events at the peasant hut earlier in the day, but a few menacing stares from Krug had been enough to warn him the affair had not been forgotten. For his part, Dieter had not decided whether he should report the two men's behaviour to Sergeant Bohlen. He was inclined to ask Gerhardt or Rieger for their opinion, but for the present he thought he should let the matter rest. There were far more pressing issues ahead of them.

'The rest of the regiment will withdraw in stages, file by file,' Bohlen said. 'The captain has already sent runners ahead to take news of the orcs to our army. But, if they don't make it, it is the duty of every man in the regiment to make sure the news gets through. If not, there's the danger the greenskin bastards will catch the encampment unawares. We all have friends and comrades back at camp. I take it I don't need to tell you what'll happen to them if the orcs overrun it?'

No one among the men of the file tried to answer his question. The glum expressions on their faces were answer enough.

'It's our job to cover for the others so they can escape,' Bohlen continued. He pointed to a trail that cut through the trees and led over the lip of the valley. 'There aren't enough of us to form a line and guard the whole area, so we'll position ourselves in the place where the greenskins' scouts are most likely to emerge. This trail here seems the easiest way up from the river. We'll set up on either side of it and hope for best.'

* * *

'WELL, THAT'S IT,' Holst said, ten minutes later. 'It's in Sigmar's hands now. We'll just have to trust to his mercy.'

'Sigmar's mercy?' Rieger lifted a sardonic eyebrow. 'I suspect you would've had to have lived a more virtuous life, my friend, to have any hope of that.'

In accordance with Sergeant Bohlen's instructions, the ten men of the file had split into two groups of five and hidden themselves on either side of the trail that led up from the river. Preferring to avoid any further entanglement with either Krug or Febel, Dieter was relieved when Bohlen ordered him to join the men on the opposite side of the trail to theirs.

He had been assigned to the left side of the trail, to a five-man group commanded by Gerhardt, alongside Holst, Rieger and Kuranski. Given that an entire enemy army was probably headed towards them, it seemed a pitifully small force with which to meet their advance.

Still, the Scarlets had done their best to make sure any impending battle was not wholly one-sided. Expecting the leading elements of the enemy army to be scouts or fast cavalry, they had laid a length of rope across the trail, camouflaging its existence with fallen leaves. Other than that, they could only wait.

'At least I'm better off than Kuranski,' Holst said. 'Admittedly, I'm no theologian. But I can't see Sigmar performing any miracles on behalf of a Kislevite.'

Holst turned to Kuranski with a mischievous smile.

'What gods do they worship in Kislev anyhow, Kuranski? Whoever they are, I'd say you'd better start praying at once. Of course, you're so far away from your homeland, they might not be able to hear you.'

'You can kiss my backside, Holst,' Kuranski hissed back. 'I keep telling you, I'm only half-Kislevite. My father was from Kislev, but my mother was born in Hergig – just like I was. That means I'm as much a Hochlander as you are. Assuming you ever knew your parents well enough to be able to tell where they came from.'

'Personally, I'd always assumed Holst was raised by wolves,' Rieger offered. 'It would account for his atrocious table manners.'

'Hnn, we can't all be born with a silver spoon in our mouths,' Holst grunted. 'You are so fastidious about everything, Rieger, it surprises me you didn't try to become a tax collector when they wouldn't let you be a priest. You have the personality for it.'

'Quiet,' Gerhardt said, his quiet voice commanding instant authority. 'I think I heard something. Listen.'

Straining his ears as the others fell silent, Dieter wondered initially whether Gerhardt was hearing things. Then, distantly, he heard a series of unfamiliar sounds coming from further down the trail. It was a soft sound, more like the padding of giant paws than the harsh echo of hooves.

Whatever was making the noise was coming nearer. Without realising it, Dieter's hand tightened on the hilt of his sword.

'Wait for the signal,' Gerhardt whispered, noticing his behaviour. 'And keep it quiet, all of you. Their ears will be sharp.'

Even as Dieter tried to guess what manner of creatures were approaching, their identity was abruptly revealed as a pack of a dozen or so giant wolves appeared at the end of the trail. As a small boy, grow-ing up at the mill, he had occasionally seen the paw prints left by such creatures on the edge of the forest. However, it was the first time he had seen wolves of such great size in the flesh.

Even more remarkably, the wolves had riders. He supposed, given the animals were the size of horses, it made sense that goblins had long ago decided to use them as mounts. Certainly, both species shared a common savagery and cunning.

If anything, the goblins he could see riding down the trail on wolfback were more savage and barbaric than the ones he had already encountered. Perhaps it was a measure of the confidence that came to them from riding their wolfish mounts, but in their behav-iour they seemed more reminiscent of orcs than goblins.

Each wolf rider was festooned with grisly trophies, presumably taken from vanquished opponents. Dieter saw leather cords that held severed heads, dried animal claws and other unpleasant objects, dangling from the riders and their mounts. The riders themselves were well-armed, each carrying a spear, shield, bow and a quiver of arrows.

Watching them, Dieter realised Captain Harkner had been right to be wary of the threat of enemy scouts. There was no doubt the wolf riders had been sent ahead of the main greenskin army to scout the terrain. If Dieter and the other men of Sergeant Bohlen's file attacked them, there was every chance some of the wolf riders would escape to bring back reinforcements. There was no other option, however.

They could not let the wolf riders get past them for fear the goblins would discover the rest of the regiment.

Dieter understood the logic of the situation. It was better for a ten-man rearguard to be exposed to danger rather than to run the risk of the greenskins riding down their fleeing regiment. If he and the men around him were destined to be the sacrificial lambs in order to keep their retreating comrades safe, so be it. It was the soldier's way.

The wolf riders were coming closer. Dieter would have expected them to advance more cautiously through unknown terrain, but their mounts moved down the trail at a loping gallop. Suddenly mindful of the keenness of a wolf's sense of smell, Dieter glanced at the leaves around him to see which way the wind was blowing. If the wolves sensed their odour, it would ruin everything.

Seemingly unaware of the human presence, the wolf riders kept coming. The lead riders were almost abreast of Dieter and the others' hiding place. He could feel his heart pounding in his chest, so loud it seemed a wonder no one else could hear it. The air felt charged with invisible tension.

A shrill whistle sounded from the other side of the trail. It was the signal to attack.

'Now!' Gerhardt yelled, as the Scarlets emerged from hiding.

On either side of the trail, two men pulled hard on the rope, lifting it to head height as the goblins rode past. Riding into the rope, the three leading goblins were thrown back from their mounts and sent tumbling to the ground. Meanwhile, the other men of the file had charged from cover, catching the wolf riders by surprise.

Dieter was among them. Attacking the nearest goblin to him, he parried its spear thrust and jerked the creature from its saddle, pulling it down forcefully enough to dash the goblin's head against the hard ground. Almost immediately, he realised his mistake as the goblin's mount turned and snarled. Too late, it occurred to Dieter that fighting wolf riders was not like fighting men on horseback – not when the mount was potentially more dangerous than its rider.

Jumping out of the way as the wolf whirled and snapped its jaws at him, Dieter cautiously backed away from the animal. Hoping to draw it into making a lunge, he shook his shield at it and stepped forward as though he was going to charge it.

The wolf took the bait. Leaping forward, it tried to pounce on him and knock him from his feet, but Dieter was faster. Correctly gauging the animal's angle of attack, he sidestepped it and stabbed his sword deep into its side, just behind the wolf's front leg.

Howling, the wolf turned back on itself and tried to bite Dieter, but the lethal blow had already been struck. Overcome by sudden weakness, it collapsed to the ground and died.

Startled, Dieter heard another howl as a figure charged towards him from the side. Expecting another wolf, he was surprised to see it was a goblin – the rider of the wolf he had killed. Its head bleeding from the wound inflicted when Dieter had pulled it from its saddle, the goblin let out a weird, undulating cry as it closed to melee distance and attacked. Dieter knew nothing of these creatures and their ways, but it seemed to him the goblin was reacting with some deep emotion as though the death of its mount had moved it to rage.

Whatever the case, it hardly mattered. Without its wolf, the goblin was a less fearful proposition. Almost as an afterthought, Dieter dispatched it with a quick stroke of his sword.

Looking about him, he saw the skirmish was over. The other men of the file had killed the rest of the wolf riders and their mounts without sustaining any serious injuries. More importantly, none of the goblins had escaped to raise the alarm.

'All right,' Sergeant Bohlen said, once he was sure all the enemy were dead. 'We drag the bodies back into the undergrowth and set up as before. If we're lucky, we'll take the next group of scouts along this road in exactly the same way.'

The men moved to follow his orders, but before they could finish their labours a commotion from further down the trail grabbed their attention.

Another half-dozen wolf riders suddenly appeared at the end of the trail. Spotting the Scarlets as they were busily dragging away the corpses of the goblins they had already killed, the wolf riders let loose a hasty volley of arrows, turned tail and galloped away in the direction they had come. The arrows fell short, leaving the Scarlets unharmed, but the damage was already done.

'Rhya's teats!' Bohlen cursed as the scouts rode away. 'That's torn it! Inside a quarter of an hour every

111

greenskin in the area will be on us like dung on a bull's arse.'

The sergeant scanned the trail in both directions, casting watchful eyes at the looming shapes of the trees in the forest around them.

'We've got no choice,' he said, after he had considered the matter for a few seconds. 'Now the greenskins know where we are, they can come at us from every angle and tear us apart. Our position on this trail is no longer defensible.'

'There's a woodsman's hut further along here,' Holst said, pointing vaguely eastwards. 'One of the local huntsmen mentioned it to me last night. I didn't see it when we came this way earlier because of the mists, but from what the huntsman told me, I'd say it's over in that direction.'

'There'd be a wood pile there,' Gerhardt said. 'Maybe some bigger logs. Assuming we can reach it before the greenskins, it wouldn't take us long to create a barricade we could fight behind. That way, we could make more of a stand. Give the rest of the regiment more time to escape.'

'We could even set fire to the hut itself,' Rieger picked up the theme. 'It would make it more likely the orc army would be drawn toward us rather than tracking the regiment. Orcs love nothing more than some smoke and fire. It would attract them to us like moths to a flame.'

Long seconds passed in silence as the sergeant thought it through. Standing nearby, Dieter wondered whether they were talking about the same hut where he and Krug had nearly come to blows. He

worried whether he should say something to someone about the old woman's body, but a murderous
glare from Krug made him hold silent. It was not so
much that the other man frightened him; more that it
seemed an inappropriate time to bring the matter up,
given they were likely to be fighting side by side
against the orcs at any moment.

'We'll head for this hut,' Sergeant Bohlen said,
finally. 'It sounds like a better place to make a stand.
Holst, you lead the way. Breitmeyer, you're our rearguard. Right then, there's no time like the present.
Quick time, two men in tandem. Let's get going.'

Following the sergeant's lead, the men formed up
two-abreast, with Holst at the front of the short column and Breitmeyer at the rear. At a signal from
Bohlen, they began to jog down the trail in search of
the hut.

Uncomfortably close to Krug and Febel in the
marching order, Dieter wondered what would happen at the hut when they found it.

IN THE END, they didn't make it.

Having first encountered the hut when the forest
was still shrouded in early morning mist, Dieter had
no clear idea of where it was. He would have had a
better chance of finding an obscure tavern on the
docks of Talabheim, a city he had never visited, than
of finding his way back to the hut.

Similarly, having only the half-remembered directions he had heard from a huntsman to go on, Holst
showed no great aptitude in leading his comrades to
their destination. Nor did Krug or Febel volunteer any

information – if they had any. However, the greatest
obstacle the men of Sergeant Bohlen's file faced in
reaching the hut was not a lack of directions. It was
that the orcs did not leave them alone long enough to
be able to find it.

The first attack came after only a few minutes.
Bohlen's men were jogging along the trail when
they heard the sound of wild whoops and war cries.
A new group of wolf riders had appeared on the
trail behind them. Foregoing any attempt at subtlety, they seemed intent on riding the Scarlets
down.

'Form up on me,' Bohlen said, his eyes narrowing
as he saw the enemy. 'I want two ranks of five,
spread across the trail with the first rank in skirmish
formation. First rank, you're to let the riders pass
you. Second rank, stay tight enough to lock shields
with each other. You're the wall that breaks their
charge. When they see you, they'll have to pull up.
That's when we'll skewer them.'

Following the example of the other men around
him, Dieter took up a position in the second rank.

They readied to meet the wolf riders' charge in
exactly the way that Sergeant Bohlen had directed.
The first rank of five men stood strung across the
trail, posted far enough apart to let the goblins ride
through the gaps and pass by the side of them.

The second rank adopted a tighter formation. The
men stood close together, each man's shield edge-
to-edge with the shields of the men on either side of
him. With their swords held thrusting outward in a
high guard position, the five men had created a

shield wall – making an impenetrable barrier across the centre of the trail, studded with sharp points.

The shield wall was an unusual tactic for a group of swordsmen. Mostly utilised by units of spearmen who could make better use of the longer reach of their weapons, it was one of the most ancient and venerable manoeuvres in the tactical lexicon of the armies of the Empire. Legend had it the shield wall was one of the many innovations the god Sigmar had brought to human warfare when he still walked the land as a man.

In his youth, Dieter had practised the shield wall often. Helmut Schau had insisted on it. As the only experienced soldier in the village, Helmut had been commander of the local militia as well as a miller. He had drilled the other members of the militia in the tactic relentlessly, telling them the strength of their shield wall might one day stand between them and certain death.

For Dieter, today was that day. Using the formation now, to fight mankind's natural enemies the greenskins, he felt part of an unbroken line of human achievement and succession stretching back over two and a half thousand years to the founding of the Empire and beyond.

'The strength of the shield wall is the collective strength of every man in it,' Helmut had taught him. 'Each man must do his duty. He must hold the line in face of the enemy charge, in face of his own fear. He must hold the line, or else the wall breaks and he dooms his comrades.'

Mindful of the lesson, Dieter ignored the nervous butterflies fluttering in his stomach and set himself to receive the goblins' charge. As the wolf riders came closer, it occurred to him it took a special courage, or a special madness, for a soldier to hold his ground when cavalry were charging towards him.

Setting aside their bows, the goblins held their spears couched under their arms like lances as they charged. As they closed the distance to the infantry, the sound of wolf paws padding on the hard ground of the trail grew louder until it resembled a strange kind of thunder accompanied by the noise of claws scratching in the dirt. It took every ounce of bravery in Dieter's soul to hold the line in the face of the charging enemy. It was the wolves, not the goblins, that he found most frightening. With slavering jaws and hungry eyes, they seemed the nightmare creatures of his nursery dreams given wicked flesh.

'First rank! Let them pass!'

Sergeant Bohlen shouted out the order a split second before his men came within range of the goblin spears. Acting with well-drilled precision, the men of the first rank abruptly stood aside to let the goblins pass, melting away before the wolves or their riders could touch them.

Carried on by the momentum of their charge, the wolf riders found themselves bearing down on the second rank's shield wall with its line of gleaming sword-points. Not unnaturally, they tried to halt their advance, the charge coming to a shuddering halt as the wolves at the back collided with the wolves further forward.

'Now!' Sergeant Bohlen's voice sounded among the din of shouting goblins and snarling wolves. 'Shut the gate!'

The men of the first rank charged into the back of the wolf riders while the second rank advanced forward at their front. Caught between the two groups of swordsmen, hemmed in on top of each other in an ever-decreasing space, the wolf riders' superior numbers counted for nothing.

The Scarlets made short work of them, swords stabbing again and again into the confused enemy mass. Having learned a lesson when fighting the last group of wolf riders, Dieter was careful this time to always strike for the wolf first and not the rider.

Even as he joined in with the others, his sword stabbing mechanically back-and-forth as blood sprayed into the air and fell to drench the hard earth, he was amazed at how quickly he had become accustomed to the grisly nature of warfare. He had never been squeamish, but once he might have felt uneasy at having to slaughter an enemy who had no chance to escape, to hear their dying screams, to feel their slick blood underfoot.

In the face of war with the greenskins, all his kinder emotions had left him. It was not so much that he hated them, though in common with most people in the Empire he believed it was the destiny of orc and man to be eternal enemies. He was moved by a simpler, less complex imperative. He killed them because it was the nature of war; kill or be killed.

More quickly than he would have thought possible, it was over. As the last of the enemy fell, the Scarlets walked among the fallen bodies of wolf and goblin, making sure they were dead and dispatching any that were not with quick, merciless strokes.

Following the lead of his comrades Dieter joined in with their work, but he had no real stomach for it. Now the heat of combat had left him, he felt queasy about such tasks. He recognised that any enemy left alive might later try to strike them down, but it was harder to kill in cold blood – even when the target was a goblin. It was the way of war between human and greenskin. Neither side took prisoners. No quarter was given, nor was it asked for. For all that though, Dieter found it hard to be the one who had to do the bloody work of killing a wounded enemy.

Looking for some mental respite, he gazed at the forest around him. It occurred to him that the section of trail where the Scarlets had made their stand was particularly narrow. At the same time, the trees on either side of the trail were thicker and positioned more closely together. Realising that Sergeant Bohlen must have intentionally chosen the best place for his men to take a stand once the wolf riders were spotted, Dieter was filled by an admiration for his sergeant.

'Look lively,' Sergeant Bohlen said, his voice snapping Dieter out of his reverie. 'There's more of them.'

Another group of goblins had appeared at the end of the trail. This time, the enemy were on foot. There were more of them as well. Several dozen were in sight already, with more in a long line snaking away in the distance along the trail.

'They're not scouts,' Gerhardt said. 'It's a goblin mob, could be a thousand strong or more. And, if they're here, the rest of the army won't be far behind. It'll take more than ten men and a shield wall to deal with that lot.'

'What do we do, then?' Dieter asked. He looked to the faces of the men around him. 'If that's true, they'll have us outnumbered a hundred to one. How do we hold them back?'

'We don't,' Sergeant Bohlen said. 'We've done our best, held back the enemy scouts long enough for the rest of the regiment to escape. But that lot there will roll over us like a grinder over oats. We'd last maybe ten seconds against them. We've done our duty.

'Now, we run.'

THAT NIGHT, AND for many nights afterwards, the next hour would serve as a source for Dieter's nightmares. Where earlier the Scarlets had jogged along the trail trying to maintain an even pace, they now ran as fast as they could.

With the goblins behind them, they ran for their lives.

Lungs burning, his breath rasping like sandpaper through his throat, Dieter tried to keep up with the others. He had thought himself in good shape, full of youthful energy and vigour, but before they had covered barely three hundred paces he found himself flagging.

His body was bathed in sweat, soaking through his clothes, the salt of his own perspiration itching at his skin like acid. The weight of his weapons, shield and armour seemed unbearable. He wanted to cast them away, to lighten his load, but he saw the other Scarlets still carried theirs.

He refused to do anything that might make him seem weak or unable to meet the same demands as the others. He would rather face death than dishonour. He would not do anything that might give cause for anyone to whisper he was unworthy to be a member of the regiment. He realised his pride might end up killing him, but he took comfort from the thought he would die as a Scarlet.

The goblins were hard on their trail, dogging their tracks. Dieter heard a cacophony of shrill whoops and war cries as the goblins egged each other on. The enemy seemed to be right behind them, breathing down their necks. It seemed impossible they would not catch them.

Afterwards, he could not have said how long the pursuit lasted. It felt like it went on for hours, but it could not have been more than half an hour at most. The men were perhaps only a league away from their encampment. Ordinarily, it was the kind of distance a man might run in eight or nine minutes. Encumbered by armour, hampered by the broken, uneven terrain of the forest, it took the men of the file considerably longer.

In the end, Dieter supposed that fate – or even Sigmar – played a role in their salvation. If there had been any more wolf riders with the goblins chasing them, if Dieter and the others had not already killed them, the enemy would have been able to run them down. As it was, the Scarlets managed to stay ahead of the goblins by the skin of their teeth. Running as though all the powers and principalities of the damned were on their trail, the men finally found their way to the edge of the forest.

'Come on!' Gerhardt breathed hoarsely. Seeing Dieter catch his ankle and stumble over a tree root, he caught him and pulled him to his feet. 'We're nearly there! They won't dare keep chasing us once we're past the tree line.'

Following numbly in Gerhardt's wake, it was all Dieter could do to keep going. The last part of the pursuit was the worst.

Ahead, he could see sunlight breaking through the trees. The tree line, where the forest met the open ground of the clearing in which their army had made its encampment, was only a couple of hundred paces away. They seemed the slowest steps Dieter had ever taken. It felt as though he was running underwater, his legs leaden and unresponsive. Behind them, the screams of the goblin mob were terrifyingly loud.

In his nightmares, this would always be the moment when he realised he was no longer making any progress. Looking down, he would see his legs flailing uselessly in the mud, unable to make progress or gain any purchase no matter how hard he ran.

Thankfully, in this case, reality diverged from his dreams. Given an extra boost of acceleration by the fact he was so close to escape, he emerged out of the forest and into the clearing with a speed that belied his exhaustion.

Breaking into the open, he staggered a further handful of steps before casting a nervous glance over his shoulder to see whether Gerhardt was right. He could no longer see them clearly through the trees, but it was apparent the goblins had halted their pursuit. Wary of being caught out in the open within sight of the human encampment, they stopped, glowering angrily after the men who had escaped them.

'What in the name of Sigmar...' Dieter heard Sergeant Bohlen's voice, its tone raised by a note of astonishment. 'What the hell happened here?'

Looking around him, Dieter was glad to see that the other men of the file had survived – even Krug and Febel. At first, he was at a loss to work out what had caused Bohlen's astonishment. When he turned toward the encampment he thought that everything was as it should be.

It was clear the army was in the middle of packing up. Even from a distance, Dieter could see the camp fires had been doused and the tents were in the process of being packed away, ready for transit. It was no more than he would have expected. With such a large army and so many supplies to be transported, it was best to get a jump on things so that when General von Nieder gave the order to break camp everything would be ready.

Then, looking at the camp more closely, Dieter realised something was missing. There should have been a perimeter of wooden pickets set around the camp, guarded by sentries. The pickets had been there last night, but this morning there was no sign of them. Appalled, Dieter realised the pickets and their sentries were not the only parts of the camp's defence that were missing. The cannons he had seen in emplacements last night, designed to support the pickets, were nowhere to be seen.

Without pickets, sentries or artillery to guard its perimeter, the camp was left open and unprepared. Turning back to look at the forest, he wondered how long it would be before the orcs they had seen crossing the river arrived at the clearing and realised the human camp was ripe for attack. With thousands of orcs potentially about to come screaming from the tree line, the Hochlanders' camp was next to defenceless.

Dieter found he was wondering the same thing as Sergeant Bohlen. When the Scarlets had left in the pre-dawn light to sweep the woods, they had left behind an encampment that was ready to face an enemy attack. In the meantime, inexplicably, the camp had packed away its defences, all but inviting the orcs to attack them.

What the hell had happened?

From
The Testimony of General Ludwig von Grahl
(unexpurgated text):

…In all the annals of battle in Hochland, it is hard to think of a more disastrous decision. For reasons best know to himself, General von Nieder ordered his army to break camp without first waiting to hear the reports of the units he had sent to sweep the surrounding woodlands for greenskins.

Granted, von Nieder was not to know the entire orc army was within a few leagues of his encampment. But, by refusing to wait until the woods had been completely scouted and pronounced clear, he needlessly exposed his forces to danger.

By the time the first messengers arrived with news the enemy were on their doorstep, the pickets and other defensive measures designed to protect the camp from attack had already been removed and packed away. Similarly, the army's artillery had been taken from their positions and prepared for transit.

Worse, earlier in the morning, von Nieder had sent all his cavalry – including his knights, outriders, pistoliers, mercenaries and other assorted mounted troops – on ahead in advance of the rest of the army.

With the greenskins about to attack, there was no time to recall the cavalry, nor to re-deploy the artillery and pickets. Although the infantry hurried to deploy in battle formations, the situation left the entire encampment severely exposed.

Afterwards, in an attempt to explain his decisions, von Nieder would claim he had been badly advised. He would insist he had checked with his staff and they had told him the woods had been cleared. Given such circumstances, he argued the decision to break camp was entirely reasonable.

Obviously, von Nieder's story was a tissue of lies designed to deflect blame on to others. For myself, I suspect his decision to break camp was largely based on a misreading of orc intentions. Despite the scale of the invasion, von Nieder assumed the enemy had come to Hochland as raiders. Accordingly, he expected them to move comparatively slowly as they paused to pillage every village and township along the way.

The reality was different. The greenskins moved swiftly. No one would ever know the reason, but it seemed Morgoth Ironfang was intent on utterly destroying Hochland – not by inflicting piecemeal devastation, but by striking southwards to the very heart of the province. Perhaps Ironfang saw himself as some re-embodiment of the great orc warlords of old, come to sweep away mankind and reclaim the orcs' ancestral homelands. Perhaps he was just a greenskin with a grudge. Who can say why an orc does anything?

Whatever the case, through his premature decision to break camp, von Nieder had played right into Ironfang's hands...

CHAPTER SIX
BATTLE LINES

By the time Dieter and the others sprinted across the open ground that marked the boundary between the edge of the forest and the beginning of the encampment, it was clear matters were worse than they expected.

Inside the perimeter, the entire camp was in a state of pandemonium. Everywhere Dieter looked, confusion reigned. Officers and sergeants shouted contradictory orders. Messengers ran in every direction. Soldiers raced around like headless chickens.

Clearly, news of the greenskin presence had come before them, but there seemed no coherence to the army's response. Much of the artillery was already packed away, but as Dieter watched he saw some gunners hurrying to unpack their guns while others continued to make their artillery ready for the road as though nothing had changed.

In front of his disbelieving eyes, Dieter saw two captains of artillery come to blows as they argued the point. Soon, a gaggle of gunners had gathered around them, cheering their respective captains as they wrestled in the dirt. Despairing of splitting them apart, a master engineer fired a warning shot from his repeater pistol into the air. It was to no avail.

'Idiots,' Holst rumbled angrily once he saw the fight. 'An army of orcs about to break from the trees and our artillerymen are fighting amongst themselves.'

Abruptly, a familiar figure arrived to adjudicate the matter. Pushing his way toward the combatants through the cheering throng of gunners, Captain Harkner kicked one of the struggling officers in the groin and punched the other in the face. Having got their attention, he remonstrated with them swiftly, before turning back to the crowd of gunners.

'This is an army, not a tavern,' he said, his voice carrying despite the fact he spoke quietly. 'And you are soldiers, not a bunch of drunkards. Any man who fights his comrades is derelict in his duty, as is anyone who stands by and watches them fight without trying to stop it. You all know the punishment for dereliction.'

He stared the gunners down, allowing his words to sink in.

'Get back to work. Get those guns unlimbered and set them to cover the tree line. The orcs are coming, and it could be the artillery is all that will stop this camp from being overrun.'

Cowed, the gunners hurried back to their duties, their bruised captains lagging shamefacedly behind them. Satisfied, Harkner turned away.

'So, you made it then?' Harkner said, greeting Sergeant Bohlen as the men of the file rushed to meet him. 'And you, Gerhardt. And Holst and Rieger and the rest. I see even our new recruit Lanz made it. Good job, all of you. As you can see, you came back just in time.'

'What in the name of Ranald's arse is going on?' Bohlen asked. 'You'll have to excuse my language, sir, but we arrived back here to find it looks like the whole camp has gone mad. Where's the pickets? Who ordered the artillery packed up? There's a horde of greenskins about to break screaming from the trees and the camp is next to defenceless.'

'Ranald's arse is right, sergeant,' Harkner replied darkly. 'Somewhere, the trickster god must be laughing his guts out over this mess. By the time I arrived back at camp with the rest of the regiment, I learned orders had been issued for the army to break camp while we were still in the forest.'

Seeing Bohlen was about to comment, Harkner raised a hand to quiet him.

'I know, sergeant, you needn't say it. It is rank stupidity. What's the point of sending men into the woods to scout for the enemy, if you don't wait for them to report back before you break camp? No doubt someone's head will end up on a pike by way of atonement when all this is over. But, in the meantime, we have more pressing business. How far away were the greenskins last time you saw them?'

'Right on our heels,' Bohlen answered. 'We didn't see any orcs, but the woods were thick with goblins like flies on a cow's backside. They eased off when we reached the tree line, but they'll still be there, watching us. And you can bet with the goblins here already the orcs won't be far behind.'

'Then we'll just have to make sure we have a warm welcome waiting for them,' the captain said. 'I'll warn you now, our position is even more exposed than you may have gathered. If the orcs do attack, we won't have any cavalry to help us. General von Nieder sent the knights and other mounted units on ahead first thing this morning. They are supposed to be scouting the trail for the rest of the army to follow. Naturally, the general sent messengers to recall them when he heard about the greenskins. Though whether they'll get back in time to help us is anybody's guess.'

'No knights?' Bohlen shook his head in disbelief. 'Just when I was thinking things couldn't get worse…'

'I wouldn't worry too much, sergeant,' the captain smiled, trying to make light of the situation. 'Everyone knows it's the infantry who wins the Empire's battles. If anything, we should thank whoever it is that sent the knights away. Finally, we have been granted an opportunity to show our true character.'

'By facing off against an army of greenskins without any cavalry to help us and with most of our artillery still packed away? Frankly, sir, I have always preferred showing my character in less arduous circumstances.'

'Agreed.' The captain shrugged. 'But the situation is what it is, sergeant. We will have to make the best of it we can.'

He pointed west, to an area further along the encampment's perimeter.

'I left the rest of the regiment over there, plugging a gap in the line between two units of spearmen. Take your men to join them. You'll be in command in my absence, Bohlen. Seeing as no one seems to be doing much to prepare the army against the enemy advance, I intend to do what I can to get things organised. I'll return to the regiment when I can.'

'Understood, sir.'

Saluting, Sergeant Bohlen made to turn away, only to pause and glance back at his captain.

'Sir? I'll see you later. Sigmar willing.'

'I'll see you later too, sergeant,' Harkner nodded. He looked toward the trees and the hidden horde of greenskins sheltering somewhere out of sight, before he turned to the men of the file.

'I'll see you all later. Sigmar willing.'

THE SITUATION WAS as dire on the western perimeter as it was everywhere else inside the encampment. Rushing through the camp with the other men of his file, Dieter saw the same scenes of disorder repeated in a dozen varying locations.

Outside a supply tent, a sergeant commanding a unit of handgunners argued heatedly with a quartermaster as he tried to requisition a supply of black powder for his men. Elsewhere, a great cannon had slipped its axle in the middle of one of the thoroughfares through the camp, blocking access; its gunners appealed fruitlessly for help in moving it, but no one listened. Nearby, a messenger dashed from tent to tent and regiment to regiment, searching for a particular officer with a vital dispatch, only to learn no one could help him find the man he was looking for.

The army seemed less a coherent whole, and more a collection of confused individuals. Everyone was caught up in their own personal dramas, following a tangled web of contradictory and frequently out of date orders.

Dieter found it strange that the army's senior commanders were almost nowhere to be seen. It was now, when the army was in crisis, that their role was paramount. In their place, it had fallen to individual sergeants and captains to try and make some sense out of the confusion around them. It was plain they were doing the best they could, but with no clear strategy or coherent plan to follow, their efforts were often incompatible and frequently at odds.

'Look at this,' Holst grumbled as they hurried to find the rest of their regiment. 'Someone needs to give the entire army a kick up the arse, sort things out.'

'So says General Holst,' Rieger said, beside him. 'Perhaps you should take matters in hand. "Sort things out", as you put it.'

'I couldn't make a worse job of it than whoever's responsible for this mess,' Holst snorted.

'Careful what you say,' Gerhardt cautioned him. 'Whatever you may think, you are talking about our commanders. Remember, the punishment for insubordination is having your tongue drilled through with a hot iron.'

'Do they really do that?' Dieter asked. He was out of breath from running, but the idea was so gruesome and frightening he had to hear more. 'Helmut told me about such things, but I wondered sometimes if he wasn't exaggerating.'

'Exaggerating? Hardly.' Holst shook his head. 'I've seen it done. You wouldn't believe the stink of hot fat and burned flesh when you drill a hot iron through a man's tongue. It takes seven men to do it: three to hold the victim down, two to force his mouth open, another to pull out his tongue with a pair of pliers, and the seventh to wield the drill. Even then, the victim's troubles aren't over. A quarter of them don't survive it: they die during the punishment, or afterwards from infections.'

'It's a bad business,' Gerhardt agreed. 'The hole they drill in the tongue never heals fully, so the man speaks with a whistle forever after. That's why they use it as a punishment, as an example to others. You've heard the expression "mind your tongue", haven't you?'

'Yes,' said Dieter.

'Well, now you know where it comes from.'

They had reached the spot where the rest of their regiment was stationed. Bohlen ordered the men of his file to join the ranks while he went to consult with the other sergeants.

'Talking of bad business,' Holst said, once they had greeted their comrades and taken a place to the left of the regimental line. 'I feared for the worst when I heard Captain Harkner say he had posted the regiment to plug the gap between two groups of spearmen. You know there are hard hours ahead when a regiment of swordsmen are posted to the front of the line.'

Dieter immediately understood what he meant. The second they joined their regiment it had become clear the Scarlets had been stationed in the front rank of units positioned to guard the western approaches to the camp. The fact they had been stationed so far forward was a sign of the confusion in the Hochlanders' battle line.

Thanks to Helmut Schau's frequent lessons on strategy and tactics, Dieter knew exactly how the army should have lined up. There was no great secret to the battle plans used by most provincial armies, including Hochland's. Most generals favoured one or more solid blocks of infantry at the centre of their line, supported by cavalry and missile troops on either wing. Other generals preferred to make use of a central body of knights, or alternating blocks of infantry and cavalry set behind a skirmish line of missile troops, but the current absence of the army's knights left no place for such delicate variations. By necessity, the battle line would have to be built around the infantry.

It was the precise composition of the infantry forces making up the battle line on the west of the camp that had caused Holst's disquiet. Ordinarily, units of halberdiers and spearmen would be placed at the front of the line in order to meet the enemy's charge with a forest of spearpoints and the longer reach of their weapons. Regiments of swordsmen were used to support these front rank units, either positioned just behind them as a mobile reserve, or divided into smaller detachments assigned to fight in unison with larger groups of spears or halberds. The fact that the Scarlets had been pressed into service as a front rank unit was a measure of the confusion and desperation currently convulsing the Hochlander army.

'We'll just have to make the best of it,' Gerhardt said. He looked at Dieter, standing beside him.

'You know, you don't have to stand here at the front of the line with the rest of us old hands. You're new, and you haven't been drilled. You can take up a position in the rear rank of the regiment, further back from the action. You needn't worry about repercussions. No one will think bad of you because of it.'

'I'm not worried,' Dieter told him. 'But I'm not moving.'

'You see?' Holst said, almost fondly. 'I told you the boy was all right. He's like a young bull. He's got balls the size of–'

'Quiet, Holst,' Gerhardt cut him off.

He stared at Dieter intently, as though trying to search out any hidden defect of character from among the angles of his face.

'Understand, this is serious, Dieter Lanz. As far as I've seen, you've not put a foot wrong as a soldier. You've done everything that's been asked of you, when it's been asked, and you've done it well. You're handy with a sword. That's good. You've got brass and iron inside you. That's even better. But, so far, you've only faced skirmishes. This is a battle. A real battle. It's a different kettle of broth entirely.'

'It makes no difference,' Dieter replied. 'We're in the same file, so that means we fight side by side. Unless

I hear differently from an officer or a sergeant, I'm not moving. I'll hold the line with the rest of you.'

'Big as cannonballs,' Holst said, proudly. 'You have to admit I unearthed a diamond this time, Gerhardt. Of course, he's a fool for wanting to stay in the front rank when he could go rearward. Then again, we're all fools. You have to be to join the infantry. Now, if I was a knight, I wouldn't even be here. I'd be far away from this battle, along with the rest, on whatever easy errand General von Nieder sent them on. And, to make it even sweeter I'd be sitting on a horse's back, letting him take the strain rather than relying on my poor, tired feet.'

'An unlikely scenario, Holst,' Rieger put in. 'You have to be of *noble* birth to become a knight.'

'And who says I'm not? Didn't I ever tell you the story of my dear mother and her encounter on a Talabec riverboat with the Graf Erich von Doppelfell?'

'Better leave it until later,' Gerhardt told him. 'The enemy seem set on interrupting your tale.'

There was movement from the tree line. Watching wide-eyed while the other men talked and argued amongst themselves, Dieter had seen shadowy figures moving through the forest. A group of orcs riding on the back of enormous boars emerged from among the trees. As yet, he could see barely a handful of riders, but the crashing sounds and boarish snorts coming from the forest behind them indicated they were only the advance party of a much larger force.

'Looks like they're going to hit us with some of their best fighters first,' Gerhardt said. 'They know they have the advantage and want to make the most of it.'

'But I thought orcs were supposed to be stupid?' Dieter said. 'From the way you talk, you make it sound like they know what they're doing.'

'They do know,' Gerhardt grimaced. 'Don't ever believe anyone who tells you that orcs are stupid. Granted, they're not much good when it comes to building towns, planting crops, making pots or doing any of the other things that human beings rate themselves highly for achieving. The truth is, orcs have no interest in those things. They're only clever when it comes to the areas they are interested in. Which, generally, means fighting and killing their enemies.'

'Besides, it doesn't take a genius to see our army is in trouble – not even an orcish one,' Rieger commented, agreeing with Gerhardt. 'The second they caught sight of our camp, the orcs would've noticed our lack of cavalry. Once they saw that, it stands to reason they would've decided to send their boar riders forward, to try and roll us over.'

The number of orcs visible at the tree line was growing. As Dieter watched them, he became wary of the size of the enemy forces arrayed against them. The greenskin army they had seen crossing the river had been huge; big enough to outnumber General von Nieder's army, even before the knights were sent away.

Then again, Dieter reminded himself of one of Helmut Schau's tactical dictums – an army fighting from a strong defensive position held the advantage over an attacker, even when outnumbered. But how strong was the Hochlanders' position, really? Remembering the disorder he had seen in his own army's encampment, Dieter found it hard to believe they were ready to meet the enemy in battle.

The horde of boar riders visible at the tree line was growing ever larger. From further along the camp perimeter, Dieter heard the sound of sporadic artillery fire as the few cannons in position tried to put a dent in the enemy numbers.

The orcs seemed to view it as a sign. Riding into sight before the massed ranks of riders, an orc chieftain galloped to the head of his troops and held up a long spear festooned with skulls. Opening his lips wide to reveal a mouth full of tusk-like teeth, the chieftain threw back his head and screamed out a command in his brutish inhuman tongue.

It was the signal the orcs had been waiting for. Acting as one, the boar riders spurred their ill-tempered mounts into a gallop and charged toward the human lines.

'Form a shield wall!' Abruptly, Sergeant Bohlen appeared among the men of the Scarlets' front rank and began issuing orders. 'Second, third and fourth ranks, be ready to push! Rear ranks, be ready to fill any gaps in the line and shore us up at the sides if the other regiments fall back! Musicians, play me a tune! Make it something lively, something to relieve the boredom while we're waiting for the greenskins to amble their way over.'

In response to the sergeant's orders, Dieter heard the regimental fife-player and drummer strike up a martial song as the Scarlets raised their swords and interlocked their shields. Within moments, their efforts were all but drowned out as the orcs galloped closer. Dieter could still hear the drum, just barely, but the thin reedy sound of the fife was lost among the thunder of hooves coming nearer.

The boar riders were bearing down on them, clouds of dust rising to envelop them as the boars pounded their way toward them.

'Push!'

Dieter was barely able to hear Sergeant Bohlen's voice above the din. The command caught him by surprise. As the orcs closed to melee range, Dieter felt hands on his shoulders, bracing him against the impact as the boars at the front of the enemy charge hit the Scarlets' shield wall head-on. Feeling the impact judder through his body, unable to escape or turn away due to the hands of the second rank pressing him forward, Dieter felt like the meat in a most unpleasant sandwich. It amazed him that he was not instantly pulverised.

'Push!' He heard Bohlen's voice above the sounds of battle. 'Push! All hands to the front! Give it some shoulder.'

Even as he struggled to breathe, caught between the giant boars bearing down on the shield wall at the front and the pressure of his own comrades pushing him forward from behind, Dieter realised the Scarlets' tactic was working. The support of the second, third and fourth ranks pushing forward from the rear had stopped the orcs from using the superior weight and strength of their mounts to punch through the shield wall.

Instead, the orcs were caught in a trap of their own inadvertent making. Their advance was stalled, the riders and mounts at the front caught between the shield wall and the other boar riders galloping into the back of them.

Seeing a boar directly in front of him struggling to extricate itself from the morass of bodies as its orc rider whipped its back in frustration, Dieter joined the men on either side of him in stabbing the creature repeatedly with his sword. Giving an enraged howl the boar collapsed, animal and rider disappearing beneath a flurry of lethal hooves as another boar was pushed forward to take the place of the one that had fallen.

All along the line, the same drama was repeated. Swordsmen and spearmen stabbed their weapons into the boars and their riders, the enemy rendered all but helpless by the crush of their own bodies.

It was grim, bloody work, but Dieter did not flinch. Following the lead of his comrades around him, he stabbed his sword backwards and forwards, working the blade with mechanical monotony, attacking any target that presented itself. It was hard to keep track of time, but it seemed to him that within minutes the ground beneath his feet was sodden with the enemy's blood.

As further minutes passed, he became acutely aware of the hot, stifling conditions. Caught in the press of bodies, face-to-face with the enemy at the coal face of battle, there was no relief from the butcher's work of killing. Sweat poured from his body, his muscles ached from the constant effort.

Distantly, he could still hear the sound of music; the lilt and rhythm of fife and drum as the musicians of various regiments continued to offer encouragement to their comrades. Louder still were the other noises of battle. He heard the roars of boars and their riders, screams of pain, the cries of dying men. He heard the clash of steel against steel, the crunch of sinew and bone as they struck against the shield face, the wet ripping sound a blade makes as it saws through flesh.

Suddenly, just as Dieter had begun to wonder how much longer he could bear it, the pressure around him lessened. Sooner than he would have thought possible, the enemy withdrew. The surviving boar riders turned tail and ran, leaving their dead and wounded comrades behind them, lying in the dirt.

'Tenth rank, mercy duty!' Sergeant Bohlen shouted once he was satisfied the enemy withdrawal was genuine and not a trick. 'First rank, retire! Get the wounded men back to the rear to see the surgeons. The rest of you, step forward!'

Confused by the staccato series of orders, for a moment Dieter stared dumbly around him, unsure what was expected of him. At the same time, he experienced a rush of relief at having survived his first battle.

'I wouldn't stand there taking in the air for too long,' Holst said. The big man had seen out the fighting mostly intact, as had Gerhardt and Rieger. He favoured Dieter with a broad, personable smile. 'Come on, didn't you hear the sergeant? We are ordered to retire.'

'I...' Abruptly, Dieter felt himself acutely aware of his ignorance. Even with all the things Helmut Schau had taught him, it was becoming plain there were gaps in his knowledge. 'I heard the command. But I wasn't sure what it means.'

'It means we are to pull back to the rear of the regiment,' Gerhardt said, chivvying him along. 'The men of the second rank will take our place, while the third rank takes their place, and so on. We change ranks this way at regular intervals throughout battle. It allows the men who have done the fighting to take a rest, replenishing themselves before their next turn in the front rank.'

'No, I understood *that*,' Dieter said. He glanced back toward the killing ground in front of the Scarlets' position, a place littered with enemy corpses. 'But I couldn't see why we are doing it. I mean, shouldn't we be pursuing the orcs? The battle's over, isn't it? The orcs have fled. We've won.'

'Won?' Holst rolled his eyes, before looking towards Rieger. 'Do you hear that? Sigmar protect us from war virgins and babes-in-arms. He thinks we've *won*.'

'Hardly that, Dieter,' Gerhardt said, while Rieger looked at him sadly. 'Granted, the orcs have withdrawn for now. But it's hardly the end of the battle.'

He gazed around him, at the battlefield and their own lines, and his eyes hardened.

'Believe me, there's more killing to be done in these fields before the day is done.'

'STAND FAST THE 3rd! Stand fast for Hochland! Stand fast the Scarlets!'

By the time midday came and the sun was high overhead, it seemed to Dieter he had heard those words a thousand times. He was exhausted beyond any tiredness he had ever known. Like the men around him, his face and clothes were daubed with splattered gore courtesy of the countless enemy they had killed already. His hand was sore from holding his sword. His shoulders ached from bracing his shield. His throat was dry. He wanted nothing more than to sleep.

And, still, the orcs kept coming.

Since the first charge by the enemy earlier in the morning, the fighting had continued on for what seemed like hours. With that initial attack, the shape of the battle had been revealed. In the hours since, the orcs had not varied in their strategy at all. They attacked in wave after wave, sending their boar riders to repeatedly assault the same section of the western perimeter.

For the Scarlets and the other infantry units guarding that region, it had swiftly become a war of attrition. No matter how many times the orcs charged to battle, the Hochlanders held the line – though only at tremendous cost.

Dieter had barely had time to become acquainted with many of his comrades, but already he had seen several of them die. Breitmeyer, one of the men of his file, had been killed at an early stage of the battle, gored by a boar tusk when a section of the shield wall had briefly given way during an enemy charge. Impaled on the tusk, Breitmeyer had been thrown in the air when the boar tossed its head up. He had landed disembowelled, dying in the stink of his own shit and blood as his intestines unspooled from his belly like a tangled coil of rope suddenly cut in two.

Rosen, another man from the file, had died later. By then, Dieter had lost count of how many times the orcs had attacked. Rosen, it seemed to him, had suffered an unlucky death. There was no glamour to it, no glory. Moved by fury at his riders' inability to break the Hochlanders' line, one of the orc chieftains had thrown his horned helmet into the human ranks in a gesture of pique. The helmet had hit the shield rim of the man in front of Rosen and tumbled end over end through the air, the sharp point of one of its horns transfixing the unlucky Rosen through the eye as he looked up to see where the helmet would land. Appalled, Rosen's comrades had rushed him to the surgeons, but there was nothing to be done. Rosen had suffered a mortal wound and, with it, the sad ignominy of a ridiculous death.

Alongside Breitmeyer and Rosen, at least another dozen or more Scarlets had died, not counting the men who had been wounded too badly to continue and had been evacuated for treatment in the surgeon's tents at the centre of the encampment. Even at that cost, Dieter realised the regiment had been lucky. They had held the line, as had the other units guarding the perimeter, meaning they had suffered their losses in piecemeal fashion. If ever the line broke, the effects would be catastrophic: the current trickle of casualties might well become a torrent.

'Stand down!' Sergeant Bohlen's voice called out as the latest orc attack faded. Glowering after the enemy as they turned their mounts and retreated once more to the safety of the tree line, Bohlen barked out a familiar series of commands.

'First rank, retire! Get any wounded men back to the surgeons! The rest of you step forward! Gerhardt, you and your men are on mercy duty. Look lively, the lot of you! You needn't worry you'll have time to be bored. The orcs will be back soon enough!'

Following the sergeant's orders, the men of the regiment rearranged themselves accordingly. The men who had borne the brunt of the orcs' latest assault pulled back to the rear of the regiment, taking their wounded comrades with them. From there they would be allowed to rest briefly in relative safety, rebuilding their strength before taking up their new position as the rear rank of the regiment. In the meantime, the men of the second rank had taken their place, while the third rank stepped up, ready to move forward in turn and face the enemy when it came their time to do so. War as an infantryman, Dieter was learning, combined the varied aspects of a procession and a slaughterhouse.

'And so it goes on,' Holst chuckled darkly. 'You'd think the damned greenskins would've learned their lesson by now. Sigmar knows, we must have killed ten of them for every man we've lost. But that's the way with orcs. They never seem to know when they are beaten.'

'I'm not so sure,' Rieger warned him. 'It could be the orcs know something that we don't. Either way, it doesn't do to get too cocky.'

'You are a cheery soul as ever, I see,' Holst rolled his eyes in sarcasm. 'I'm glad to see all this fighting hasn't dented your eternal optimism.' He glanced toward Dieter. 'You have to be wary of this one, young blood.

Rieger has a tendency to always look on the dark side of everything. If you hand him a refreshing cup of spring water, he's bound to ask you how many men have pissed in it upstream before you got there. He's the kind of man who can never see the silver lining for the black cloud around it.'

'It is a matter of perception,' Rieger replied. 'I see it differently. In my opinion, I am a realist and you are an oaf.'

Dieter had not known the two men long, but he suspected Holst and Rieger's mock quarrel was as much a method of distracting their minds from the task at hand rather than any real disagreement. In accordance with Sergeant Bohlen's orders, they had followed Gerhardt and the other men of their file as they advanced out into the no-man's-land in front of the Scarlets' shield wall. It was now their turn to perform an unpleasant task in the short period of grace before the greenskins attacked again.

They called it 'mercy duty'. Having refused to hide anything of the grim nature of the soldier's life from Dieter when he was growing up, Helmut Schau had described the procedure to him on several occasions.

'When you put an enemy to flight, he doesn't usually have time to go collecting up his wounded – even if he has a mind to,' Helmut had told him. 'Most of them get left on the battlefield. Now, when you're fighting civilised men, it's not too much of a problem. You leave those with mortal wounds to die, and the rest become your prisoners. But, when you're fighting orcs, or beastmen, or marauders, matters are different. Wounded or not, they'll cut your throat given the chance, and neither side takes prisoners. So you finish them. In the lull between attacks, you send out men on mercy duty. They don't mess around trying to sort the wounded from the dead. They just take a weapon and stick each body in the head or heart, to make sure the job's done right.'

Following the example of the other men around him, Dieter performed his allotted task. The area immediately in front of the Scarlets' position was littered with the bodies of orcs and boars. Here and there, a fallen orc still had enough life to pose an obvious threat. Roaring when it sensed the soldiers' presence, the creature tried to raise itself to attack, only to be chopped down by Dieter and his comrades.

Otherwise, the work was easy. Dieter might have expected it to be more harrowing, but the long drawn-out struggle of the battle had begun to inure him to slaughter. He had been killing orcs all day. The fact he was now ordered to turn his attention to slaying those too wounded or helpless to presently harm him did not seem to make much difference. They were orcs. It was a good enough reason to kill them.

Dieter was wiping sticky gore from his sword and about to advance on the next orc body, when he heard a warning cry behind him.

'Back to the lines!' It was Gerhardt, shouting out a warning. 'Get back to our lines and make it fast. The orcs are coming.'

Having regrouped their forces, the orcs appeared at the tree line as they made preparations for another charge. Even as he hurried back to safety with his comrades behind the Scarlets' shield wall, Dieter noticed a difference in the nature of their enemy.

This time, in place of boar riders, the orcs massing at the tree line were all on foot. They seemed larger than the orcs Dieter had seen before. They were taller, more broadly built, their bodies pitted with scars while their green skin was darker in hue.

'And now the battle really begins,' Gerhardt said. Seeing Dieter look at him in confusion, he explained. 'Those orcs you can see over there are the greenskins' veterans. It's said that orcs are like snakes or lizards: they never stop growing. As they grow older, they get bigger, stronger, *tougher*. The orc warlord must have decided his boar riders were never going to break our line. So, now he's sending his best troops against us.'

He smiled.

'You needn't look so worried, Dieter Lanz. This is good news.'

'Good news?' Dieter looked doubtfully toward the gathering mass of the enemy. 'Are you sure of that?'

'Very sure,' Gerhardt nodded. 'It means we are winning the battle. Now, all we have to do is kill the orc veterans and it will all be over.'

Out by the tree line, the enemy preparations were complete. A particularly large and battle-scarred orc pushed his way to the head of his fellows and bellowed a guttural commandment. The orcs broke into a run and charged towards the Hochlander line.

It seemed remarkable to Dieter, but there seemed to be a greater impact from the charge of the orc veterans on foot than there had been from the orc cavalry riding boars. Dieter and the other men of his file were stationed six ranks back, but even in their withdrawn position he felt the shiver that ran through the shield wall as the orcs charged into it.

Within seconds, Dieter found himself face-to-face with the enemy. The Scarlets' front rank buckled, unable to bear the strain of the veterans' charge. Unable to resist it any further, the second and third ranks quickly followed suit. Where once there had been disciplined, implacable ranks of human soldiers facing a brutish enemy, the situation quickly degenerated into an open melee. Equally swiftly, the Scarlets' small corner of the battlefield dissolved into a confused disorder in which any pretension to military formation was lost. In place of order, there was barbarism. Orcs and men mingled and killed each other with abandon.

The line was breaking. That panicked thought leapt into Dieter's head as an enormous, scarred orc loomed up before him. Ducking underneath the swipe of the creature's axe, he thrust his sword up into the orc's chin, the blade stabbing through the soft portion behind the line of the jaw and burying itself in the monster's brain.

Pulling his sword free with an effort as the orc fell, Dieter hurried to help an unknown Scarlet defend himself against another orc. In the wake of the veterans' charge, everything was confusion. At times, he found himself fighting side by side with Gerhardt, Rieger, Holst, even Krug, the tides of battle throwing men together like flotsam washed ashore on a beach.

The situation was so desperate, Dieter had no idea who was winning. Similarly, he was blind to the progress of the wider battle around him and his comrades. His war had become one of simple survival.

He could not swear to it, but he had the feeling the Scarlets were holding their own. The shield wall had broken, but the regiment had not crumbled with that reverse. They had held their position, willing to fight to the last man to prevent the orcs from gaining any more ground. Caught in the thick of the conflict, Dieter hoped it would not come to that.

Then, suddenly, just as it seemed the pressure of the orc attack was irresistible, the Scarlets' fortunes took a turn for the better. Dieter heard a great commotion come from his left: a cacophony of Hochlander battle cries and shouted voices raised in the praise of Sigmar. With unexpected suddenness, the orc advance began to ebb as the enemy came under attack from their flank.

For long seconds, Dieter had no clear idea what was going on. He heard orcs scream out in pain. He smelled the stench of burning flesh. The ranks of bestial orcs in front of him abruptly turned and ran, their threat evaporating like early morning dew in the face of the rising sun. Dieter stood uncertainly, watching with his mouth opened as he wondered what could have possibly put the enemy to flight. Then, he saw them.

A warrior priest of Sigmar strode across the battlefield with a hammer in each hand. He was clad in burnished plate mail, his armour shining with a shimmering golden light as though some heavenly power had set its sign upon him.

Evidently, the priest had taken it upon himself to lead a counter-attack. He moved at the head of a rag-tag band of warriors. Dieter saw free company men, halberdiers, swordsmen, spearmen, flagellants, even cooks and ostlers, all following the priest's lead.

More remarkably still, a wizard walked beside them. It was clear he was a member of the Golden Order. He wore gold-coloured robes covered in runic inscriptions, while he had long strands of gold and silver wire woven into his long beard and hair. With a gesture here, an enchantment there, the wizard unleashed carnage on the enemy, releasing sprays of acid and showers of molten metal from his open palms and directing them at the orc horde.

Together, the priest, the wizard and their followers tore into the greenskins. Heartened by their display, the Scarlets and the other units around them redoubled their efforts. With all thoughts of strategy and tactics forgotten, they gave chase to the fleeing orcs.

For a moment, it seemed victory was near. It was clear the enemy morale was crumbling. The orc veterans had been forced to flee. Soon, the rest of the greenskin army would likely follow their example.

Emboldened by the sight of the enemy in disarray, Dieter raced to be at the head of his regiment as they gave chase to the greenskins. After all the hardships and terrors of the battle and the day so far, he wanted nothing more than to have vengeance for the comrades he had lost, for the innocents the orcs had slaughtered, for all the terrible things the enemy would do to the province of Hochland and its people if they were not stopped.

In that instant, it seemed to him the war was won. Human arms had been victorious. The orcs were beaten. They were broken, running. There could be no coming back for them.

In another instant, everything changed and he learned how wrong he was.

In their eagerness to get to grips with the enemy, the warrior priest and his followers had moved far in advance of the rest of the army. Supported by the wizard's magic, they were almost at the tree line. Dieter was still some distance behind them, but he could see a new force of orcs had emerged from the trees to try and stem the greenskin retreat. At their head was the most horrifying creature Dieter had ever seen, more terrible even than the beastmen he had fought the day before.

It was a troll, he was sure of that at least. It stood twice as tall as any of the orcs around it, its blue-grey hide covered in a profusion of warty, rock-like lumps. It moved with an odd, rolling gait as though its limbs were not quite shaped for smooth locomotion.

Despite the weirdness of its gait the troll moved forward swiftly, easily outdistancing its orcish companions in its eagerness to close with the onrushing human host.

Spotting the threat at once, the wizard responded. Chanting a terse incantation, he extended an arm and pointed his palm at the troll. A stream of fiery liquid metal materialised and shot from his hand, only to dissipate as it made contact with the creature's stonelike skin.

Mouth widening to show an awful row of sharp teeth, the troll changed direction and charged toward the wizard. Refusing to flee, the mage unleashed another enchantment and sent a globule of molten metal flying toward the troll. It had no more effect than the previous spell: the metal seemed to disappear even as it struck the troll, as though by some strange quirk its skin had an ability to nullify magic that was more than the equal of the wizard's ability to cast it.

Seeing his doom striding towards him the wizard tried another spell, but it was too late. The troll closed in on him and tore the man's head from his shoulders, bathing its face in the geyser of blood that erupted from the wizard's sundered neck as he was decapitated.

In the meantime, the warrior priest had met his own doom. Turning to face the newly-arrived force of orcs as they charged forward, he was overwhelmed as a swarm of much smaller greenskins emerged from among the trees and caught him unawares. There were dozens of the creatures, each no higher than a man's thigh, armed with an array of sharpened sticks and flint knives as though they had equipped themselves by copying the example of their larger, orc cousins.

Dieter had heard that large groups of such diminutive creatures, called *snotlings* by men, often accompanied greenskin armies when they went to war. From Helmut Schau's description of them he had expected them to be quite comical beings, but there was nothing funny in the way they set upon the warrior priest. As he struggled to shake them off, some of the snotlings leapt to hang from his armour while their fellows grabbed at his legs. Dieter's last sight of the brave priest was as he fell to the ground. The snotlings swiftly covered him, their crude weapons quickly becoming stained with blood as they took advantage of the gaps in his armour.

With the fall of the priest, the Hochlanders' counterattack faltered. Bereft of their leader, the priest's followers seemed to lose their nerve even as the new hordes of orcs arriving from the forest smashed into them.

Within seconds, prayers and triumphant battle cries were replaced by the sounds of panic. Fleeing as the orc veterans had done only a few minutes earlier, the dead priest's followers now turned to run blindly away from the enemy, crashing headlong into the other Hochlander units moving in support behind them. With a swiftness that Dieter would have barely believed possible, the Hochlanders' charge turned into chaos. All pretension to order or discipline was lost as the battle briefly dissolved into a thousand separate conflicts of orc against man, or man against snotling, or goblin against man.

The army had lost all cohesion. Appalled, Dieter realised the Hochlanders were now engaging the greenskins on their own level; not as cogs in a smoothly functioning military machine, but as individual warriors meeting brawn with brawn, hate with hate, and savagery with savagery. In such a battle, they could not help but lose. Once the battle became a contest of strength of limb rather than discipline and strength of mind, the orcs held the advantage. Unless someone was able to rescue the situation quickly, all would be lost.

But there was no rescue. Even as Dieter heard the sound of sergeants and officers calling out commands and trying to restore discipline, he became aware that the confusion in the ranks of the army around was growing steadily worse.

At first, he was uncertain as to its cause. Then, he realised the same panic that had gripped the dead priest's former followers had spread to encompass the troops immediately *behind* Dieter and the Scarlets. Just as the priest's followers had turned and run blindly into the forces following behind them, now the troops behind the Scarlets had suddenly begun to run through the Scarlets' ranks with the same heedless abandon.

Dieter was confused at first, until he saw a glimpse of goblin wolf riders moving behind the rearward units that were fleeing towards the Scarlets. As cries of alarm spread through the army and the musicians began to sound the retreat, Dieter came to a horrifying conclusion.

Somehow, the enemy had managed to flank the Hochlander troops guarding the western approaches and get behind them.

There could be only one explanation. The rest of the encampment had fallen. Dieter, the Scarlets and the other units around them were currently the only Hochlander forces still holding out against the enemy.

As an almost palpable sense of panic surged through the ranks of men around him, Dieter realised they might only be seconds away from being encircled and completely annihilated by the greenskins. If the enemy were behind them it meant the battle was lost. For better or worse, all that was left now were the most basic questions of survival.

All around him, men began to break ranks. The few fifes and drums left to signal orders to the troops began to beat out the retreat. In the wink of an eye, every last vestige of discipline was lost. Men ran, willing to stumble over the bodies of dead and wounded comrades in order to escape. The army had become a frightened animal, desperate to elude its pursuers.

As for Dieter, he had long told himself he would never turn from his duty as a soldier. If ever it came to the choice between fleeing in disgrace and facing certain death, he would choose death every time. It quickly became apparent he had lied to himself, however. As his comrades turned to flee around him, the thought of staying to face a brave and noble death on his own did not once occur to him.

The army ran. Cursing his own lack of valour, counting himself as a coward and a traitor, Dieter ran with them.

PART TWO
HUNTER'S MOON

(Late Erntezeit – Mittherbst – Early Brauzeit)

From
The Testimony of General Ludwig von Grahl
(unexpurgated text):

...It would become known as one of the blackest days in Hochland's recent history. Von Nieder's army was utterly routed. Von Nieder himself escaped, but many of his men were not so lucky. The greenskins killed thousands, spilling enough blood to stain the earth red.

In the wake of victory, with his enemies in disarray, Ironfang decided to press home his advantage. Splitting his forces, the orc chieftain sent his wolf riders and other light troops to pursue the fleeing human infantry. Meanwhile, he led the rest of his army in search of the Hochlanders' missing cavalry.

They found them two days later. Having learned via messengers of the defeat suffered by their comrades in the infantry, the Hochland cavalry attempted to withdraw to safety, to regroup their forces. Ironfang was too wily to let them elude him, however. Forcing the cavalry to meet him in battle, he scored another crushing victory

– slaughtering the knights and other riders almost to the man.

In the aftermath of the two defeats, Hochland was plunged into crisis. Despite my fears for the province's safety, I found much to admire in Ironfang's generalship. Certainly, the enemy chieftain displayed a remarkable cunning and military sophistication for an orc.

Of course, in the days that followed, many in Hochland tried to diminish the enemy's triumphs. It became fashionable to claim the greenskins had 'just got lucky'.

To my mind, such opinions were no more than the mouthings of idiots. A good general must be able to recognise an able opponent when he sees him. Moreover, it was certainly the case that part of the reason for the defeat of Hochland's army in the field was that von Nieder had underestimated Ironfang's abilities.

In the meantime, the change in the military situation had led to a reappraisal at the Elector's court. Within days of the army's defeat becoming known, I was summoned unexpectedly to Hergig, ordered to report for an audience with His Excellency Count Aldebrand with all due haste.

Naturally, I made my way to Hergig as quickly as possible. Arriving at the palace, I heard that the Reiksmarshall Kurt Helborg was also there. We were old comrades, having served together on several campaigns long before either of us rose to the status of general.

Apparently, the Reiksmarshall had come to Hochland on a state visit. Although the fact his visit had been announced suddenly, with little time for the functionaries in the Count's palace to prepare for it, had led many to gossip Helborg had come in response to the province's recent reverses on the battlefield. It is an open secret the Emperor Karl Franz sometimes sends his envoys on such 'state visits' to the provinces in order that they can communicate his displeasure on some matter to the local count.

That Helborg had come on such a mission was soon made clear. As I was taken to an anteroom to await my audience with the Count, the Reiksmarshall contrived to arrange an 'accidental' meeting between us in the corridor. Greeting me as an old comrade, he insisted we should go for a walk in the palace's ornamental gardens, to 'catch up on old times'. Wary of provoking an incident, the Count's servants were powerless to dissuade him. They waited unhappily, out of earshot, as Kurt and I walked in the gardens.

'It's a mess and no mistake,' Kurt said to me, once he was certain no one was listening. 'I needn't tell you the Emperor is furious. Naturally, he respects the Elector's independence, but he thinks your Count has made a right pig's ear of the situation. Who was this idiot von Nieder, anyway? I don't remember him from the old days. Someone's brain-rotted cousin or bastard son, no doubt?'

I said nothing. Reading my mood, Kurt smiled.

'Heh, it's all right, Ludwig. I know how loyal you are. I don't expect you to say anything against your Count or his officers – not in public anyway. But this is just two old comrades having a private conversation.'

His face changed, growing more serious.

'Tell me, how bad is it? Can the situation be saved?'

'You have to understand I am no longer part of the command staff,' I replied. 'I haven't seen any of the dispatches from the front, nor read the scouting reports. All the information I have is second or third-hand, most of it gossip.'

'Yes, yes,' Kurt waved a hand impatiently. 'But you must have an opinion? You're forgetting I know you of old. You'll have been following the progress of the war, even if you have to interrogate some general's wife's scullery maid's husband to get information.'

'We stand on the brink of disaster,' I said. There seemed no reason to coat the facts in honey. 'Von Nieder's cavalry have been slaughtered, while his infantry are broken and scattered. With this defeat, the better part of the province's standing army is no longer available. If we are going to fight on against the orcs, the Count will have to call a general muster, conscripting every able-bodied man between the ages of sixteen and forty. Of course, such a muster creates its own problems.'

'Go on.'

'It is autumn. Harvest time. If the Count calls all the men away to fight in the army, the fall in manpower will affect the harvest. Crops will rot in the fields. The Count has no choice – if he doesn't call a muster, the orcs will overrun the province and it won't matter about the harvest. But, by calling the muster, he risks creating a famine.'

'Agreed,' Kurt nodded. All through my speech he had looked at me intently as though trying to read something in my face. 'But you said there were problems. Plural.'

'I did. The other problem is that it may all be too late. You don't create an army overnight. Even if the Count musters every man he can, it will take time to train and equip them. And time is the one thing we don't have at present. Based on his behaviour so far, the orc chieftain Ironfang isn't stupid. Having defeated Hochland's army in the field, he'll press south. It's only a matter of time before his army is at the gates of Hergig.'

'Is there no way to stop him?'

'Certainly. The orcs may have been victorious against von Nieder, but they are hardly invincible. Hochland will need help from her neighbours, however. If the surrounding provinces agree to create an expeditionary force and come to help us...'

'No.' Kurt shook his head. 'It won't happen. Count Aldebrand has already contacted the neighbouring provinces, asking for help. He has also contacted the grand masters of several of the knightly orders. So far, all he has received are apologies and excuses. Frankly, your neighbours realise Hochland is on its knees. They don't want to commit troops to what may be a losing cause. Then, there is the matter of self-interest. They are hoping the orcs will exhaust themselves and sate their bloodlust on Hochland, then disappear back into the mountains with their booty. I wouldn't expect help from anyone, at least not anytime soon. Do you have any other ideas?'

'Perhaps. Strictly speaking, defeating the orcs is not the issue at the moment. We need to buy time for a muster to be called, and for the new recruits to be trained and equipped.'

'And if the Count asked you for an opinion on this? If he asked you how he should buy this time, what would you tell him?'

'I'd tell him that even after the defeat of von Nieder's army, Hochland still has men under arms. All the major towns and forts have their own garrisons. Then, there is the garrison of Hergig itself, as well as the city watch, the Count's greatswords, the Talabec river patrol, the sewerjacks, the road wardens, and so forth. Add in the local militias. If you scoured the taverns and brothels in this city you'd find a fair number of men who know one end of a sword from the other – adventurers, bounty hunters, mercenaries, criminals and the like. Put them all together and you'd have a pretty sizeable force. You could march them north, with orders to press-gang every man they meet along the way – most villagers out in the wilds know how to use a bow to hunt with, if nothing else.'

'And you think an army like that could defeat the orcs?'

'Not defeat them, necessarily. Remember, all they have to do is slow the greenskins down in order to create more time for the muster. At the same time, if you sent a new army north, they should be able to collect up the remnants and survivors from von Nieder's force.'

'A rattlebag army, then. A ragtag force of garrison troops, undesirables, peasants, ne'er do wells, and the demoralised, exhausted soldiers of a defeated army. Not a very promising prospect for their commander. Who would you recommend to lead them?'

'I don't know. He'd have to be charismatic, a good leader and a good tactician. And he would need to be tough. A man ready to do whatever it takes to achieve his objective.'

'That's what I thought,' Kurt smiled again. 'That's why I recommended you for the job.'

I should have seen it immediately, but I was not summoned to Hergig to be consulted on matters of strategy. I was summoned to be given a new command.

By the time they ushered me into the Count's presence, it was clear he was quietly furious. I do not know how much of the new strategy was of the Count's devising, and how much was forced on him by Kurt Helborg acting in the Emperor's name, but it seems I am to get everything I spoke of in my conversation with Kurt.

Whatever the reasons, I am reinstated to active duty. The task ahead of me is dangerous and onerous, but still I rejoice. I am a soldier once more.

Before he sent me on my way, the Count made a couple of grand gestures – perhaps hoping to reassure me my plans had his blessing. He assigned me an escort – a dozen templars from the Knights Panther. There is a long-standing pact between Hochland and the Panthers, whereby the order sends a group of knights to act as the Count's personal bodyguards. Effectively, the Count was giving me his own bodyguards – a brave gesture in time of war.

Secondly, he has ordered his personal prognosticator – a wizard of the Celestial Order named Emil Zauber – to travel with me. Zauber seems a shy, bookish man, more a scholar than some mighty wizard, but I am assured he is a powerful mage. I hope he will prove useful.

Given the scale of the task ahead, I fear I shall need all the help I can get...

CHAPTER SEVEN
QUESTIONS OF SURVIVAL

THE WOLF STOOD at the head of the trail, its nose raised as it warily sniffed at the air. The goblin rider on its back waited patiently, eyes darting quickly from left to right as it scanned the forest on either side of the trail.

'Move, you bastard,' Holst said, whispering quietly so neither the wolf nor its rider would hear him. 'Get a move on, before the wind changes and it ruins everything.'

Finally, the wolf came to a decision. Satisfied, it lowered its nose. Taking its behaviour as a sign, the goblin spurred his mount on down the trail, simultaneously turning to signal to the other unseen riders behind him that the way ahead was clear.

'Now we wait,' Holst said, his voice barely audible. 'Give them time to draw abreast of us, then it's wolf stew on the menu.'

Crouched beside him as they hid concealed in the undergrowth at the side of the trail, Dieter waited with bated breath. The situation brought back memories of the times in his childhood he had spent on hunting trips with Helmut Schau, stalking deer and other wild game through the forest in the lean seasons when the summer was over and the harvesting was done. The difference was he had never known such danger when they were hunting deer, nor been so hungry as he was now.

'Nearly there,' Holst spoke in a barely audible murmur as the goblin scout and his mount padded past them. 'Let Rieger take the scout. We'll take the leading riders in the war party, and let the others take the rest.'

Following behind the scout, another half a dozen goblin wolf riders rode into view. They came down the trail at a brisk pace, unknowingly moving closer to the ambush.

Dieter heard a sound like the cry of an owl come from further down the trail. Confused at hearing a nocturnal bird make its call during the day, the wolf riders looked dumbly around them. Too late, the significance of the call dawned on them.

'There's the signal!' Holst yelled. 'Attack!'

Dieter was already ahead of him. Leaping from the undergrowth, he attacked the nearest target. The wolf and its rider tried to turn to face him, but he was already thrusting with his sword. The blade caught the wolf in the side of the neck, silencing the growl building in its throat. Raising his shield to ward off the blows of the goblin rider, Dieter thrust his sword forward again, stabbing the wolf deep in the heart. As the creature fell he lashed out his sword at the falling rider, killing the goblin before it hit the ground.

Elsewhere, his comrades had been just as successful. It was over quickly. Along the trail, the wolves and their riders were dead. The ambushers had killed their victims without suffering a single casualty.

'All right, that's good work,' Holst said, casting an eye back to the head of the trail to see if there were any more goblins following behind the ones they had killed. 'We'd better get to business. Throw the goblins into the undergrowth at the side of the trail. We'll take the wolf carcasses with us and butcher them back at camp. Now, get a move on. I don't like to be out in the open like this.'

IT WAS THE wolves they had wanted. Later, as the men marched back to the camp with the limp bodies of the dead animals strung upside-down from carrying poles, Dieter wondered at the ironies that had made him a huntsman so soon after he had finally achieved his dream and become a soldier.

He had survived the army's defeat in battle by the orcs. He thought it did him no credit, but by joining in the general flight and panic once the enemy got behind them, he had managed to save his life.

Dieter and his fellow Scarlets had been lucky, he supposed. Although they had lost men, the regiment had survived the defeat and the subsequent massacre in a better state than most.

Of the men who had been lost, the one whose absence was most keenly felt among his men was Captain Harkner. No one had actually seen the

captain die. He was missing, presumed killed, but
currently there was no real expectation among the
soldiers of the regiment that their commanding officer would ever be seen alive again.

In the wake of defeat the Hochlander army had
scattered, its once-proud ranks splintered into ragtag
bands of survivors whose main concern was staying
ahead of the pursuing orcs and their goblin allies. In
the weeks since the defeat, questions of survival had
been the most important consideration. No one
talked about fighting the greenskins any more. No
one talked of their duty to Count Aldebrand or to the
people of Hochland. No one talked of the honour of
the regiment. No one cared, or if they did care, they
put the value of staying alive above any such insolid
and intangible notions as duty and honour.

In common with many of the other demoralised
groups of soldiers they had met on their journey, the
Scarlets were headed southwards. There was no great
tactical thinking behind the choice; it was simply that
the province's capital and more populous towns lay
in the same direction. It stood to reason they might
find safety there, behind stone walls that they hoped
would prove impervious to orc siege. In a time of
defeat it was hard to argue against even such forlorn
hopes.

It took no more than an hour for Dieter and the
others to find their way back to camp. Given that they
were carrying fresh meat, they were greeted with
something approaching eagerness by the dirty-faced
dispirited men who were all that were left of what
had once been a proud, imperious regiment. The

thought he had joined the Scarlets just in time to see their decline and destruction bit painfully into Dieter's heart. He knew it was nonsense, but some small part of him wondered if he was somehow to blame. He had joined the Scarlets and from that point forward everything had gone wrong.

'Well done, all of you,' Gerhardt said, striding forward to greet the hunting party as they returned to camp. He cast an appraising eye over their catch. 'At least we won't starve tonight. Did you have any troubles?'

'Nothing worth reporting,' Holst shrugged. 'We slew the goblin scouts and their mounts to the last, so we've no worries of their carrying news of our location to their chieftains. Still, it would be better if we move on tomorrow. I wouldn't like to be here longer than tonight, just in case they send more riders to see what happened to their scouts.'

'Don't worry, we won't be,' Gerhardt replied. 'I've just been discussing the matter with Sergeant Bohlen. We break camp first thing in the morning.'

'How's Kuranski?' Holst asked.

'No better,' Gerhardt shook his head sadly. 'I've given him food and water, as much as he could hold down, but it seems to make no difference. He's starting to develop a fever.'

Kuranski was the Scarlets' last remaining casualty. The other wounded men who had escaped from the battle had either recovered from their injuries or already died on the march southwards.

With Kuranski, it had been different. The half-Kislevite swordsmen had sustained a deep wound in his thigh from a boar tusk during the protracted struggle with the boar riders. He had managed to limp away from the battle otherwise intact but in the weeks since, the wound had become infected. Kuranski's condition had worsened to the degree that he could no longer walk. For the last week, his comrades had been forced to carry him everywhere on a makeshift stretcher.

'The wound has started to develop pus,' Gerhardt said. 'I'm sure it's treatable, but since we don't have a surgeon with us, there isn't much we can do. We just have to try and keep him comfortable, and hope for the best.'

'It's not the *only* choice we have,' a voice interrupted their conversation.

It was Krug. He had survived the battle along with the toady Febel. The two men walked over now, drawn by the discussion of Kuranski's condition.

Dieter had always heard that war was unfair. He supposed it was an example of that unfairness that Krug and Febel still lived, while better men like Captain Harkner had been lost.

'There is another choice,' Krug said. 'A more practical one.'

'We have discussed this already, Krug,' Gerhardt's eyes narrowed. 'I have talked to Sergeant Bohlen about it and he agrees. Kuranski is one of us. He will be given every chance to recover.'

'You ask me, you're making a mistake,' Krug continued. 'You said yourself, Kuranski has a fever. He's only going one place from now on, and that's downhill. Besides which, it is slowing us down having to carry him everywhere. At the very least, we should put the matter to a vote. With that in mind, why don't we ask the young blood what he thinks?'

Krug turned toward Dieter, his eyes glittering with malice. Ever since Dieter had stood up to him at the old woman's hut, he seemed to delight in trying to needle him.

'You're a country boy, Lanz – aren't you? You must know all about these things. What happens when a farmer has a lame horse or dog? He doesn't carry it around with him everywhere, does he? Now, don't get me wrong. I'm not suggesting we just bash Kuranski's brains out like we would with a dog. We can be more humane. I'm sure we can scare up some strong drink from among the men in camp. Then, we get Kuranski good and sodden, and one of us does the job when he's insensible. Maybe the farm boy here could do the dirty work, if he's got the stones for it.'

'Shut up, Krug,' Gerhardt said, tightly. In the course of the argument, Rieger had come to join Holst and Gerhardt in standing beside Dieter, backing him up. 'I've warned you before. Now, I'm going to make myself very clear. There will be no more loose talk about Kuranski. He is a comrade, a fellow soldier, and he will be treated in the same way as we would hope to be treated if we were in the same position. Do you understand me?'

'I understand you.' For a second, Krug held Gerhardt's gaze as though he was willing to push the dispute further. 'I think the decision is foolish, but I suppose I will have to let it pass. For now.'

Averting his eyes, Krug walked away. Febel scurried behind him.

'Someone should teach him a lesson,' Dieter said, after a moment had passed. 'I've half a mind to call him out. Challenge him to duel–'

'Shut up, boy,' Gerhardt said quietly.

He rounded on Dieter.

'You are young and full of vinegar, so I make exceptions. But if I hear you say anything on the subject of challenging Krug to a duel again, I will clip you around the ear and give you a boot up the arse. What do you think is more important – a few harsh words between comrades, or the survival of the regiment?'

'I…' Dieter's tongue seemed frozen in his mouth. His words were stymied. Facing the full force of Gerhardt's anger, a man he looked up to, he felt the colour drain from his face.

'In case you haven't noticed, we're in a bad situation' Gerhardt continued. 'We've lost a lot of good men. Our commander is missing and most of our sergeants are dead. Just like the rest of our army, the Scarlets are in tatters. We are like hunted animals, alone and on the run, our every step dogged by the enemy. What's worse, the entire province is at risk. We were supposed to defeat the orcs and protect our people. Right now, we couldn't protect a privy pit from a company of pigs. And what do you want to do, at this, our worst hour? You want to pick a fight with a fellow soldier. You want to fight a duel in which one or both of you could get killed, at a time when your province needs every fighting man it can get. Well? Are you ashamed of yourself and your big mouth, Dieter Lanz? You should be!'

With that, Gerhardt stalked off, leaving Dieter white-faced and open-mouthed in embarrassment.

'I wouldn't take it too personally,' Rieger said, after a decent interval had passed. 'With most of the sergeants dead, Gerhardt has been forced into a position of command alongside Sergeant Bohlen. With things the way they are, the two of them are struggling to hold the regiment together. We've lost over half our men. That means there's a lot of pressure on Gerhardt's shoulders.'

'I didn't mean to make it worse,' Dieter said. He shook his head, still taken aback by Gerhardt's outburst. 'I was just sounding off.'

'I wouldn't worry about it,' Rieger commiserated. 'Don't brood on the matter too long. Least said, quickest mended, as some sage once put it. Anyway, we'd better get to work.'

He indicated the bodies of the dead wolves they had brought into camp. Already, the smell of woodsmoke in the air had intensified. Glancing at the centre of the camp, Dieter noticed men had started building up the fire, adding more wood to increase the temperature ready for roasting meat.

'These wolves won't get to butchering themselves,' Rieger said. 'And I don't know about the rest of you, but I'm so hungry I could eat them pelts, teeth and tails in all.'

LATER, WHEN THE cooking was done and the Scarlets had feasted on roasted wolf meat, Dieter considered their position. With his belly full, the situation seemed less bleak than it had earlier, but he realised it was an illusion born of his temporary contentment.

The wolf meat was the first real meal the men had shared in a week.

It was not so much the fact that they were camping in the wilderness which had led to their lack of food. Summer had given way to the autumn in the time since the army of Hochland had suffered defeat in battle. In the deep woods it was a period of comparative plenty. If a man knew where to look, there was a surfeit of easily gained provender in the form of wild mushrooms, edible berries and other fruit, not to mention small game like rabbits and birds.

What was more, having been raised in the country, Dieter knew exactly where to find this bounty. Like every other child in his village, he had spent the majority of his autumns helping to gather from among the available foodstuffs in order to increase his family's stores in preparation for winter.

In the last few weeks, such hard-won knowledge had proven invaluable. Most of the rest of the Scarlets had been born and raised in an urban setting, either in the slums of Hergig or in the latticework of towns and villages that surrounded the capital. They were the sons of soldiers and whores, of innkeepers, of craftsmen, of scribes, even of minor landowners.

With the exception of Dieter, none of them knew how to best lay snares for rabbits, or knew how to tell the edible dwarf's cap mushroom from the almost identical, and deadly, brown shade. One made a good meal when cooked in the hot ashes of a fire, the other meant a lingering painful death of the kind Dieter would not have wished on his most hated enemy, not even Krug.

In the last few weeks, Dieter's knowledge had allowed him to prove his value to his comrades on numerous occasions. Even with such knowledge, however, it had been hard to find enough food to keep body and soul together. The greenskins were on their trail constantly, meaning there was little time for gathering food. Most of the time, the Scarlets had been forced to concentrate on keeping ahead of the enemy's scouts, rather than being able to spend the hours needed to find food for themselves. It was not that there was a lack of food. Simply, the Scarlets lacked the time to find it.

Even the feast they had just shared was a fleeting resource. If they had been able to salt the meat, pickle it in brine or smoke it, there was enough left that it might have lasted them for the best part of a week. As it was, they had no salt or brine, and they could not afford the days needed to build a smokehouse and put it to work. They could take the remains of their feast with them, but it would probably only last a day or two before it began to spoil. Then, they would be back exactly where they had been before they had killed the wolves. Hungry.

In the aftermath of the army's defeat by the orcs, Dieter had come to realise precisely how dependent a human army was on the assorted supply train that trailed in its wake. Unlike the greenskins, a human army could not afford to forage for their food. Without a small subsidiary army of cooks and victuallers to provide for them, along with the requisite provisions, any force of human soldiers existed forever on the brink of starvation.

Dieter remembered the victualler Otto, and how certain the man had been of his importance to the army. Time had proven Otto's words were correct. Having lost the cooks and victuallers, along with all their cookware and provisions, had proved to be more of a blow to the Scarlets' hopes of survival even than the number of fighting men the regiment had lost.

However Dieter looked at it, the future seemed dark and uncertain.

CHAPTER EIGHT
FIELDS OF GOLD

THE NEXT DAY, as the sun rose high in the midday sky, the Scarlets came face to face with temptation.

It did not take the same shape as any of the temptations they were usually prey to; the pitfalls endangering their souls that the priests were always swift to warn them against. It did not take the form of strong drink, the various games of chance, or of a beautiful woman of uncertain virtue. It was a temptation of a more subtle character.

It took the form of a gently swaying field of wheat.

'There has to be enough there to feed the regiment for a month,' Holst said, as they sheltered among the trees of the forest at the edge of the field, watching with hungry eyes as the wheat swayed gently in the breeze. 'I never thought I'd be so excited to see some farmer's field. Look how golden it is. It has to be ripe. We could use it to make bread.'

'We'd have to grind it first,' Rieger said from the side of him. He turned to look to Dieter, who was standing beside them. 'Well, what about it, Dieter? Helmut Schau was a miller. Do you think you could grind us the flour to make some bread?'

'It would take too long.' Dieter shook his head. 'Besides, we'd need to thresh the wheat first, and make a grindstone. And we'd need an oven if we were going to make bread properly. But we'd only need some water to make porridge from the wheat. It's better if you let the wheat grains get wet first, so they will sprout over night. Then, you mix them with water and boil it to make porridge the next day. The taste is a bit dull without salt, but Holst is right. There's enough in that field to feed the entire regiment for weeks. We wouldn't have to go hungry again. Each man could carry his own supply of grain with him.'

The three of them, alongside another half-dozen men, had been on scouting duty. Sent on ahead of the rest of the regiment, they had encountered the wheat field first. Holst had sent a runner back to notify Sergeant Bohlen of their find. Now, turning to look deeper into the forest, Dieter saw Bohlen and Gerhardt hurrying towards them.

'I DON'T LIKE it,' Gerhardt said, staring into the field. 'It could be a trap.'

Several minutes had passed since his and Sergeant Bohlen's arrival. In that time, Holst had given them his report on the situation, leading to a discussion among the men present as to the best way forward.

In the meantime, the rest of the regiment had taken up a position a little way back from the edge of the field. Wary that there might be greenskins in the area, Sergeant Bohlen had ordered the rest of his men to wait in silence.

'Still, we can't just bypass the field,' Holst argued. 'Think of all that food. Even without any scythes, Dieter thinks it wouldn't take more than a couple of hours to harvest the grain. And we'd be set up for weeks. No more going hungry.'

'Better hungry than dead,' Gerhardt said. 'By now, every village and farmstead in the region will have heard that the greenskins are coming. The people will have fled south. There's no way a farmer would leave his crops behind like this. Either he'd harvest them and take the food with him before he left, or he'd burn them so the enemy couldn't have them. He wouldn't leave it ripening in the field like that.'

'Perhaps he didn't have time,' Dieter said. 'For all we know, the orcs may have already been through this area. Perhaps the farmer was forced to flee at short notice and he didn't have time to set light to his fields.'

'Then, the greenskins would have done it for him,' Gerhardt said. 'Whether it was orcs or goblins, any greenskins that came through here would have destroyed anything they couldn't take with them. I don't know whether they eat wheat, but if they don't, they wouldn't have left it behind for us to find it. After they'd finished stealing everything they wanted, they'd set fire to the rest. It's the way they do things. What do you say, sergeant?'

All eyes turned to Sergeant Bohlen. The sergeant had been uncharacteristically quiet throughout the discussion. Looking at him, Dieter saw an unsettling degree of uncertainty in the sergeant's eyes. It was there for only a moment before Bohlen covered himself by turning to gaze thoughtfully at the wheat field. He stared intently at the swaying crops as though considering the matter at length.

Abruptly, Dieter realised the sergeant was unsure of his ground. Usually, this kind of decision-making was the task of the company commander. As a sergeant, it was Bohlen's job to make sure that his commanding officer's orders were enacted; he was not normally responsible for the fate of an entire regiment. In the command void left in the wake of the army's defeat by the orcs, Bohlen had been forced into an unfamiliar position. Dieter could only hope he came to grips with his new responsibilities as quickly as possible.

'Gerhardt is right,' Bohlen said, at last. 'The situation is suspicious. We'll send scouts to check the edge of the forest all around the field to make sure there are no greenskins lying in wait. We'll only enter the field itself if it turns out the surroundings are clear. Any questions?'

'It is a good plan, sergeant.' Rieger had been silent, but he suddenly spoke and pointed towards the field. 'But I don't think we'll have to send out scouts to see if there are any greenskins around. Someone else has decided to do it the easy way – by offering themselves as *bait.*'

Following the direction of Rieger's gesture, Dieter saw a party of men had emerged from the forest and entered the field. There were about forty or fifty of them. At first, seeing the ragged state of their clothing, he mistook them for a group of flagellants. Looking more closely, he realised they were soldiers, their uniforms much the worse for wear after weeks on the road. Although they wore the red and green livery of Hochland, he did not recognise their regiment. He could see them well enough, however, to spot the long barrels of their weapons. They were handgunners. Apparently, they had been as captivated at the presence of the wheat field, and its promise of an extended food supply, as the Scarlets.

Hurrying deeper into the field, the handgunners began to forage among the crops. Running their hands along the stalks of wheat, they started to pull away grain in great handfuls, depositing the golden treasure in the dozens of ammunition pouches that each man carried dangling from a bandolier across his chest.

'Fools,' Gerhardt said. 'They obviously haven't scouted the area – otherwise, they'd have found us here. Don't they realise they could be wandering right into an ambush?'

Even as Gerhardt spoke, a movement among the tall stalks of wheat indicated he was not wrong in his fears. A few hundred paces away from the handgunners, the wheat started moving violently, swaying in a direction at odds with the breeze. Too late, one of the handgunners noticed the movement. He called out to his fellows, even as a thin piercing note rose high on the wind.

It was some kind of signal. All around the handgunners, the wheat started moving. Catching a glimpse of green skin and furred bodies among the sea of wheat, Dieter realised the ambushers were goblin wolf riders.

The handgunners had started running, but the trap was already closing. Swift shapes furrowed towards them through the wheat like sharks in a golden sea.

'We have to help them!' Bohlen shouted.

Confronted by a situation of imminent danger, he was back to the sergeant of old. His voice rang out in clear commanding tones, bringing the rest of the regiment running to his call.

'Forward!' Drawing his sword, Bohlen stepped out into the field with Dieter and the others at his side. 'Forward the 3rd! Forward the Scarlets!'

It was the first time Dieter had heard those words in many weeks. They thrilled him. For a moment, it was as though all the fears and anxieties of the last few weeks had fallen away. He was a soldier again. He was a Scarlet, not a member of a broken regiment, nor a coward running for his life.

Then, as he joined the others in charging across the wheat field, he remembered where he was. His regiment's numbers were depleted. The last weeks had taken their toll. They were exhausted men. Worse, they were facing an unknown number of the enemy. For all they knew, there might be *thousands* of goblins hiding in the wheat field.

Somehow, it did not matter. From the instant he had heard the call to arms, he was a Scarlet once more. Though he might well face death, he would do his duty.

'Forward the 3rd!' he took up the cry with the other men of the regiment as they charged across the wheat field's golden expanse. 'Forward for Hochland! Forward the Scarlets!'

Perhaps the enemy's blood was up, or the wolf riders miscalculated the number of soldiers charging towards them. Either way, instead of fleeing, the goblins continued pursuing the handgunners even after the Scarlets broke from cover.

Meanwhile, seeing the Scarlets appear from the forest to charge to their aid, the handgunners began to angle their run toward their fellow Hochlanders and safety. Here and there, a man paused to fire a snap shot toward the pursuing wolf riders, but for the most part the handgunners sprinted through the field, hoping to reach the Scarlets before the enemy caught up with them.

Some of the men did not make it. As the goblins closed on them, their wolfish mounts pounced on fleeing men, snapping jaws hamstringing their prey and leaving them open for the kill. Others were shot down in their tracks by goblin arrows. By the time the Scarlets closed to melee range with the enemy, as many as a third of the handgunners were already dead or wounded.

Outraged to see their fellow Hochlanders fall before they could get close enough to save them, the Scarlets tore into the wolf riders with a savage ferocity. Goblins were pulled from their saddles and cut to pieces, their wolves brought down by dozens of flashing blades.

It was over quickly. Realising they were heavily outnumbered, the surviving wolf riders turned and ran.

Some of the handgunners fired their weapons, bringing down their targets, but the wolf riders quickly escaped while their enemies on foot could only curse after them.

In the aftermath, the field seemed almost preternaturally quiet. The two groups of soldiers regarded each other warily. Much of the crop around them had either been torn from its roots or trampled to the ground by the brief intensity of the fighting. In places, the ground and the golden wheat were stained red with blood.

'Who's in charge here?' Bohlen demanded, breaking the silence. He gazed back and forth among the faces of the handgunners, waiting to see which of them answered.

'I am.'

A tall, rangy figure strode forward. He was clad in the same uniform as the rest of his fellows, but in place of a handgun he carried the greater length of a Hochland long rifle. Staring at the newcomer, Dieter thought he had the look of a huntsman about him. He had a hawkish nose that put Dieter in mind of a bird of prey, but it was more than that. The man's grey eyes had a fixed and distant quality to them, as though he was accustomed to seeing the world from over the sights of a gun.

'At least, I suppose I am,' the man shrugged, but from him it did not appear a gesture which indicated any degree of weakness or uncertainty. 'Our captain and all our sergeants are dead. I guess most everyone is dead when you come to it. I'm Markus Brucker. Marksman. I shoot things.'

He smiled in greeting, but Bohlen ignored it.

'What the hell did you think you were doing – entering the field without scouting it first?' the sergeant asked angrily. 'You walked right into the wolf riders' trap. You do realise, if it wasn't for the fact we were here to save you, all your men would be dead by now.'

'I realise it,' Brucker responded. 'And I am grateful. We all are. As for entering the field… I counselled caution, but the others were so hungry they decided to go into the field and to hell with the consequences. As I say, I'm a marksman. I shoot things. I'm not a sergeant. I don't have what it takes to command a group of men. It's part of the reason I'm glad you're here.'

'All right. We'll leave it there, then. For now.'

As quickly as it began, the storm of Bohlen's anger had abated. He looked at the scene around them as though considering his options.

'Help them with their wounded,' Bohlen said, gesturing his men forward. 'I want us ready to get under way again as quickly as possible. All of us – that's handgunners and Scarlets. Anyone who's not helping the wounded can take a couple of minutes to gather up as much grain as they can. But, after that, we're leaving. We can't afford to hang about gleaning food. The goblins that escaped are bound to bring back reinforcements. I want us to be long gone from the area by the time they get here.'

'You didn't tell me what your regiment is called?' Bohlen turned back to Brucker as the men around them hurried to their tasks.

'The Hergig Long Gunners,' Brucker replied. He glanced at the men around him. In all, perhaps twenty of the handgunners had survived. 'Not much of a regiment any more, of course. And, in case you're wondering, we're short of lead balls and black powder, not to mention food and water. We're short of pretty much everything it takes to survive.'

'Then, it's a good thing we found you. For *you*, I mean. We may not have lead balls, but we've got the other kind – the kind it really takes to survive when everything is against you.'

Bohlen fixed the man with a steely gaze.

'Welcome, Markus Brucker, marksman. Welcome to the Scarlets.'

CHAPTER NINE
UNDER THE STARS

'JOIN THE COUNT'S army and you are set for life,' Holst said, making no effort to hide his foul humour. 'That's what the recruiting sergeant told me, all those years ago when he came to our town. Join the Count's army and freeze to death would be more like it. Join the army and eat a meal of raw wheat. Sleep under the stars without a blanket or camp fire. Wait for the greenskins to come and kill you. You can bet the recruiting sergeant forgot to mention any of those things in his speech.'

'And, no doubt, you are planning your vengeance?' Rieger asked sarcastically. 'Any minute now, you'll tell us you remember the man's face. If you ever see him again, you'll kick his arse from here to Hergig and back again, stopping only to have lunch at a favoured hostelry while you leave him tied to a hitching post, out in the rain. That's the way you usually end it when you launch into one of your diatribes on the Count's recruiters and their lack of truthfulness.'

'Hmm, maybe; it depends,' Holst said doubtfully. 'What's a diatribe?'

'A long, bitter speech criticising something or someone.'

'Really? So that's what this is, then? Ah, the value of an education. The next time you're in Hergig, you should remember to thank whichever brothel keeper taught you that one.'

'It wasn't a brothel keeper,' Rieger told him. 'It was a priest. Although, frankly, given the old man's morals, it was difficult to tell the difference at times.'

'Shut up the pair of you,' Gerhardt interrupted. 'Or at least quieten it down. Some of us are trying to sleep.'

They were lying out beneath the stars. In the summers of his childhood, when the weather had been hot and humid, Dieter had sometimes climbed to the roof of the mill where he lived with Helmut Schau and his family, to sleep there and escape the heat.

There had been no such imperative operating on this night. In common with the rest of the men in the regiment, whether they complained of it or not, Dieter was cold. He was shivering. In an effort to conserve warmth, he rolled his body into a ball under his cloak and tried to wriggle himself into a comfortable position on the cold, hard ground. It made very little difference.

Two nights had passed since their encounter with the handgunners at the wheat field. Markus Brucker

and his men had joined the Scarlets in their journey
southwards, but their presence did not account for
the fact the last two nights had been the most miserable Dieter had ever known. At least, not directly.

Having been unable to stop most of the wolf riders
from escaping after the skirmish in the wheat field,
the Scarlets and their handgunner allies had been
forced into an even more desperate situation than
they had been before.

Wary of attracting the attention of any new scouts
the greenskins might have sent out to hunt them
down, they could no longer risk lighting a fire at
night to either cook their food or warm their bodies.
In its place, on each of the last two nights, the soldiers had been forced to bed down in the forest after
a meal of uncooked grain. Without blankets or tents
to shield them from the cold it had been a miserable
experience.

If there was one bright spot in the otherwise
gloomy situation, it was that it was not yet winter.
The autumn nights might be chilly, but Dieter would
not have liked to camp out later in the year. The win-
ters in Hochland could be notoriously harsh, the
northern winds bringing down heavy snows from
Kislev and the Middle Mountains.

All in all, he supposed things could have been
worse. Still, he knew better than to try and share that
particular insight with his comrades. If his time
among the Scarlets had taught him nothing else, it
was that all foot soldiers were inveterate complain-
ers. Granted, given recent events, they had plenty of
reasons for a sour disposition, but Dieter suspected

some among his fellow soldiers would have complained even if they had a roof over their heads and warm food in their bellies.

'You are wrong, Rieger,' Holst said, continuing the discussion, though more quietly out of respect for the others. 'There's no way I'd kick the bastard's arse from here to Hergig. It would involve too much walking, and Sigmar knows I've had enough of that ever since I joined the damn army. I was actually thinking, if I ever meet that recruiter again, I'd tie him behind a pair of wild horses and let them drag him to death. Or, maybe, I throw him into a latrine pit with some rabid rats and see who comes out alive. Of course, then I'd need to find some rats, or wild horses for that matter. Perhaps I'd just kick him in the balls. It's not as permanent. But it is a more immediate solution, and it requires less effort.'

'So speaks a great philosopher,' Rieger yawned tiredly. 'What about you, Dieter? Admittedly, you actually sought out army life, rather than being tricked into it by a recruiter. Do you regret joining the army now? Well? You're very quiet. Orc got your tongue?'

'I'm sorry, I wasn't listening,' Dieter said. 'I was looking at the moon. At Mannslieb.'

'The moon?' Holst grunted. 'What about it? It's still there, isn't it?'

Their interest piqued, Holst and Rieger joined Dieter in looking up at the heavens.

There was no sign of the second moon, Morrslieb, in the night sky. Instead, its brother Mannslieb held the heavens to itself. The moon was full. It hung in the inky blackness of the northern sky, broad and beaming, its light brilliant and white.

'Yes, it's still there,' Holst snorted. 'I know you're a country boy, Dieter. But really, there's not that much of interest to be seen in old Mannslieb is there? Or are you about to tell us you've read our futures in the movements of the celestial bodies? If so, I hope it involves some warm food, good beer and women of easy virtue. Ideally, sooner rather than later. At least for the food and beer, anyway. It's so cold out tonight, if a woman came by – no matter what the state of her virtue – I'm not sure there'd be much I could do about it.'

'Actually, I was just struck by how bright the moon is tonight,' Dieter said. 'It's the first moon after the autumn equinox – Mittherbst has been and gone. I guess that makes it the hunter's moon.'

'Hunter's moon?' Rieger's voice sounded a quizzical note. 'I'm not sure it's an expression I've heard before.'

'It's what people call the first full moon after Mittherbst. The brightest full moon of Mannslieb always comes just before Mittherbst. They call it harvest moon because it's the signal to begin harvesting the crops from the fields. The moon *after* Mittherbst is called hunter's moon. It's the second brightest moon of the year. By then, the crops are all harvested and put away for winter. In the country, the men of the village make use of their time to go hunting. Wild game is abundant in autumn, and the light of the moon gives them plenty of light to hunt by at night.'

'Hunter's moon, eh?' Rieger said. 'I can't say I like the sound of it. It seems too ironic, given our current situation.'

'Ironic?' Dieter was perplexed. 'I don't know what you mean.'

'I mean, you've just told us this is the time of year for hunting,' Rieger replied. 'You said the bright moon makes it easier to hunt by night. The irony of your words didn't occur to you? Right now, we are the ones being hunted, Dieter. We are the prey. If your hunter's moon is going to help anyone, it will help the greenskins who are pursuing us.'

'Oh…' Briefly, Dieter was silent. 'I hadn't really thought of it like that.'

'Yes, well, no harm done,' Rieger shrugged. 'A word to the wise, though. I wouldn't go sharing the fact with any other men in the regiment. The situation is dire enough, without you telling them things are worse than they think. I'd keep your own counsel on the moon and what it means. Anyway, get some sleep. I know it's cold, and the ground is hard. But we'll be off again tomorrow at dawn. Better to get some rest while we can.'

HE COULDN'T SLEEP. At least, not then.

Eventually, despairing of the cold, Dieter decided to get up and walk around in the hope the movement would get the blood flowing and bring some warmth back to his limbs. Bundling his cloak around him against the chill night air, he stood up and picked his way through the sleeping bodies of his comrades.

Nodding in greeting to the men on sentry duty as he passed them, Dieter decided to use the fact he was awake to check on Kuranski.

The injured soldier's condition had grown worse over the last two days. No one discussed it aloud, but the general consensus was the man was dying. The wound on his leg had turned gangrenous. The best efforts of the man's comrades to keep the wound clean and regularly change his dressings had achieved little effect. Increasingly, it looked like the amputation of his leg was Kuranski's only hope for survival. None among the Scarlets possessed the necessary skill to perform such an operation – at least not with any realistic chance of success. They all knew therefore, before it came to hacking off Kuranski's leg, the man would have to be as good as dead already and lacking any other option.

In the meantime, his comrades took turns caring for him. To Dieter, it seemed to speak well of the Scarlets, and the sense of brotherhood between them, that they were willing to do so much for one of their wounded fellows. Ready to do his bit, he decided he would offer to replace whichever of the Scarlets was currently nursing Kuranski. It seemed the least he could do: since he could not sleep himself, it made sense that another man was able to sleep in his stead.

The Scarlets had placed Kuranski on the southern side of their makeshift encampment, within the shelter of an old oak whose bulk would serve to hold off the worst of the weather if it rained. Using the bright moonlight to guide him, Dieter headed for the oak.

As he came within sight of it, he saw Kuranski lying in the shadow of the tree. The dark shape of a man was crouched beside him, leaning over the sleeping figure. Thinking it was one of his comrades on nurse-maid duty, ministering to Kuranski's wounds, Dieter called out softly to him.

'Hallo. It's Dieter. I thought I'd relieve you for a while, let you get some sleep.'

The nursemaid started at the sound of Dieter's voice. Startled, the man turned to look back over his shoulder.

It was Krug. He had a guilty expression on his face, as though he had been discovered unexpectedly in the midst of a crime. In the moonlight, Dieter saw that Krug had a balled-up piece of cloth in his hand. He had been holding it over Kuranski's face, pressing it down over the unconscious man's mouth.

Horrified, Dieter realised he had caught Krug in the middle of trying to choke Kuranski. Drawing his sword, he charged over and tried to kick Krug away from the wounded man. But Krug was faster. Darting out of the way of Dieter's kick, he dropped the cloth and drew his own sword.

The two men faced each other, steel glinting in the moonlight.

'You were trying to murder him!' Dieter accused Krug, appalled. 'You bastard!'

Krug's only response was a venomous smile. Provoked beyond endurance, Dieter stepped forward and slashed out with his sword. Krug parried the blow, the sound of clashing steel seeming almost deafening amid the silence of the sleeping camp.

'So, what of it?' Krug sneered at him, his voice barely above a whisper. 'What use is he? He's like a lame animal, country boy. You'd kill a dog after it went lame, wouldn't you? I was just doing Kuranski the same favour. He was slowing us up anyway.'

'I think you do it because you like it,' Dieter said angrily. 'You're a monster.'

'And you're a fool.' Krug's smile widened. 'You know, you should really be more careful of your flank if you want to be a soldier, country boy.'

Suddenly, Krug snapped a glance over Dieter's shoulder and called out as if speaking to someone standing there.

'Well? You have a knife, Febel. Use it. Stick the bastard.'

It was a trick, but Dieter was wise to it. Even as Krug suddenly charged forward, hoping his words had unsettled his opponent, Dieter was ready for him. Among Helmut Schau's many lessons, he had taught Dieter to make maximum use of his hearing and peripheral vision to keep aware of his surroundings.

'Remember, a battle goes on all around you,' Helmut had said. 'It's not just the enemy you are facing you have to worry about. There's also the enemy behind you, and the one to your flanks. Keep your ears open, use your eyes fully, don't let yourself become too focused on the man standing in front of you. Stay aware of all that's going on around you. Do that, and after a while it's like you've got a sixth sense. You won't have to ask yourself if there's a man behind you. You'll know when he's there, or you'll know when he *isn't*.'

As ever, Dieter always tried to put Helmut's good advice into practice. He did not need to glance behind him to know there was no one standing there ready to ambush him.

As Krug charged forward, Dieter raised his blade to parry the clumsy thrust of the other man's sword. Taking inspiration from a manoeuvre he had seen Holst use in battle, he let Krug's momentum bring them face to face. Then, as their swords locked and Krug struggled to free his blade, Dieter head-butted his opponent across the bridge of his nose.

Blood spurting from his broken nose, Krug fell backwards onto the ground. Despite the shock of the impact, Krug had managed to keep a grip on his sword, but as he looked around him it was clear he was at a disadvantage.

Dieter loomed over him. Cautiously staying outside the reach of Krug's sword, he raised his own weapon and made ready to charge forward to administer the killing thrust.

'Wait!' Krug held up his hand in a warding gesture. He lifted his face to look at Dieter and begged for his life. 'Whatever you think of me, we are members of the same regiment. We are Scarlets. We are comrades. Please. You can't just kill me…'

Distracted, Dieter hesitated. Around them, the rest of the regiment was stirring, roused from sleep by the sound of the fight. Abruptly, it occurred to Dieter that if he ran Krug through it might seem to the others he had murdered him. Dieter would have nothing to support his story that Krug had tried to kill Kuranski.

Reading Dieter's hesitation as weakness, Krug's face took on a crafty gleam. Before Dieter could stop him, he began to call out loudly.

'Help! Murder! Someone please help me! He's trying to kill Kuranski!'

Within moments, the sentries had raced onto the scene. The rest of the Scarlets soon followed them. Dieter found himself surrounded, his sword pulled from his hand, as men rushed forward to interpose themselves between him and Krug.

'What in the name of Sigmar's holy arse is going on here?' Sergeant Bohlen roared as he arrived onto the scene.

'It was the young blood!' Krug said, as the assembled men tried to hold him and Dieter back from each other. 'He's gone mad! I found him trying to smother Kuranski! Then, when I tried to stop him, he attacked!'

'He's a liar!' Dieter yelled, pushing against the hands of the men who held him back. 'He's the one who was trying to murder Kuranski! I stopped him!'

'Shut up, both of you!' Bohlen growled. 'Before we go any further with this, has anyone thought to check the supposed victim?'

'I did,' Gerhardt said. While everyone else's attention was on the fight, he had knelt down beside Kuranski. He stood back up and turned to Bohlen.

'He's still breathing, but he's unconscious. I can't rouse him. Whether that's because of his fever, or because someone tried to choke him, I don't know. But I found this lying on the ground beside him.'

He held out the balled-up cloth.

'Yes, that's it!' Krug shouted. 'That's the cloth I saw in the young blood's hands. He was trying to force it into Kuranski's mouth while he held his nose shut with his fingers.'

'Liar!' Dieter yelled, pushing even more fervently against the hands that restrained him.

It occurred to him abruptly that he had no way of proving his story. It was his word against Krug's.

To make matters worse, Krug was a polished liar. Dieter suspected it was proof his opponent had been in such situations before, but Krug was so convincing in his story that Dieter would have been tempted to believe him himself if he hadn't known better.

'You see how he keeps going for me,' Krug said, insidiously. 'That's what he was like before. I tell you he's a madman.'

'Pushing a cloth into the mouth while holding the nose shut is an old bodysnatcher's trick, isn't it?' Rieger said, pushing his way through the crowd of gathered soldiers. 'I hear they kill people that way because it doesn't leave marks. And you have already argued that Kuranski should be "put out of his misery". You can't deny that, Krug. Everyone heard you.'

He cast a significant glance at Krug, who glowered back at him in silence.

'I don't care who did what, or how they did it, or what they did it with,' Sergeant Bohlen said at last. 'In case no one noticed, we are up against it. We are on our own. For all we know the greenskins are on our trail. They could attack tomorrow. They may even attack tonight. That being the case, I don't have the time to pick over the bones of your squabbles. I don't care which one of you is guilty. I don't care which one is innocent.'

He let the point sink in. Then, he continued.

'We don't have time for private duels. With the greenskins breathing down our necks, I need every man I've got. That means you two don't get to kill each other – no matter how much you want to. Try it again and I'll have you both executed for breach of discipline in a time of war. You'll be hung from the nearest tree branch, and I'll make sure there's not enough slack in the rope to break your necks. You'll die slow, your feet kicking in the air. You understand me?'

The two men nodded.

'Good, because there's more. I'm putting you both on warning. If anything happens to either of you now, even if one of you dies mysteriously in his sleep, I'm going to assume the other man killed him. And I'll hang the survivor. So, congratulations, you are both now responsible for each others' lives.'

Bohlen turned to look at the men holding Dieter and Krug.

'All right, release them. And give them back their swords. I won't ask the two of you to shake hands and pretend everything is dandy. But remember my words. I consider both your lives a small price to pay if that's what it takes to keep discipline in the regiment. Bear that in mind. Now, get back to sleep, all of you.'

With that, Sergeant Bohlen turned away and headed back to his sleeping place. Krug glowered at Dieter for a moment. Then, he turned away himself, Febel trailing after him like a faithful dog. Soon, the rest of the men had dispersed, leaving Dieter standing with Gerhardt, Rieger and Holst.

'I wasn't lying,' Dieter said quietly. 'When I came upon him, Krug was trying to kill Kuranski.'

'I don't doubt it,' Gerhardt said. His face was grim. 'Before, when I told you to stay away from Krug, I didn't envision him doing something like this. Don't get me wrong – he's always been a bastard. Normally, you make exceptions for a man's flaws when you are in the same regiment together. But I never thought he'd go so far.'

'It was lucky you came on him when you did,' Holst said. 'Otherwise, Kuranski would be murdered and no one would be any the wiser. That's the thing to remember. You did good here, Dieter.'

'Still, I would take the sergeant's words to heart,' Rieger added. 'Bohlen is not the kind to make idle threats. Make sure you stay away from Krug. The three of us will watch your back, so you needn't worry about Krug or one of his cronies sticking a knife in it.'

'But what about justice?' Dieter asked. 'Krug tried to murder a comrade. Are you telling me he just gets away with it?'

The three men looked at each other uneasily. Eventually, it was Gerhardt that answered.

'For now he does. It is not a perfect world, Dieter Lanz. Sometimes, it is beyond our powers to see that evil men are punished. We are soldiers, not kings or lawmakers. Sometimes, it is best to let sleeping dogs lie. You do your duty. And you hope for the best. As for justice, that is not within our reach.'

Gerhardt shrugged.

'Soldiers must see to soldiering, Dieter Lanz. Leave justice for the gods.'

CHAPTER TEN
A SORT OF HOMECOMING

'WELL, IT LOOKS quiet enough,' Holst said. 'Although I suppose there's only one way to know for sure.'

He was crouched beside the log of a fallen tree alongside Dieter and Rieger. Ahead of them lay a water mill, nestled cunningly among the trees so it was all but invisible from the forest trail that ran by the side of it. Having spotted the place while they scouted ahead of the rest of the regiment, the three men had immediately crept toward it for a closer look.

In accordance with its isolated position in the forest, the mill was fortified against attack. It was surrounded by a high wall on all sides. The deep and fast-flowing stream that fed the mill's waterwheel crossed the wall courtesy of a tunnel beneath it that entered underneath the western section of the wall and emerged from under the east. The only entrance past the wall was through a set of impressive wooden gates, fashioned from thick timber planks and held together with iron bands and nails. The windows of the mill building itself that were visible from over the wall were covered in wooden shutters, while there were a series of murder holes, designed to allow missile fire against a besieging enemy without exposing the archer to counter-fire, set near the top of the exterior wall.

From the outside, the mill appeared to be deserted. In the quarter of an hour that Dieter and the others had stood watching it, there had been no sign of movement from inside.

'It'd be a tough nut to crack,' Holst said. 'Look at those iron spikes at the top. You can bet there'll be sharp stones and blades set into the top of the wall to make it harder to climb.'

'Hopefully, we won't have to,' Rieger said. He cast a quick look at the forest around them. 'We should pull back, tell Sergeant Bohlen what we've found. It's up to him what our next move will be. The place looks deserted, but who knows? It's locked up tighter than a merchant's strongbox. Even if the mill is empty, we could find it's a hell of task to get in there.'

'Hallooo!' Gerhardt called out for the fifth time. 'Is anyone there? We are Hochland troops! There's nothing to be scared of!'

He was standing in front of the mill's gates. After Dieter and the others had made their report, Sergeant Bohlen had decided the mill needed further investigation. He had ordered the men of the regiment to take up positions surrounding the mill, ready to fight if the situation should turn unexpectedly violent.

'Nothing,' Gerhardt said, once he returned to the place where the sergeant was waiting, beneath the branches of an old, shady oak. 'Either they're deaf or there's nobody in there. The gate is barred from the inside, but that means nothing. The last man to leave could have locked the bar, then dropped down over the wall to exit the place.'

'Could there be greenskins in there?' Bohlen asked. 'Or other ambushers?'

'I wouldn't think so,' Gerhardt said. 'I made myself a decent target standing out in the front of the gates like that. I can't imagine any orc or goblin possessing the self-control not to take a shot at me. Or beastmen either, for that matter. Of course, there could be someone inside, biding their time. There's only one way we'd find out.'

'Hmm, there could be food in there,' Bohlen said, considering the matter aloud. 'And blankets, cook-ware, salt, other supplies. Then, there's the fact that the place is fortified. If we got inside, we could spend the night there. It would be nice to spend a night in relative comfort for once, in a place of safety. Good for morale as well.'

'And then, there's the question of Kuranski,' Gerhardt added. 'His condition is worse. The wound has developed gangrene. Right now, I'd say his only chance is if someone amputates his leg, removing the source of infection. It would easier to do that in a place where there is a table, lanterns, sheets for bandages, perhaps even some medical supplies.'

'A messy business, that. Not for the squeamish. Say we did spend the night in the mill, who would do the operation? You?'

Gerhardt nodded. His face was grim.

'You are sure you can manage it?' Bohlen asked. 'You know what you're doing?'

'I've never amputated a man's leg before, if that's what you're asking. But I've assisted in the medical tent when a surgeon was doing one. I've seen how it's done.' He shrugged his shoulders. 'I can't say I'm looking forward to it. But I don't see how there's any other choice. Even then, Kuranski's chances are slim.'

'Very well,' Bohlen nodded slowly, considering the issue a few seconds longer. 'In that case, the decision is not a difficult one. See if you can find the young blood – Lanz – and bring him to me. If we're going to break into a mill, it makes sense to use a soldier who used to live in one.'

'IT'S EITHER CLIMB over the wall, or break down the gates,' Dieter said once the sergeant had told him what he wanted. 'If this place is anything like the mill I grew up in – and from all appearances, it is – then those are the two best ways into it.'

'Breaking down the gates is no good,' the sergeant said. 'We might not be able to lock them again afterwards, while we're spending the night. What about the mill stream? Couldn't a man wade through the tunnel under the wall, holding his breath when it gets deep?'

'It wouldn't work,' Dieter told him. 'There'll be an iron grille part way through the tunnel to block that kind of thing. There may even be hooks set into the grille and the walls to catch any swimmers and make sure they drown. These mills in the wilds are always well fortified against raiders. They have to be, or the miller and his family would never survive.'

'All right,' Bohlen said. 'We will make ourselves a makeshift rope and grapnel. We can use it to send a man over the wall. Does that meet with your approval, Dieter Lanz?'

'It does... I mean, it should work, sergeant.'

'Good. I am glad you are happy with it. Especially because you are the one who will be doing the climbing.'

IT WAS NOT a difficult climb, even given the jury-rigged nature of the rope and grapnel he had been given to help him. Still, Dieter found he was nervous at the thought he could be about to climb over the wall and come face-to-face with the enemy.

Granted, there was not much chance of that. At least, that was what he told himself as he made ready to launch his one-man assault against the mill's outer wall. Holst and Rieger were beside him, ready to offer moral support and an initial physical lift, as he stood at the foot of the wall considering his options for ascent.

'It's not that tall, really,' Holst said. 'I'd estimate it as no more than two and half times, maybe three times, the height of a man – and not a particularly tall man, either. Frankly, he was a bit of a short arse, whoever he was. And it could be worse. It's not like you're climbing a siege ladder under fire, while the enemy pours a rain of stones and boiling oil down on your head. In comparison, this should be easy.'

'Be careful when you get to the top,' Rieger said beside him. 'Don't put your hand on the top of the wall to pull yourself up until you've checked it's clear. When a wall like this is built, the builders will often leave sharp stones, old rusty blades, caltrops, broken glass and pottery shards set into the top – anything sharp. And make sure you stay alert for loose stones. The wall may not be that tall, but it's big enough for the fall to break your skull if you lose your footing. And remember, if you encounter any trouble, don't worry about opening the gates. Get out of there as quickly as possible and any way you can.'

In place of real climbing equipment, Dieter was forced to make do with a rough approximation of a rope that had been created by tearing off pieces of cloth from his comrades' uniforms, twisting the pieces around each other and knotting them together. A short section of stout tree branch, tied to the end of the makeshift rope, served duty as a grapnel.

Twirling the tree branch above his head from the end of the rope with one hand while he held the slack with the other, Dieter held his breath and threw the grapnel. He struck gold with the first cast, the wooden branch wedging itself between two of the iron spikes at the top of the wall. Tugging on the rope to make sure it was set firmly in position, Dieter took another breath and started climbing.

'Good luck,' Rieger said, pushing on Dieter's backside to help him up the wall. 'Sigmar go with you.'

'Aye, good luck,' Holst echoed his companion as he pushed Dieter with him. 'See you when you open the gates.'

As a child Dieter had loved climbing trees, so the wall presented no great barrier. Reaching the summit, he saw Rieger had been right to warn him: sharp pieces of broken glass and old iron nails were dotted among the small stones at the top of the wall. Grabbing hold of the base of the iron spikes on either side of him, he carefully levered himself up onto the wall and looked cautiously around him.

The courtyard that separated the mill house from the fortified wall around it was deserted. Satisfied that there was no sign of life anywhere in the parts of the mill in front of him, Dieter gestured the all clear to Holst and Rieger below him. Leaving the rope still in place, he eased himself onto the narrow rampart that ran around the inner circumference of the wall. Finding the rampart to be little more than some planking shored up with packed earth intended to give extra strength to the wall, Dieter looked about him and saw a wooden ladder leading down from the rampart to the courtyard. Scanning his surroundings one more time to reassure himself, he followed the ladder downwards.

Reaching the courtyard floor, he felt relieved to see there was no horde of goblins charging out to meet him. If anything, the mill seemed eerily quiet.

Hurrying to the gates, he removed the wooden bar holding them closed and pulled the gates open.

'You took your time, country boy. I was starting to think you must have fallen and broken your stupid neck.'

Dieter was unpleasantly surprised to see Krug's sneering face waiting for him when he opened the gates. Krug stood at the head of a small scouting party of Scarlets. Despite Sergeant Bohlen's instructions to the both of them on the previous night, it was clear Krug maintained nothing but hatred for Dieter.

'Get out of the way, country boy,' Krug sneered as the others in the scouting party pushed past Dieter. 'Or were you waiting for some kind of reward just because you managed to climb a wall? A pat on the back, perhaps? A celebratory cheer?'

Still sneering, Krug rejoined the rest of the scouting party as they fanned out across the courtyard. With swords drawn and shields at the ready in case of trouble, they moved to investigate the mill house and its outbuildings.

'Everything clear?' Dieter heard Gerhardt's voice behind him as he stood in the shadow of the gates and watched the scouting party go about their duties.

Turning, Dieter saw Gerhardt, Rieger and Holst approaching the open gates at the head of a mixed group of Scarlets and handgunners.

'The scouts are still checking everything,' Dieter told them. 'But, so far, the place looks empty.'

'Good,' Gerhardt nodded. 'Sergeant Bohlen will stay back with the main body of the regiment until we are certain the coast is clear. If and when we are, he'll bring the rest of the men forward and we'll start sweeping the place for food and supplies. As long as the mill still seems defensible once we've scouted it, we'll be spending the night here.'

'Well, thank the gods for that,' Holst snorted. 'It will be good to have a night's sleep with a roof over our heads. Who knows? Maybe this is a sign? Maybe the worst of it is over now, and from now on it will be clear sailing all the way to Hergig.'

'I wouldn't tempt fate,' Rieger cautioned. 'Nor count your chickens before they've hatched.'

'Feh, you're too grim, Rieger,' Holst grunted. 'Always looking on the dark side. Believe me, I have every reason for confidence. There is a pattern to these things, you know. And, after all we've been through so far, it stands to reason our luck has got to change some time.'

CHAPTER ELEVEN
SENTRY DUTY

'ALL RIGHT, YOU needn't say it,' Holst muttered as the rain fell in great torrents and soaked their clothes to their skin. 'I should have kept my big mouth shut.'

They were standing on the ramparts of the wall encircling the mill. Several hours had passed since the mill buildings had been scouted and pronounced clear. Night had fallen and, much to Holst's displeasure, he had been among the men posted on first watch alongside Dieter and Rieger. While the rest of the regiment slept, the three of them manned the walls on sentry duty along with another dozen men.

'Of course, how was I to know I was putting my foot in it?' Holst grumbled, continuing his diatribe. 'How was I to know the gods are spiteful, thrice-damned bastards? How was I to know they were listening? Imagine. They hear a man make a perfectly innocent comment in the heat of the moment along the lines that things can only better. And what do they do? They unleash the heavens and piss in his eyes just to show him who's in charge.'

'Let us accept for a moment that all of that is true,' Rieger said, his body huddled under his cloak in the shadow of the wall as he tried to escape the worst of the downpour. 'Let us assume for the sake of argument that the divine powers spend all their time listening to you and trying to find ways to spite you. I don't see how calling the gods "thrice-damned bastards" is likely to improve things.'

'I suppose it won't if you think about it,' Holst said, glumly. 'Do you think I just damned us to another month of rain? Although, actually, when you consider the facts it is really Sergeant Bohlen who is at fault here. It would hardly matter to us how hard it is raining if it wasn't for him putting us out here on sentry duty.'

'Surely he did that because he trusts us?' Dieter said. He was as wet and as cold as the others, but he was struggling to find some cause for optimism. 'It is a weighty responsibility being on sentry duty, after all. Especially considering that those wolf riders could still be pursuing us.'

'Feh. You'll excuse me if I fail to see that as a subject for great rejoicing at the moment.' The rain was so heavy that Holst's usually luxurious moustache hung down limply by the sides of his face, adding to his hangdog look. 'Right now, I'd prefer not to be trusted. Especially if it meant I could be with the rest of the men, where it is warm and dry.'

Privately, Dieter had to admit he could see Holst's point. The rain showed no sign of abating, while their comrades inside the mill house luxuriated in what had seemed like relative comfort after the deprivations of the last few weeks. The miller and his family had evidently taken as much food and milled grain as they could carry when they fled the mill, but that had still left plenty of supplies to be looted when the Scarlets arrived.

In the course of scouring the mill and its buildings for any usable foodstuffs, the Scarlets had found a few forgotten sacks of grain, some churned butter, a few vegetables, salt and some dried meat, alongside a variety of other useful supplies including lanterns, lamp oil and blankets. After the Scarlets' recent experiences since the army's defeat by the orcs, the mill seemed like a palace.

What was more, they had eaten well for once. Demonstrating an unexpected culinary ability, one of the handgunners – a man named Groetsch – had combined some of the food found in the mill to create the most delicious stew Dieter had ever tasted. Frankly, he suspected his opinion of Groetsch's cooking might have been unduly influenced by the lack of appetising food over the last few weeks, but he had enjoyed the meal tremendously all the same.

Even granting the rain, which drummed down relentlessly, Dieter found it was difficult to be entirely pessimistic when his belly was full – not that he was much inclined to pessimism anyway. In the wake of a decent meal, the world seemed brighter somehow.

In some ways, literally so.

Despite the fact they had every reason to fear the wolf riders might still be on their trail, Sergeant

Bohlen had decided to forgo the fire and light discipline of the last few nights. Light shone through the shutters from several of the mill house windows. The combination of the rain and a cloudy sky meant they could see little luminance from the moon, but in comparison to the gloomy night the mill house seemed like a shining oasis of light.

Then again, Dieter was well aware there was a reason Sergeant Bohlen had decided to allow so much light in the farmhouse. It had been agreed that Gerhardt would amputate Kuranski's leg. To stand any chance of successfully completing the operation, Gerhardt would need a great deal of light to see what he was doing.

'At least, that's one advantage of being outside.'

Noticing that Holst and Rieger were staring at him, Dieter realised he had spoken the last thought aloud.

'I was thinking about Gerhardt operating on Kuranski,' he said, trying to explain. 'I was almost glad in a way when the sergeant sent us outside on sentry duty. I wouldn't like to be in the mill house when the operation starts. Poor Kuranski. I know Gerhardt found a bottle of wine and has tried to get him drunk. But can you imagine the pain Kuranski is going to have to go through?'

'They are poor bastards – both of them,' Holst said sombrely. 'Kuranski, for being on the verge of death. Gerhardt, for having to hack at a comrade's leg with a knife and hope for the best. Right now, I wouldn't want to be either of them.'

Just then, a scream came from the mill house. The scream went on for long seconds before it fell silent.

Suppressing a shudder, Dieter mentally said a prayer for the suffering Kuranski.

'A bad business,' Holst said. His face darkened. 'If you have to die, I've always thought it is better to go quickly – say from an arrow through the heart or having your head split open by an axe. Anything has to be better than getting a wound infected and suffering a long, lingering death.'

'You don't think the operation will be successful, then?' Dieter asked. 'You don't think Gerhardt can save Kuranski?'

'Miracles happen, but I wouldn't count on them,' Holst answered. 'It would be wrong to gamble money on whether or not a comrade will die. But, if I was asked to make odds on it, I'd say Kuranski's chances are no better than one penny for compared to twenty against. Still, he is a comrade. A fellow Scarlet. Even with the odds stacked against him, there is no harm in doing everything we can to give him a fighting chance.'

'Despite that, though, you believe Gerhardt is wasting his time?'

'That is not for me to say,' Holst shrugged. 'Anyway, that is the kind of man Gerhardt is. He's not the kind to give up. He'll always risk life and limb to try and save a comrade, even if everyone else thinks it is a hopeless cause. He puts others first, before himself. He couldn't be more different from Krug in that regard.'

'Krug is an animal.' Dieter spat the words out with venom.

'He's more cunning than that,' Holst said. 'Be wary of him, Dieter. You can rest assured that me, Rieger and Gerhardt will watch your back, but keep your eyes skinned all the same. It doesn't matter what Sergeant Bohlen said – I wouldn't put it past Krug to risk cutting your throat in the hope he'll be able to talk his way out of the hangman's noose later. It's only gossip, but rumour has it Krug made his living as a grave robber and bodysnatcher before he became a soldier. That tells you what kind of man he is. Don't trust him with your back.'

'I wouldn't have anyway,' Dieter nodded. 'How does a man like that become a Scarlet?'

'I don't know,' Holst shrugged again. 'Bear in mind, the regiment may be well thought of – but we're not the nobility. The pistoliers and the knightly orders may ask to see proof of a man's wealth and breeding before they allow him into the ranks, but in the infantry we keep these things more simple. If a man can use a sword, show some brass, and carries some steel in his britches, like as not the recruiters won't turn him away. You've met the Ripper, of course?'

'Sergeant Rippner?' Dieter remembered the scowling face of the Scarlets' recruiting sergeant in Hergig.

'Yes. In your brief acquaintanceship, you may have noticed the Ripper is a bastard of the highest order. A fiend in human form. Still, even fiends occasionally make mistakes. Even with the best efforts of men like the Ripper, sometimes a bad apple slips into the regimental barrel.'

'And that's what you'd call Krug? A bad apple?'

'Well, admittedly, I can think of less pleasant things to call him. But bad apple will suffice for now.'

Throughout their conversation, Rieger had stayed silent. Keeping to his own counsel, he had remained huddled under his cloak. Dieter had almost wondered whether the man was falling asleep.

Suddenly, Rieger stood up straight. Turning to look hawkishly over the wall's ramparts, he stared into the darkness.

'Did you hear something?' Rieger said.

'Yes. Raindrops. Lots of them,' Holst replied. 'But then, it is raining. I mention this just in case you hadn't noticed.'

'Quiet.' Rieger raised his hand. His every movement was tense, his posture alert and watchful as he stood facing the blackness of the night. 'Dieter, get the lantern.'

Complying, Dieter bent forward to collect an oil lantern from under a cloth on the rampart floor. It was one of the lanterns they had found in the mill house.

The lantern was already lit – Rieger had seen to that earlier. To prevent its light giving away their position on the wall, the lantern's shutter was closed and its wick had been turned down, while it had been hidden under the cloth to further obscure its brightness.

Picking up the lantern in his left hand, Dieter pulled open the shutter and fiddled to turn up the wick. The lantern flared more brightly, its light gleaming through the raindrops as they fell in front of it.

'Use it to have a look on the other side of the wall there,' Rieger said, his finger pointing. 'I'd swear I heard a scratching sound.'

Following the other man's instructions, Dieter moved toward the spot Rieger had indicated. Leaning over the top of the wall, he lifted the lantern to shed more light on the area and looked downward to see if anything was below him.

He saw a half a dozen dark shapes clinging to the wall, with more waiting on the ground below them. The creatures' eyes glimmered redly in the light as they looked back up at him. His breath catching in his throat, Dieter realised they were goblins.

For a moment, the goblins seemed frozen in the light as though they were uncertain whether to flee or continue climbing. Reacting more quickly, Dieter pulled out his sword and shouted a warning to the other men manning the walls.

'Goblins!' he yelled. 'Look to your swords!'

Spurred into life by the noise, the goblins hurried to finish their climb. Slashing one of the goblins savagely across the face as it tried to climb over the iron spikes at the top of the wall, Dieter found he was forced to take a step backward as two more of the creatures vaulted over the spikes onto the parapet. Mindful of the parapet's narrow nature, Dieter met them head-on before they could get their bearings.

The goblins were armed with wicked, curved-edged knives. Dodging a wild slash from one of the greenskins, he responded with a well-aimed blow that split the head of the first goblin down the middle. Turning to face the second one, he parried another slash, before dispatching it with a fast thrust of his blade to the creature's heart.

As the second goblin fell, Dieter realised the fight was over. Holst and Rieger had made similarly swift work of their own opponents. Looking around him, Dieter could see other sentries running to join them, but it appeared the short-lived crisis was already at an end.

'Shine a light over the wall again,' Rieger said. 'Quickly, before the rest of them withdraw.'

Doing as his comrade asked, Dieter saw the remaining goblins scurry off into the night. It was difficult to be sure, but he counted about another dozen. Like the goblins that had climbed the wall, the ones on the ground wore black cloaks and hoods. He supposed it could be considered a sacrilegious thought, but the creatures' appearance brought to mind some manner of species of stunted, ugly, greenskinned monk.

'Night goblins,' Rieger said, watching them flee. 'The ones we killed must have been scouts, sent to test out our defences. We'd better tell the sergeant.'

He glanced back at the mill house. Already, soldiers were pouring out from inside it, drawn by the sound of battle. Sergeant Bohlen was visible at the head of them.

'I suspect he won't like the news any better than the rest of us,' Rieger continued. 'But if the night goblins we killed were scouts, there will be more of them waiting somewhere nearby. A lot more.'

He turned to Holst.

'You thought we were having a bad night before? I suspect it's about to get a great deal worse.'

CHAPTER TWELVE
ENEMY AT THE GATES

'WE SHOULD GET out while we can,' Krug said. 'Head out under the cover of darkness and make a run for it before they begin the attack.'

'And run where?' Rieger said. 'There's nowhere for us to go, Krug. Never mind the fact the enemy are night goblins. You're forgetting they can see in the dark. The cover of darkness works in their favour – not ours.'

'Then, we should set fire to the mill as a diversion,' Krug said. 'It will ruin the goblins' night sight. We can use the confusion it creates to slip away without them seeing us.'

'You ask me, you are clutching at straws,' Holst joined the argument. 'You say the fire would ruin their eyesight? How do we know that would even work? We can hardly call out to the goblins and ask them.'

'At least it would give us a fighting chance,' Krug spat back. 'Anything is better than staying here like rats in a trap.'

They were standing in the kitchen of the mill house, part of a gaggle of a dozen men who were busily debating the merits of various responses to the goblin threat. No more than a quarter of an hour had passed since the skirmish with the night goblin scouts at the wall, but the revelation of the enemy's proximity had thrown the entire group of Scarlets and their handgunner allies into a state of consternation.

Every man in the mill took it for granted that the goblins were only part of a much larger force. Since it was obvious, even from a distance, that soldiers occupied the mill, there was only one reason a small group of goblin raiders could have for trying to sneak over the walls.

Dieter had less experience of greenskins than some of the men assembled around him in the kitchen, but even he understood the basic laws that operated among such creatures. No goblin would willingly put itself at risk facing a numerically superior foe in a fortified position – not unless it had been compelled to by a leader whose orders it was afraid to refuse. In this case, it probably meant they had been sent by an orc warlord or goblin chieftain. A much larger greenskin force was probably nearby.

From the back of the group a man cleared his throat, the sound causing the other men in the room to turn their heads to see the source. It was Markus Brucker, the handgunner marksman. He had been listening quietly to the discussion from the back of the room. Now, he offered his opinion.

'We'd be better off here than out in the open,' Brucker said. 'I've fought night goblins before. It's not just the fact that they can see in the dark while we can't. It's their custom to trap and train the monsters that live underground with them. At the very least, they'll have squigs with them. Maybe other creatures besides.'

'What's a squig?' It was Dieter who asked the question.

'Imagine an ugly ball of muscle with a pair of short, clawed legs at the bottom of it. Then, imagine that its most prominent feature is a mouth nearly as wide as its body, full to the brim with sharp fangs, any one of which is the size of a man's thumb. That's a squig. The small ones are about as wide as a doorway, though I've seen 'em as big as a bull. They're good hunters, when it's dark, and they move by jumping. They're the strangest animal I've ever seen, not to mention the ugliest and probably the meanest. The goblins use them like we use dogs.'

'So?' Krug glowered at the marksman. 'You're saying we should be scared of these squigs, is that it?'

'Not scared so much.' Brucker shook his head. 'They're animals, and a bullet or sword will kill them – just like anything else. But you said you thought we should make a break for it and try to slip away to escape the goblins. I'm telling you it won't work. All they'd do is set their squigs on us like hounds after a fox. We wouldn't have a chance. We stand a better chance of surviving by staying right here and defending the mill walls. That way, night or not, we'll see the night goblins and their squigs coming at us. Doing that, we can keep the fight on our terms, not theirs.'

'I'm with the handgunner,' a familiar voice said.

Turning with the others to find out the identity of the speaker, Dieter saw Gerhardt step through the doorway into the room with Sergeant Bohlen beside him. Gerhardt looked tired. There were fresh bloodstains on his sleeves and hands.

'How did it go?' Holst asked. 'With Kuranski, I mean?'

'As well as can be expected, I suppose,' Gerhardt shrugged in exhaustion. 'I got the leg off. Hopefully, that will deal with the infection. Kuranski passed out. He's sleeping now. We'll just have to hope for the best. But I know one thing. There's no way we can move Kuranski now – not without killing him.'

'Again with this nonsense,' Krug scowled. 'I can't believe you're saying you think we should all stay here just because Kuranski can't be moved. It's madness. I have nothing against Kuranski, but we can't put all our lives at risk for one man. We should get out of here and leave Kuranski to look after himself. That's what I say.'

'Then it's a good thing your vote doesn't count for anything,' Sergeant Bohlen grumbled. He fixed his eyes on Krug for a moment, staring him down, before he turned to look at the faces of the other men around him.

'The problem here is that you all seem to think this is a council chamber or some kind of debating society,' the sergeant continued. 'Because it isn't. It's a regiment of soldiers and that means only one man is given the luxury of having an opinion – *me*. So, let me tell you what I've decided. We are staying here. If the goblins come, we will make our stand behind these walls – at least for tonight. In the morning, when there's light, I'll look at the situation again and decide whether there's any chance of us making a withdrawal. But, until then, we stand and fight. From now on, this place isn't a mill. It's our fortress. Any questions?'

He gazed at the men around him almost as though daring them to contradict him. No one spoke. After a few seconds, the sergeant nodded in satisfaction.

'All right, then. We have a fight to win. Let's get to work.'

ANOTHER TWO HOURS passed by the time the goblins made their first attack. By then, it was midnight. The rain had stopped, leaving the ground outside the mill walls muddy and sodden. To Dieter's mind, muddy conditions underfoot were something that could only work in the defenders' favour.

As he was learning, the time before a battle was the hardest part. It was the waiting that bothered him. He supposed he did not like being unable to know what the enemy were planning. Out in the darkness, away from the feeble light cast by the Scarlets' lanterns, it felt like the goblins could be hatching all manner of diabolical plans. Whatever they were up to, it would only become clear once the battle began in earnest.

In the meantime, the Scarlets tried to make the best of the waiting. Efforts were made to strengthen the mill's defences. The long table of the mill house kitchen was cleared while the room was made ready to serve duty as a makeshift hospital. Stones were gathered from the courtyard and piled on the ramparts, ready to be sent crashing down on the heads of any besiegers. Swords were sharpened. The remaining butter and grease from the kitchen was applied to the iron spikes on top of the mill's exterior wall to stop climbers from gripping them. Empty grain sacks were filled with soil and used to construct a small redoubt ten paces behind the main gates in order to give the defenders a strong point from which to resist the enemy advance if the gates were breached.

The space for men on the wall ramparts was limited, but Sergeant Bohlen posted as many soldiers as possible to defend them, with his remaining forces stationed in the courtyard as a mobile reserve. In order to maximise the firepower of the soldiers guarding the wall, a handgunner was posted after every fifth man. The handgunners were low on lead shot and black powder, but they promised to do as much damage as possible to the enemy before their ammunition was exhausted.

Markus Brucker took up a position alongside Dieter, Holst, Rieger and Gerhardt. Having never seen a long rifle up close before, Dieter watched captivated as Brucker made a series of minute adjustments to the weapon. The man's manner seemed strangely prayerful in the run-up to battle, as though he was communing with his rifle on an almost religious level.

'How far would you say it is to that tree over there?' he asked Dieter, pointing his rifle toward a gnarled and ancient oak at edge of the forest's tree line.

'I don't know… Perhaps a hundred paces.'

'Hmm. We'll call it ninety,' Brucker said, looking through the brass cylinder set on top of the barrel of his gun.

Earlier, he had explained the brass tube was like a telescope. It enabled him to see targets in more detail and improved his aim accordingly. As he stared at the tree through the brass tube, Brucker used his fingers to make a tiny adjustment to a small metal wheel at the side of his gun.

'Yes, that's right, ninety,' Brucker spoke softly, though whether to himself or his gun Dieter could not be sure. 'The wind is blowing south-westerly. The light could be better, but it will have to do. We'll kill some greenskins, Hilde, won't we? We'll shoot for the big nobs first, the shaman – if they have one – and any chieftains. Then, we'll take our targets where we can find them. We'll kill some greenskins, though. That is certain.'

As time went on, the night grew brighter. The clouds obscuring the moon moved aside, revealing a gibbous sphere. The full moon that Dieter had seen a few days ago had passed, but there was still radiance enough in the moon that was left to light the night brightly. He took it for another good omen – like the muddy ground underfoot, a bright night would favour the defenders.

From time to time, as the men on the ramparts waited for the enemy to appear, they heard movement out among the trees. Hidden in the depths of the forest, some force was massing, but at first the Scarlets could only guess at its nature. Dieter found he was eager to ask Brucker more about his experiences fighting night goblins, but the marksman had fallen quiet.

The entire mill was silent. Even in the forest the sounds of movement had stopped. It was as if the night held its breath.

Then, Dieter saw them. He heard an inhuman battle cry and an army of stunted black-robed figures appeared on every side of the mill simultaneously.

It was clear the time for waiting was past.

Dashing from the cover of the tree line, the front rank of night goblins charged toward the mill walls carrying roughly-made scaling ladders. The handgunners responded with an opening salvo of shots – all except for Brucker. Looking through the brass tube atop his rifle, he scanned back and forth among the trees.

'Patience, Hilde, patience,' Brucker whispered. 'There's plenty of targets, but we'll save the first shot for one that's worth it.'

Somewhere, from among the trees, a ghastly green bolt of magical fire appeared. Shooting through the air, it hit an upper section of the wall about twenty paces to Dieter's right. Dieter heard men screaming, their flesh shrivelled by the unearthly fire.

'And there he is,' Brucker said, his voice low and calm among the noise around them. 'A shaman. You shouldn't have used such a spectacular spell, my green friend. You think you are too far away for us to hurt you, but you just gave away your position. Now, it's mine and Hilde's turn.'

The rifle barked once, the sound almost lost among the reports of gunshots fired from elsewhere along the ramparts.

Satisfied, Brucker began reloading his rifle.

'Did you get him?' Dieter asked as the marksman opened the powder horn he carried at his side and began to carefully tip out a precise measure of powder into the barrel of his gun.

'Of course, I got him,' Brucker replied, his expression suggesting he could hardly believe Dieter had asked him the question. 'Head shot. A quick, clean death.'

Outside the walls, the goblins with scaling ladders had reached their objective. As the enemy began to raise their ladders into position, Dieter joined his comrades in trying to drive them away. Grabbing stones from one of the piles nearby, he dropped as many as he could on the goblins' heads. Then, helped by Holst and Gerhardt, he pushed at the top of one of the ladders where it had been propped up to rest against the wall. Dislodging it, he heard a satisfying chorus of screams as the ladder fell and the goblins climbing it were sent smashing into the ground.

'Watch out!' Rieger yelled. 'Some of them are on the ramparts!'

Hearing his comrade's warning, Dieter turned to see a group of goblins had managed to get their scaling ladder into position in the gap in the wall's defences created by the shaman's magical missile. Leaving Brucker to continue sniping at the enemy on the other side of the wall, Dieter hurried to help his

fellow Scarlets repel the goblin assault before the
enemy turned their breach into a bridgehead.

The night goblins were armed with a bewildering
variety of weapons, including curved swords, clubs,
picks, nets, knives, spears – one was even armed with
something that looked not unlike a cross between a
cattle prod and a boat hook. They swarmed onto the
ramparts, exploiting the breach. Dieter saw one of his
fellow soldiers die, an unknown Scarlet whose
attempts to hold back the green tide had ended in
heroic failure. Refusing to let the unknown man's
sacrifice go in vain, Dieter pushed forward and
launched himself into the enemy with the regimental
battle cry on his lips.

'Forward the 3rd! Forward for Hochland! Forward
the Scarlets!'

With Gerhardt, Holst and Rieger beside him, Dieter
swept into the goblins. Battering into them with his
shield, swinging his sword in arcs of destruction, he
sent goblins squealing to their deaths as they fell back
over the wall or tumbled from the rampart into the
courtyard below.

Without thought for his own safety, Dieter pushed
on into the enemy, relying on his comrades to cover
his flanks. Leaping over the wall, a goblin tried to hit
him with its club, only for Dieter to smash the creature's head to pulp with his shield. Another goblin
followed it. Dieter killed it swiftly, and moved on to
the next. Instinctively, he realised this was a key
moment in the battle. If the goblins managed to push
the Scarlets back from the walls so early in the siege,
the battle would be all but over.

Cutting a bloody swathe through the goblins swarming over the wall, he managed to reach the scaling ladder that was the source of the breach. Unlike the other ladders the goblins used, this one had a metal hook at the end that had bitten into the substance of the wall and held it fast.

'Cover my back,' Gerhardt said from beside him. Without Dieter realising it, the older man had kept pace with him as he cut his way through the goblin ranks. 'I'll unhook the ladder, but I need you to cover me.'

Nodding his agreement, he took up a position directly in front of the ladder while Gerhardt hacked at it with his sword and tried to dislodge it. Wary of blunting his blade on the metal hook, Gerhardt struck at the hook's wooden housing instead. Suddenly, a goblin appeared at the top of ladder and tried to strike at him.

Slashing the creature from its perch before it could achieve its aim, Dieter realised the flow of goblins up the ladder had slowed to zero. Such was the creatures' cowardice, they stopped ascending the ladder the moment the two men had appeared at its top. Presumably, the goblins below had assumed the humans would destroy the ladder and, except for one foolhardy soul, had decided not to risk climbing it while there was the danger of the ladder being dislodged.

The situation made his and Gerhardt's task easier. Guarding the ladder as Gerhardt hacked at it, Dieter saw his comrade's sword finally smash through the housing, sending the broken ladder falling to the ground.

Looking right and left along the ramparts, Dieter saw the goblin attack was faltering. The enemy had managed to gain access to the wall in a couple of places, only to be pushed back by the defenders. Gazing down from his vantage at the goblins below him, Dieter saw that the greenskins had already started turning to run back to the safety of the woods.

As the last of the goblin attackers retreated, Dieter heard a cheer along the ramparts as the Scarlets celebrated their victory. Around him, men started to move the wounded and the dying off the ramparts, while throwing the bodies of dead goblins over the wall. Joining in to help them, Dieter was pleased to notice Gerhardt, Holst and Rieger, as well as the marksman Brucker, had all escaped the fight relatively unscathed.

Looking further up the wall, he saw that Krug had also survived – a fact he felt less inclined to celebrate. It was clear the feeling was mutual. Seeing Dieter glance his way while he talked to his crony Febel, Krug responded with a sneering smile.

Ignoring him, Dieter turned to help Holst lift a wounded handgunner down from the rampart to the courtyard. Once the last of the wounded and the dead had been cleared away, he returned to take up his place on the wall once more with Gerhardt and the others. Even as he resumed his position, however, he saw a new horde of night goblins had begun to emerge from the cover of the tree line.

At the centre of the enemy mass was a group of goblins carrying a huge battering ram. They were flanked on either side by archers. Behind them, Dieter could see other goblins, some of which herded monstrous, muscular, round-bodied animals that bobbed up and down impatiently and strained to go forward. Each animal had a mouth that extended across the full width of its body, filled with rows of sharp teeth. They were so unlike any other animal Dieter had ever seen that he could not help but find them disturbing. Looking more closely, he realised they could only be the creatures called squigs that Brucker had talked about.

It looked as though the battle was far from over.

THE NEXT ATTACK took the form of an assault on the main gates.

Showing more tactical organisation than Dieter would have credited them with, the second wave of night goblins attacked with a definite battle plan. While the goblins carrying the battering ram advanced on the gates, their archers unleashed a rain of arrows obviously intended to force the defenders into keeping their heads down.

Sadly, from the goblin perspective, neither tactic proved particularly successful. The effectiveness of the goblin archers was blunted by the fact they refused to advance from the shadow of the forest. Given the lack of power and relative lack of range of their short bows, the archers' refusal to advance meant the majority of their arrows fell pitifully short, while the few that made it to the ramparts or the courtyard were easily deflected by the Scarlets' shields.

In the meantime, having suffered several casualties from the sporadic gunshots of the handgunners, the archers abruptly withdrew, leaving the goblins manning the battering ram without any missile support.

The result, predictably, was that the assault failed. The men guarding the gates rained down stones and gunfire on the goblin besiegers. Within a short space of time, the goblins fled, leaving the battering ram abandoned behind them.

'So much for that,' Brucker said, watching the goblin retreat. He glanced up at the moon overhead. 'But there's at least another four hours before sunrise. They'll attack again, and again, trying to wear us down.'

'Is the sunrise that important?' Dieter asked him. 'You think they won't attack in the daytime?'

'I can't say it for definite, but usually they don't like attacking by day,' Brucker told him. 'They know they have the advantage when it's dark. Deep down, all goblins are cowards. If we can hold 'em off until sunrise, there's every chance they'll give up – at least until tomorrow. Even then, there's a chance they might give it up for good. Goblins don't do sieges well, not unless there's an orc about to keep them at it.'

'Get ready,' Gerhardt called out, having spotted movement in the forest. 'Here they come again.'

All at once, dozens of small glowing lights appeared amid the darkness of the trees. At first, Dieter wondered if the goblins had lit candles for some unfathomable reason. Then, the true source of the lights was revealed as the enemy archers emerged from the forest once more.

Each goblin archer had a burning fire arrow strung in its bowstring. Raising their bows, they sent them arcing towards the mill. Evidently, having failed twice to take the mill by frontal assault, they had decided to burn them out.

'Pathetic,' Holst grunted as they watched from the rampart as the fire arrows streaked through the night sky. 'I know they're goblins, but you think they'd realise this is no different from the last time they used arrows.'

His words were quickly proven right. The majority of the fire arrows fell short and petered out in the mud below the exterior walls. The few arrows that hit the mark were swiftly extinguished by the mill's defenders.

'Incredible,' Holst shook his head in weary amazement. 'I know greenskins are supposed to be stupid, but you'd think they'd notice there's a stream running through the mill. Even if they had managed to set the building alight, we've got a ready supply of water to douse the flames.'

'I think they did notice,' Rieger said, drawing his comrades' attention to a commotion further along the wall. 'In fact, I'd say they are trying to make use of it.'

Turning to look in the direction Rieger had indicated, Dieter saw the activity was among the men guarding the section where the mill stream went under the wall. The source of their concern seemed to be something that was happening at the foot of the wall.

At first, Dieter was at a loss to understand what was going on. Then, he saw goblins moving by the entrance to the mill stream tunnel and realised what had happened. Unaware of the presence of the iron grille that barred entrance to the mill via the tunnel, the goblins had apparently sent a raiding party to enter it under cover of the fire arrow attack.

Predictably, the attempted assault had ended disastrously. Dieter saw a few wet and wounded goblins stumbling away from the tunnel as the Scarlets made mocking catcalls and threw rocks and stones after them.

'So much for greenskin subtlety,' Rieger said. 'They've tried three different ways into the mill in the last half hour, and so far all they've managed to do is give most of us a breather. I can't imagine they'll leave things that way for long, though. We'd better get ready. It's only a matter of time before they revert to the standard greenskin way of solving every problem – outright physical force.'

IT SOON BECAME clear Rieger had called the situation correctly. Having briefly adopted a more subtle approach in their siege of the mill, the goblins swiftly reverted to type. They launched a full frontal assault again, attacking from all sides at once and, this time, combining the use of scaling ladders with a simultaneous assault by battering ram on the front gates.

'Well, if at first you don't succeed,' Rieger said as hordes of goblins emerged from the forest and the enemy strategy was made clear. 'Try again.'

Dieter was calm as he watched the night goblins approach the mill, but still he found it almost extraordinary that the other men around him could greet an attack of such magnitude with so limited a show of emotion. The goblins had overwhelming numbers on their side, even if the walls and other defences of the mill gave the Scarlets and their allies the advantage. Everywhere he looked it was as though they were surrounded by a sea of goblins. The mill was an island in a broiling green ocean filled with hate and malice.

Yet, despite the situation, Gerhardt and the others seemed almost indifferent to danger. Dieter supposed it was a matter of experience. Each of these men had been a soldier for at least a decade, with years of hard campaigning and bloody, desperate fights behind them.

War made men different, Dieter was learning. When he thought about it, he found it hard to imagine what manner of man he would be in ten years' time.

Assuming he survived that long, of course. At the moment, ten years seemed a very distant prospect.

'Get ready,' Gerhardt said. 'We've already repulsed them the last time they used ladders. We need to do it again, prevent them from getting a foothold on the walls. Above all else, we need to stop them from thinking they are making progress. We want them to think it's hopeless and lose confidence. With so many numbers behind them, it's the only way we'll beat them.'

The battle mirrored the events of the goblins' first attack. The handgunners opened fire, doing their best to winnow the enemy numbers before they could reach the walls. Then, the Scarlets dropped rocks and stones on the goblins' heads.

When the greenskins pushed their ladders up against the walls, the mill's defenders fought them off. Even as he joined in the fight, however, Dieter noticed a difference in the enemy's manner. At times, during the first attack, it had seemed as if the goblins almost expected defeat. They had given up relatively easily, fleeing after their initial attempts to climb the wall were repelled.

This time, the goblin army seemed more determined. When the first wave of attackers failed to gain a foothold on the wall with their ladders, they were swiftly replaced by a second wave of goblins using exactly the same tactics. Then, when the second wave was defeated, a third wave of goblins appeared equipped with more ladders.

Throughout it all, the attack did not falter. It was as though the goblins had acquired new grit and determination from an unknown source.

To Dieter, it felt as if hours had passed. The Scarlets had exhausted their supply of rocks and stones, just as the handgunners had exhausted their supply of powder and shot. Bit by bit, the successive waves of goblins had begun to encroach on the territory of the mill until it was as though the enemy were permanently camped at the foot of the walls. It was no longer possible to differentiate between the different waves of the enemy assault. Instead, the assault had become one, long, drawn-out struggle. The worst of it was, little by little, it felt as though the Scarlets were being slowly overwhelmed.

Refusing to retreat despite suffering appalling losses, the goblins continued their assault. Over time, the ramparts at the top of the walls became awash with struggling bodies as the human defenders and their goblin opponents fought in savage hand-to-hand combat.

It was the hardest, most bloody fighting Dieter had ever known. No sooner did he strike down one goblin than another quickly appeared to take its place. The Scarlets had suffered their own losses, and as men fell from the ramparts other men rushed up from the courtyard to take their place.

Despite the fact they were unable to repulse the goblin attack, Dieter felt the mill's defenders were holding their own. For their part, despite the protracted fight, the goblins had not managed to take the exterior walls. As long as Dieter and the other men on the ramparts could maintain that situation there was every chance that goblin morale would eventually crumble and the battle would be won.

Still, for the moment, there seemed no end in sight. The goblins did not want for numbers. Even as Dieter killed yet another enemy, he felt gripped by a bone-numbing weariness. He was breathing hard, pushed to the edge of exhaustion by the endless bloodstained grind of the battle. He knew the other men around him must have felt a similar tiredness. The fight had gone on so long, time seemed to have lost all meaning.

Yet, abruptly, Dieter found he was reminded of time's passing. As he smashed the hilt of his sword into the face of the goblin nearest him, Dieter caught a glimpse of a gathering redness in the eastern sky.

Risking a momentary glance to confirm it, he realised the sun was beginning to rise. The dawn was coming and, with it, the prospect of victory. Remembering Brucker's words earlier, Dieter found he hoped the marksman had been right when he said night goblins preferred not to fight in the day.

For better or worse, he supposed he would soon know whether Brucker had been correct. The marksman was right beside him, forced to fight hand-to-hand with the rest of the wall guards against the goblins when his ammunition had given out. Dieter was almost tempted to call out to him, to draw his attention to the sunrise, but the close press of the enemy around them left little room for any thoughts of bravado.

Either way, they would quickly know the answer.

Then, just as Dieter had begun to convince himself the goblin attack might indeed be faltering, he saw a new horror, a terrifying sight that would remain in his nightmares until the day he died.

A dark and massive shape suddenly emerged from the forest while the goblins around it screamed out in shrieks of joy and wonder.

It was a scorpion, but a giant example of that insect, far larger than any animal Dieter had ever seen in his life before. It was hard to judge, but it looked to be at least fifteen paces long, with a body that was five paces wide – not counting the reach of its claws. It was enormous and horrifying, a busy writhing insect thing, the very appearance of which was enough to create a sick feeling in the pit of Dieter's stomach. Abruptly, he realised there was a reason bugs were normally small – it was a mercy, the work of benevolent gods, intended to preserve the human mind from ever understanding just what manner of loathsome horror each insect represented.

'Sigmar protect us,' Brucker whispered beside him. The marksman made the sign of the hammer as though he hoped it might ward off the monster. 'I had heard tales that such things existed, but I never thought it possible...'

The giant scorpion had a rider. A night goblin warlord sat on the creature's back, his squat form swathed in a black robe, chainmail armour and a weird assortment of metal oddments and bones that Dieter could only assume was meant to be some kind of regalia.

Watching the warlord prodding his mount forward while the night goblins around them cheered, Dieter realised the battle for the mill was swiftly heading for a climax. His hopes that goblin morale might collapse now looked forlorn. Buoyed by the appearance of their chieftain and his 'pet', the goblin army redoubled their efforts.

It no longer mattered whether it was day or night, whether the sun rose or set. The Scarlets and their allies had fought the good fight, but it looked to be in vain.

Death, in the form of a giant insect with snapping claws and an arching venom-laden tail, was sweeping toward them.

CHAPTER THIRTEEN
FOOLISH HEROICS

'STAND FAST!' SERGEANT Bohlen's voice roared out over the ramparts. 'Stand fast the 3rd! Stand fast for Hochland! Stand fast the Scarlets!'

'Stand fast!' Gerhardt yelled. 'Stand fast the Scarlets!'

The cry was taken up all around the mill walls and the courtyard. As men struggled to hold back the goblin tide pressing ever more keenly upon them, they joined in the general chorus. The regimental battle cry rang out over the scene of battle. From grizzled veteran to rawest recruit, the words came out.

'Stand fast the 3rd! Stand fast for Hochland! Stand fast the Scarlets!'

Even the handgunners contributed their voices. In the push and pull of battle, amid the sound of screams and the smell of fresh blood, earlier allegiances were forgotten. Today, they were all Scarlets. Facing death, they were united.

But even as the words rang out proudly and strong, there was an element of uncertainty hidden within them. A seed of doubt that had taken root in each and every heart at the appearance of the giant scorpion and its master.

'Sweet Sigmar, look at the size of it,' Holst said. 'If that's the bug, I wouldn't want to see the man whose boot heel is big enough to crush it.'

His witticism, such as it was, fell on deaf ears. On the ramparts around him, men and goblins were too lost in their individual life-or-death struggles to pay much attention.

Even as he said it, Holst knew he was whistling in the dark. It was his nature to try and deflect the seriousness of any situation with humour. Looking at the spectacle of the scorpion advancing on the mill, however, he found it difficult to think of anything that was actually funny.

A goblin charged screaming toward him brandishing a heavy, cleaver-like blade. Holst deflected its blow with his shield, then stabbed his sword deep into its chest. A second goblin followed it, and a third. Holst made short work of them, cutting one down with a sword slash to the throat while he smashed his shield into the face of the other.

'Any more for any more?' he shouted at no one in particular. 'I'm just getting started, you ugly runty bastards!'

He had no idea whether the goblins could even understand him, but it felt good to give voice to his frustration. Right now, Holst felt like screaming his anger loud enough to deafen every living thing within twenty paces. He wanted to curse the gods, to damn them all as bastards, and to hell with the consequences.

It had looked like they were winning, that was the fact which frustrated him. Only five minutes earlier, Holst had been confident of victory. Dawn's rosy fingers had begun to light up the sky to the east, while the goblin horde had not made any progress in trying to drive the mill's defenders back from the walls. In such circumstances, he had been sure it was only a matter of time before the goblins' morale failed and they turned to run.

Then, the scorpion had appeared and ruined everything.

Even with the goblin warlord riding on its back, it was clear the monster was at best only half-tamed. As it lumbered its way through the thronging goblins, it paused here and there to grab a struggling greenskin with its claws and toss it into its mouth. The goblins around it did not seem to greet this behaviour with shock, as though they expected nothing less of the creature and its appetites.

Unencumbered by any of the limitations faced by the goblins, the thing advanced on the mill wall and simply climbed over it, sweeping the men in front of it from the ramparts with its claws. Moving past the wall, the insect monstrosity advanced in the courtyard. All but immune to the attacks of the puny soldiers who scurried around it, it laid waste to its enemies with its claws and tail while the goblin warlord on its back egged it on.

Meanwhile, goblins had begun to surge through the gap in the Hochlanders' defence caused by the scorpion's attack. Although the men to the west and east of the breach tried their best to stem the flow of invaders, their efforts seemed hopeless. Despite hours of fighting, of blood and sweat, the defence of the mill lay within moments of collapse.

It will take a miracle to save us now, Holst thought to himself as he lashed out with his sword and downed another goblin. He had never really considered the prospect until that instant, but suddenly it occurred to him that these could well be the last seconds of his life.

He resolved to meet his death in the same way he had lived his life. He would go down fighting, vowing to spit in the eye of whichever goblin finally struck the fatal blow and killed him.

If there was one small comfort, it occurred to him, it was that he would die with so many old friends around him. Gerhardt, Rieger, even Sergeant Bohlen: he had known them all for years and counted each one of them as kings and princes – in spirit, if not in title. Like Holst, they would fight until the last.

Sadly, not all men were made of the same, stern stuff. From the corner of his eye, Holst saw Dieter Lanz suddenly turn and flee the ramparts. Appalled, Holst came to the obvious conclusion: the Scarlets' newest recruit evidently had a hidden yellow streak.

Given that he was already too busy fighting for his life, Holst did not try to stop Dieter's flight. The sight of it filled him with sorrow, however. He had thought the young recruit had the stuff to be a fine soldier, but it seemed he was mistaken. He understood it, naturally enough. Fear could become any man's master, especially when he was a young blood, unused to the blood, violence and sheer madness of close quarter battle. Any man could break, Holst understood that, but it didn't mean he had to forgive it. He would accept almost any flaw in a comrade, but cowardice was the one inexcusable sin in a soldier. To make matters worse, in his panic, Dieter appeared to have completely lost all sense of direction.

Instead of running away from the scorpion, he was running *towards* it.

DIETER LANDED ON the flagstones of the courtyard and was running toward the scorpion before he even had a chance to question what he was doing.

It was for the best this way, he supposed. His decision to charge the scorpion and try to kill it was born of a moment's mad impulse. He had seen the creature climb over the mill wall as though the wall was not even there. He had seen it slaughter the men guarding the wall with ease. He had seen it skitter across the courtyard, its tail rising and falling in a series of deadly arcs, its claws grabbing men and crushing them, pausing only to feed the occasional sundered body into its mouth.

He had seen the creature and he had felt a rising sense of terror and despair. Its very presence had seemed to enliven the goblin army with a new sense of energy and purpose. They followed in the scorpion's wake, surging onto the walls and into the courtyard as they tracked the creature's trail of destruction. Realising the Hochlanders' dogged defence of the mill was on the verge of collapse, Dieter had been provoked to take action. Admittedly, the fact he was not entirely sure what that action would be was possibly a defect of his decision, but he hoped to come up with something before he came within range of the scorpion's claws.

Abruptly, an idea occurred to him. In the cold light of day he was sure it would seem like madness, but at that instant any kind of plan was better than nothing.

Angling his path as he ran through the courtyard, he headed for the mill stream that emerged from underneath the exterior wall and travelled across the courtyard until it ran underneath the spars of the massive mill wheel set at the side of the mill house.

The stream was deep and fast flowing. Casting aside his shield, helmet and breastplate as he ran, Dieter jumped into the stream and swam across it. He was taking a risk, he knew. The current was strong, and if he lost control it could easily drag him into the mill wheel where he would likely either drown or be crushed by the turning wheel.

Fortunately, he was able to make the swim. Emerging from the other side of the stream, his sword still gripped in his hand, he ran toward the scorpion.

As he charged toward the creature he briefly wondered how he would attract its attention, but it quickly became clear it would not be an issue. Perhaps it was the fact Dieter was the only man in the courtyard running towards it rather than fleeing, but the scorpion immediately fixated on him as he moved closer. The monster's black eyes swivelled to regard him, while – sure of its superiority – the goblin on its back grinned down at Dieter with a smug, malevolent smile.

Wary of getting too close, Dieter came skidding to a halt. Then, turning to run away, he was pleased as he glanced over his shoulder to see the scorpion had decided to give chase.

Hoping the creature's goblin rider would not be intelligent enough to guess his plan, Dieter sprinted over to the mill house. Coming to a halt in front of the enormous brick housing that sheltered the mill wheel, Dieter watched the scorpion charge toward him.

He waited, muttering a prayer to Sigmar under his breath. If the scorpion decided to attack him with his claws, or if Dieter failed to time it correctly, the whole business would be over quickly – and, with it, any chance of defeating the goblins.

The size of the creature was extraordinary. As the scorpion loomed over him, Dieter felt like a character from a childish nursery rhyme confronting a giant. He raised his sword in a threatening gesture, inwardly aware that the blade must seem no larger than a needle to the eyes of the monster.

Lifting the bulbous stinger at the end of its tail high above its head, the scorpion made ready to strike. To Dieter, the moment seemed frozen. Seeing a tell-tale quiver run along the creature's tail, he dived out of the way as the scorpion's sting flashed through the air and smashed through the stonework of the housing wall behind him.

The creature hissed in what he could only guess was the sound of disappointment. It lashed out again, its tail striking the housing at several points along its base as Dieter rolled desperately along the ground to elude it.

Hissing even more furiously the scorpion lifted its tail to strike once more, but the damage was already done. With an awful wrenching noise, the housing collapsed, spilling an avalanche of falling bricks, splintered timbers and the entire weight of the tilting mill wheel onto the scorpion and its goblin rider.

Dieter saw the creature crushed beneath a rain of stone. Then, something struck him hard in the ribs, knocking him to the ground. He felt the breath *whoosh* from his lungs as a heavy weight pressed down on him. Realising he could no longer breathe, he began to panic, his view of the scene around him – and whatever it was that weighed so heavily on his torso – was obscured by the clouds of dust raised by the collapsing housing.

Dieter tried to call out for help, but it was too late. Trapped as surely as the scorpion under the weight of fallen stone, he lost consciousness.

'DAMNED LUCKY IF you ask me,' a voice intruded into his black, dreamless sleep. 'I've seen some foolish heroics in my time, but that was absolute madness.'

'I wonder,' a second voice said. 'I don't argue that it was foolish. But I suppose he knew what he was doing, after a fashion. He did grow up in a mill house, after all.'

'That's as may be,' the first voice retorted. 'But I'm guessing he never went out to collapse a mill wheel before. Assuming that's what he went out to do, of course. I'm still not convinced the whole thing wasn't just blind luck.'

'Who cares if it was?' a third voice joined the conversation. 'It worked, didn't it? Bravest thing I ever saw. I told you, right when I first introduced him to you, the lad has stones the size of a young bull's.'

'Actually, I believe you only said that later,' the second voice disagreed. 'When you first introduced us you said he was a dab hand with a sword, nothing else.'

Recognising the voices as belonging to Gerhardt, Rieger and Holst, Dieter opened his eyes to find he was staring up at the sky. It was daylight and the sun was high overhead.

'Careful, lad,' Gerhardt said solicitously. 'I wouldn't try to move just yet.'

'What happened?' Turning his head to look around him, Dieter saw he was lying on a makeshift stretcher outside the mill house. He saw other wounded men around him, being tended to by their comrades. Looking further afield, he saw the courtyard of the mill was littered with goblin bodies.

'You were knocked about pretty bad when the mill wheel collapsed,' Gerhardt told him. 'A broken timber fell on you. I've done my best to bind your ribs, but I think you've broken a couple of them. You'll live, of course, but I wouldn't be surprised if there are times over the next few days when you'll wish you hadn't. It's always hard going when you've broken a rib. Even breathing hurts.'

'But, what happened to the goblins?' Finding his skull felt like it was filled with old rags, Dieter tried shaking his head to clear it. He quickly regretted it, as the movement caused a shiver of pain to run through his ribs.

'They fled,' Holst said. 'After the mill wheel collapsed, burying the scorpion and their chieftain, the goblins turned tail and ran. Of course, we did our best to make 'em pay for attacking this place. By the time the general got here it was all over, bar the mopping up.'

'The general?' Dieter looked at him quizzically. 'What are you talking about?'

'Come and see,' Holst said. Then, when he noticed Gerhardt glowering at him, he shrugged. 'All right, I know you said he shouldn't move. But it can't hurt that much, not if he takes it slowly. And it stands to reason, he'll want to know what's going on. And, besides, good news makes a man heal more quickly – ask any surgeon.'

Despite further protestations from Gerhardt, Holst and Rieger carefully helped Dieter to his feet. Supporting him between them, they began to lead him toward the mill gates. After they had gone about a dozen paces, Dieter had them pause for a few seconds so he could look around him.

Now he was up on his feet, he could see the dead scorpion buried beneath a mound of bricks and timbers, the shattered mill wheel lying on top of it. Glancing at the other wounded men nearby, a sudden thought occurred to him.

'How is Kuranski?' Dieter asked.

'He didn't make it,' Gerhardt answered. 'He died while the rest of us were fighting the goblins. We were going to bury him in a little while, along with the others.'

Gerhardt turned to gaze at some of the human bodies lying among the dead goblins littering the courtyard.

'We lost some good men last night,' he said. 'We have to hope it was worth it – that, finally, things have turned the corner and we're going to start winning this war.'

'They will do,' Holst predicted confidently. 'Now we've got Old Iron Britches leading us, everything will be better. Just you wait and see.'

'Iron Britches?' Dieter asked.

'Come on,' Holst urged him forward. 'I said we had something to show you.'

Leading him slowly to the open gates, the three men helped Dieter prop himself up alongside one of the gate posts. Holst pointed to one of the areas of open ground on the other side of the mill's walls.

Turning to look in the direction Holst had indicated, Dieter saw a grey-haired man in full plate walking among the night goblin bodies lying outside the walls. The man looked to be about sixty years of age, with a grim, stoic countenance and his hair cut close to his scalp in a severe, military style. Half a dozen knights, also in full plate, walked beside the old man as an escort. Noticing that the knights wore the colours of the Count of Hochland's personal livery emblazoned on their shields, Dieter's breath caught in his throat.

'Is that him?' he asked the others. 'Is it Count Aldebrand?'

'So speaks the bumpkin,' Holst laughed and shook his head good-naturedly. 'You can tell our poor country mouse here hasn't spent much time in high society.'

'The Count is a considerably younger man,' Rieger said. 'The man you see over there is His Excellency, General Ludwig von Grahl.'

'Old Iron Britches,' Holst said. 'That's what his men call him. We must've served under him in a dozen campaigns. He's beaten the greenskins in battle before. Not to mention the beastmen, the marauder hordes and the damn Ostlanders. The finest general ever to have led the armies of Hochland, that's what they say about him. For myself, I believe it. Why, I remember at the Battle of Tannesfeld–'

'No doubt you saved his life,' Rieger cut him off before he could finish. 'I couldn't tell you whether he's really the best general in Hochland, Dieter. But, I know this. I've served under von Grahl before, and he knows his business. I'd trust him with my life.'

'Aye, I see it the same,' Gerhardt nodded. 'Von Grahl and his bodyguard arrived about an hour ago, alongside some outriders and a regiment-sized group of Kislevite horse archer mercenaries. Apparently, the General has been given command over every aspect of the province's defence. From now on, we answer to him.'

Looking at the man, Dieter wondered whether the others were right about him. His comrades' sense of joy and excitement now that General von Grahl was in command was readily apparent. Dieter wasn't quite sure if he could see it himself. Von Grahl looked to be an ordinary enough fellow in the flesh. Yet, Dieter had to admit he had a certain something. The general had an aura about him, an air of strength and decisiveness.

When Dieter had briefly glimpsed the army's original commander, General von Nieder, he had been struck by the fact the man looked like a tax collector. With General von Grahl it was different. There was no mistaking the fact that von Grahl was a soldier.

Perhaps it was another false dawn. But, for the first time in Dieter was not sure how long, he had the definite impression that things were looking up.

PART THREE:
THE KILLING TIME

(Late Brauzeit – Early Kaldezeit)

From
The Testimony of General Ludwig von Grahl
(unexpurgated text):

…Once I arrived in the north, it became clear the task ahead was even more formidable than I had feared. The remnants of von Nieder's army were spread over half the province. They were dispirited and tired men, many of whom had forgotten what it is to be a soldier. At the same time, the orcs were in complete ascendancy.

The one small factor in our favour was the fact that the orc army was likewise spread over a great distance. Apparently, it had proved beyond even Ironfang's power to make sure his troops held their discipline for long. In the wake of victory, the greenskins had split back into their tribal groupings as they pursued the flee-ing human forces. Naturally, being greenskins, some of these tribal groups had fallen to looting every human habitation in their path, hampering their chieftain's efforts to bring his army together so he could continue driving southwards. We even heard reports of greenskin tribes fighting amongst themselves as their natural animosity toward each other reasserted itself.

Thankfully, the enemy's lack of discipline gave me valuable time to bring my own forces back into order. Gathering together the various bands of soldiers we met on the way north, I ordered my troops to press-gang every man they encountered who was capable of holding a weapon. From among the columns of weary refugees fleeing the orcs, we recruited thousands of such conscripts – many of them archers, already armed with the bows and arrows they used for hunting.

In the meantime, in the course of our journey northward, I had come to realise the wizard Emil Zauber had the potential to be a valuable ally. While most men are inclined to consult the Lore of the Heavens in the hope of divining their personal future, I am more interested in Zauber's ability to predict the weather. During the long journey to the north, a plan began to form in my mind.

Sigmar willing, it may help swing the war in our favour…

CHAPTER FOURTEEN
THE END OF A ROPE

'ERICH VON NIEDER, you have been found guilty of crimes against your Count, your province and its people,' the sergeant intoned, squinting up at the man standing on the scaffold. 'Your punishment has been decreed in accordance with army tradition and protocol. Do you have anything to say before the sentence is enacted?'

'Only that this is a travesty,' the former general replied, glaring down at his questioner. The rope had been fixed tight enough around his throat that he could only speak at the volume of a whisper. Despite this, he was defiant to the last. 'I am innocent. And, even if I wasn't, you have no power to judge me.'

Raising his eyes, von Nieder took in the situation around him. He was standing on a roughly fashioned wooden scaffold, beneath the branches of a broad elm destined to be the place of his death. His hands were tied behind him. Ahead of him several regiments of infantry had been drawn up in formation to watch his execution, while a number of the army's knights and officers stood off to the side of the scaffold, among them the army's new commander, General von Grahl.

Turning his head as far to the side as he could manage, von Nieder glared viperishly at a man he hated with a passion. Surrounded by his bodyguard and the officers of his staff, von Grahl met his gaze impassively. Still unable to raise his voice above a whisper, von Nieder uttered his final words before he faced eternity.

'I am of the nobility,' von Nieder said. He knew no one except perhaps the sergeant could hear him, but he spoke the words anyway, eager to leave some record – no matter how transient – of the injustice that had been foisted upon him. 'By the ancient legal codes of the Empire I am guaranteed the right to a trial before my peers. The Count will not forgive you this breach of precedent, von Grahl. You can hang me now, but the Count will punish you for it. Mark my words. One day soon, you'll kneel before the headsman's axe and wish you had not done this thing.'

The sergeant waited until von Nieder had finished his speech. Then, he raised his hand. Three drummers stood nearby. At the sergeant's signal, they began to beat a rolling rhythm.

'The sentence will be carried out,' the sergeant said. 'May the Lord Sigmar have mercy on your soul.'

Von Nieder felt rough hands behind him. He was pushed from the scaffold.

'THERE'S SOMETHING I never thought I'd see,' Holst muttered. 'A general being hanged. Granted, he probably deserves it. But, usually, if a general does something wrong, the worst punishment he can expect is being sent home in disgrace. The last thing you expect to see is them hanging a general. They save the hempen dance for our kind – for commoners, soldiers and other assorted undesirables.'

He was standing at attention in the front rank of the regiment, alongside Dieter, Gerhardt and Rieger. Half an hour earlier, the Scarlets had been summoned from their quarters along with several other regiments to bear witness to the death of the former general Erich von Nieder – once commander-in-chief of the armies of Hochland. For days, ever since von Nieder had been captured, rumours had run rife throughout the army that he had been sentenced to be hanged. No one had believed it, however – not until they were ordered to go and watch the execution.

The army was camped in the northern forests, a few leagues west of the mill house where Dieter and the others had made their stand against the night goblin army. In the wake of General von Grahl's arrival on the scene, it seemed to Dieter that everything had changed.

The last month had passed almost as a blur, as von Grahl assembled a new army made up of a mixture of old regiments like the Scarlets and new regiments recently constituted via a province-wide muster. Many of the newly-mustered regiments were still being equipped and trained further south, but General von Grahl had managed to acquire enough men to bolster his army – even if the majority of the new recruits had yet to see any action.

'I can't believe how small and fragile he looks,' Dieter said, staring at the man standing on the scaffold. 'I mean, I know he's an old man. But, it's the first time I've seen General von Nieder up close. I suppose I expected him to bigger.'

'Ex-general,' Rieger reminded him. 'And, as for hanging him, I hear it's because when the scouts found him von Nieder was carrying over a dozen bags of gold with him. Apparently, when the orcs overran us back in Erntezeit, von Nieder decided to loot the army's pay chest before he escaped. They think he was trying to cross the border into Ostland when the scouts found him. He probably hoped to live out his remaining years in luxury while his soldiers were busy running for their lives from the orcs. You ask me, hanging is almost too good for him.'

There was a vengeful tone to Rieger's voice. Usually, Rieger was inclined to sarcasm rather than anger, but in the case of von Nieder he seemed to view the man's behaviour as almost a personal affront. Dieter had heard whispers that Rieger had once trained to become a priest before he fell under the spell of the hellfire and brimstone sermons of men like Luther Huss. Disgusted by the corruption and venality of the priests he saw around him, Rieger had decided on the life of a simple soldier, hoping to find inner peace in the task of fighting Sigmar's enemies.

'Yes, well, *everyone* has heard that,' Holst snorted. 'That rumour has been through the camp like the Bretonnian Two-Step. If you want my opinion, I'd say Old Iron Britches has decided to hang von Nieder to make an example of him. It's always the way when you get a new general – he wants to hang a few men just so the rest of the army know he's not a man to be trifled with. Although, admittedly, I've never heard of a general hanging another general before. You think he'd be worried he's setting a precedent.'

'Quiet all of you,' Gerhardt said, his voice sounding a warning note. 'A man is about to die. He was a soldier – even if he wasn't a very good one. Show some respect.'

The drummers standing by the scaffold had begun to beat a rhythm. Watching with the others, Dieter saw two men step up quietly behind the scaffold. They wore black hoods to cover their faces. Dieter had heard the two executioners had been chosen randomly by lot – the hoods were to conceal their identities from the rest of the army and save them from retribution from anyone who might have held a good opinion of the man they were about to kill.

With a shiver, it occurred to Dieter he himself might have been chosen for that unpleasant duty – as could any man. It was a nasty thought. It was one thing to be called upon to kill a man in battle, quite another to administer his execution.

There but for the grace of Sigmar, thought Dieter. He shivered again.

There was no trapdoor in the scaffold von Nieder stood on, that particular device having proven beyond the wit of the army's carpenters. Instead, his executioners moved behind him and simply pushed him from the scaffold.

Von Nieder's fall was broken with a jerk as he reached the end of the rope. His legs flailed beneath him as his body swayed back and forth under the elm. Watching the man's struggles, Dieter felt sick to his stomach. He had never seen a man hanged before. He was struck by the cruelty of it. Even as he watched, the former general's struggles seemed to grow more frantic, more desperate.

'Sweet Sigmar,' Holst breathed, making the sign of the hammer. 'They didn't give him enough rope to break his neck. The poor bastard's strangling to death.'

As von Nieder's body continued to sway under the elm with his legs kicking wildly beneath him, the two executioners looked at each other as though uncertain as to their next move.

After a pregnant pause, one of the hooded men jumped down from the scaffold and advanced on the hanging man. He turned to look toward the watching General von Grahl as though asking his permission. Then, at a nod from von Grahl, he grabbed hold of von Nieder's wildly flailing legs and pulled down hard on them, trying to add his weight to the load on the hanged man's neck in the hope it would end the matter more quickly.

Realising his comrade's aim, the second executioner leapt down to join him. Together, they pulled down on von Nieder's body. Slowly, the hanged man's struggles subsided. With the combined weight of the executioners added to the task, it ended quickly. Von Nieder's neck broke with an audible snap. With a last forlorn twitch, the body stopped moving.

'A bad business,' Holst said, once it was over. 'That's the problem when you have men draw lots to decide who will be hangman. You never know whether the men who are picked have any idea of what they are doing. I've always said, if ever I found myself scheduled to die on the gallows, I'd bribe the gaolers to give me some weirdroot or mandrake. At least that way, you wouldn't suffer.'

He fell quiet. As the drums signalled the end of the execution, and the sergeants shouted orders for the soldiers to return to their duties, the Scarlets dispersed in a sombre mood, each man made mindful of their mortality by their former general's execution.

To Dieter, it seemed Holst was right in declaring it a bad business. He would not have wished von Nieder's death on any man – not even Krug, who with characteristic tenacity had managed to survive the siege at the mill house.

The enmity between Dieter and Krug was as palpable as ever. Even as the Scarlets made their way back to their tents in the eastern quadrant of the encampment that housed General von Grahl's rapidly growing army, Dieter saw Krug glaring at him from afar. It seemed inevitable there would be a reckoning between them one day.

For Dieter's part, he hoped it would be sooner rather later. He had grown tired of having to be wary at all times, watching to ensure Krug did not slip a knife between his ribs when he wasn't looking.

He had toyed with the idea of challenging Krug to a duel. Strictly speaking, duelling between men who were not either of the nobility or officer rank was forbidden. In swordsmen regiments, however, it had long been the practice to turn a blind eye to such restrictions. Although duels to the death were rare, it was not uncommon for men to settle their disputes at the point of a blade.

Upon taking command of the army, however, General von Grahl had made it clear he intended to zealously enforce the strictures against duelling. He had issued a proclamation announcing that, with Hochland in the midst of a 'time of peril', it was no longer permissible for men to risk injury or even death in private quarrels. What was more, the general had made it plain his wishes in the matter would be enforced in the strongest terms possible. Henceforth, any men found duelling, along with any men who were found to have aided the duel, were to be sentenced to death.

The former general, von Nieder, may have been the most prominent figure to be executed, but he had hardly been the first. General von Grahl had shown no compunction when it came to assigning the penalty of death. In the last month, by Dieter's reckoning, two dozen men had been hanged from the same elm tree for crimes including desertion, looting, theft of army supplies, and a range of other offences.

It was widely understood that the general was doing this as part of a stern policy intended to restore discipline to Hochland's army. In the dark days of the retreat before the orcs, discipline had been completely lost. The Scarlets had fared relatively well in that regard. Dieter had heard rumours of units that had mutinied and turned on their own commanders. There were tales of entire regiments of deserters fleeing Hochland altogether and trying to cross the border into Ostland or Nordland. There were even tales of cannibalism, of soldiers who in their search for food had turned on each other.

Dieter was not sure whether he believed all the tales he heard. He was learning that gossip was a popular pastime among soldiers – the more outrageous the tale the better. It helped to pass the time and stave off boredom. Dieter had even heard wild rumours that the orc army had bypassed them and was already besieging the gates of Hergig. That last tale at least he completely discounted.

Still, amid all the mad tales of soldiers turned cannibal and wild rumours of the enemy advance, there had been at least one cause for celebration among the Scarlets. Despite theories to the contrary, their regimental commander Captain Harkner had turned out to be very much alive. Having been reunited with his men in the wake of the Scarlets' stand against the night goblins at the mill house, Captain Harkner had reassumed command – a fact which had come as a relief to many, not least Sergeant Bohlen.

They had lost men, and the progress of the war against the orcs was far from clear, but to Dieter's mind the fact they had their captain back could only be a good omen. Having recovered from the worst effects of the long retreat from the orcs and the draining siege against the goblins, the Scarlets were once more ready to fight. Meanwhile, all around them, the rest of General von Grahl's new army was taking shape. Come what may, they were ready to fight the greenskins.

Now, it was only a matter of time.

From
The Testimony of General Ludwig von Grahl
(unexpurgated text):

...It is never a pleasant duty to kill a man, much less order him to be executed with a rope of hemp around his neck. Still, in the case of Erich von Nieder, I maintain I had no choice.

Admittedly, I may have exceeded my authority. Von Nieder was a nobleman, with all a nobleman's rights. Among those, he had the right to be judged by a jury of his peers and the right to appeal to the Count of Hochland to reprieve his sentence. He also had the right to die on the headsman's block, not to be hanged like a common criminal.

Sadly, I had no choice. There was no question of von Nieder's guilt. The bags of gold pieces he was carrying when he was captured still bore the wax seals that identified them as part of the army paychest. I had already ordered other men hung for less serious offences. If I had let von Nieder go, or allowed him the luxury of any other death, it would have suggested I expected less of those of my own class than I do of the common soldier. If such notions were allowed to spread, it would prove damaging to morale and unity at a time when I am trying to rebuild these men into an effective army.

Von Nieder had to die. It was a hard decision, and I feel sorry for it. But there was no other decision to be made.

Still, I find I feel guilty. Not just for von Nieder, but for the others as well. He was not the first man I had ordered hanged, nor sadly is he likely to be the last. In some ways, it is a worse thing to command a man's execution than to have to see him die in battle. At least in the latter case, it is the enemy who is responsible.

In the meantime, matters continue apace. My regular consultations with the wizard Emil Zauber have begun to bear fruit. He assures me a series of heavy autumn storms are about to begin, drenching this whole area in rain. At the same time, the orcs have been reported some leagues to the east, moving towards us. With Sigmar's grace, all my plans may be about to come together.

Accordingly, I have sent a prearranged signal to Count Aldebrand who is at camp some distance southwards, overseeing the muster. I sent the message via carrier-hawk – one of half a dozen such birds the Count gifted to me before I left Hergig. The message the bird carries is brief and to the point:

'We are ready to destroy the enemy. Come north with all due haste.'

CHAPTER FIFTEEN
COMETH THE HOUR

'RAIN,' HOLST SNORTED in derision as the storm fell to earth around them. 'I'd hoped we'd seen the last of a storm like this when we fought those damn night goblins at the mill house. But, no, the curse of the poor infantryman holds good. The gods are taking pleasure pissing down on our shoulders once more.'

It was night, and they were standing guarding the entrance to the army encampment. Hugging his cloak around him as he shivered against the cold, Dieter listened to the beginnings of another one of Holst's diatribes with a weary sense of resignation.

'You know what month this is?' Holst asked, warming to his theme. 'It's Kaldezeit – "cold time". Now, I'm not saying it isn't cold, but you think they'd name these months properly. Rain time would be more apt. It would make more sense.'

'The killing time,' Dieter said, half to himself.

'Hnn? What?' Holst raised a wet eyebrow.

'The killing time. That's what they used to call it in the village where I lived. At this time of year, the farmers are making their choice as to which animals they'll keep over the winter and which ones will be slaughtered. They slaughter them now, before the worst of the winter comes, so they don't have to waste any winter feed on them.'

'Really?' Holst shook his head in mock wonderment. 'You know, you are a constant source of information, Dieter. I'm not saying any of it is actually useful. But you know some things, to give you your due.'

Holst laughed as though he had said something enormously funny. Then, squinting to see through the rain falling in great sheets around them, he stared down the trail and suddenly unsheathed his sword.

'I see lights in the distance,' Holst said, his good humour evaporating to be replaced by a more businesslike manner. 'Someone's coming. Go get the others.'

Turning away, Dieter ran to a nearby stand of trees where the rest of the men on guard duty were sheltering from the rain. Seeing the friendly faces of Gerhardt and Rieger, he nodded and hurried past them to the spot where Captain Harkner was standing with Sergeant Bohlen.

'Captain, come quickly! We saw lights in the distance! Someone is coming!'

Motioning for the other men to follow them, Captain Harkner ran with Dieter to rejoin Holst. Behind them, the other Scarlets spread out in a well-practiced pattern, doing their best to stay hidden from sight until the nature of the individuals headed towards them could be ascertained.

'There's a good few of them,' Holst said as Dieter and the captain appeared alongside him. 'They're using torches and they seem to be moving in good order, so I don't think they're greenskins. Could be they are a new batch of reinforcements.'

Further up the trail, the lights had grown brighter. As the new arrivals drew nearer, the sound of hoof-beats made it clear they were travelling on horseback. The light of their torches snaked down the trail behind them as though some fiery dragon was headed toward the encampment.

'Who goes there?' Holst called out loudly as the first of the riders came closer.

'The bodyguards of His Excellency Aldebrand Ludenhof, Count of Hochland and all related territories,' came back the gruff reply. 'Why? Who's asking?'

The riders appeared out of the rain, revealing a half a dozen knights wearing the Count's livery on their shields and panther skins around their shoulders. Coming to a stop before the Scarlets, the knights' leader raised a hand in salute and lifted his visor to look down at them.

'I am Graf Ernst von Toppel of the Knights Panther, leader of the bodyguard to His Excellency the Count of Hochland. Who's in charge here?'

'I am,' Captain Harkner stepped forward. 'Captain Harkner of the 3rd Hochland Swordsmen. Well met, sir knight.'

'Well met, captain,' the knight nodded. 'Count Aldebrand travels with us. He wishes to be taken to meet General von Grahl at once.'

'The Count is with you?' Harkner appeared surprised. Catching himself, he began again more calmly. 'Forgive my question. It is a matter for the Count as to where he goes and when. I speak only as a soldier, to whom the Count's presence here seems a good omen.'

'Let us hope so,' the knight said. 'It is a good time for omens, I think. The latest reports we have received say the orc army is only a few leagues north of here. Let us hope the Count will lead us to victory. Alongside General von Grahl, of course.'

'Of course,' Captain Harkner agreed. He gestured to his men to clear a path for the Count and his entourage. 'If you will follow me, I will send a runner to tell General von Grahl that the Count has arrived.'

From
The Testimony of General Ludwig von Grahl
(unexpurgated text):

...'You have a plan to defeat the greenskins?' the Count asked, once we were alone in my command tent. 'You will forgive our surprise, von Grahl, but we thought your plan was to contain the enemy, not destroy him. I thought you didn't have enough men to achieve that grandiose aim.'

'It is true I don't have as many men as I'd like, Your Excellency,' I replied. 'And, certainly, the plan is not without its risks. But circumstances have come together in a way which I believe will allow us to defeat the orcs in open battle, not just hold them.'

'Ah, yes, the rain.' The Count turned back to the maps spread out on the table before us, his quick sharp eyes taking in the details. 'You think it will make the difference?'

'I think it presents us with our best chance. I have chosen the battleground with the conditions in mind. The men have been drilled with a specific battle plan in mind. Nothing can ever be guaranteed in war, but they are as ready as they will ever be.'

'Good.'

Upon his arrival, the Count's servants had left a long wooden case on the table. He laid his hand across it now.

'You have done well, von Grahl. Whatever the outcome of the battle tomorrow, it will never be said that you shirked in your duty. You are a credit to Hochland. With that in mind, I wish to reward you.'

He opened the case, taking a sword from inside it. Removing the sword from its sheath, he revealed a rune-encrusted blade of obvious dwarf workmanship. It was no match for the runefang at his hip, but still the sword was a magnificent weapon.

'I took this from the province's armoury before I left Hergig. It is a mighty weapon, given to the Counts of Hochland some centuries ago in return for a service the Count of the time had performed for one of the dwarf holds. It seemed fitting that our general should ride into battle with such a blade.'

He handed the sword to me. Testing its weight, I found it light and responsive. At the same time, I could feel the power inside it, like a coiled serpent ready to strike.

'My liege... I don't know what to say.'

'Say nothing. Know only that this gift is a sign of my faith. I believe in your plan, von Grahl. It will be our honour to ride by your side tomorrow.'

He turned to look back at the plans.

'The battle lines are drawn. Now, the fate of Hochland is in the hands of the gods...'

CHAPTER SIXTEEN
FACING THE ENEMY

'MEN OF HOCHLAND,' the general had said earlier that morning as he delivered a final speech to the assembled troops under his command, 'today is a day that will live long in the memory of our people. Today is the day when we will sweep the greenskins aside. Today is the day when we will win a crushing victory.'

At those words, a cheer had rung out among the men. In his place among the ranks of the Scarlets, Dieter heard a word repeated by the soldiers around him, chanted almost, until it became like a heartbeat to which the entire army responded.

'Victory!' they said, cheering. 'Victory! Victory!'

A few hours later, he remembered those words as the Scarlets stood on a low ridge overlooking open fields. Last night, after a conference with Count Aldebrand, General von Grahl had abruptly ordered the army to break camp. He had marched them north, telling his men to take up position on a line of hills and ridges set facing a broad expanse of open country. On the other side of the fields, the greenskin army was already massing.

Looking down at the enemy army, Dieter was struck by how greatly the Hochlanders were outnumbered. It was hard to judge the matter with any accuracy, but by his rough estimate he reckoned the greenskins outnumbered them at least two to one – perhaps by as much as a factor of three to one if his estimate was out. Whatever their precise numbers, the sheer scale of the enemy force arrayed against the Hochlander army was terrifying.

As he waited for the battle to begin, Dieter cast his mind back to the previous night and the encounter with Count Aldebrand. If anything, calling it an encounter flattered the event. In reality, Dieter had caught nothing more than a brief glimpse of the Count as a party of Scarlets escorted the Count and his bodyguard to meet General von Grahl. The moment they got within the camp, the Scarlets had been dismissed and told to return to guard duty while a phalanx of greatswords took up escort duty in their stead.

Dieter supposed it was a matter of protocol. Despite their illustrious reputation as a fighting unit, the Scarlets were apparently judged too humdrum a regiment to be allowed the prestigious task of escorting their ruler. For Dieter's part, he took no offence at the snub. It was enough to him that, after eighteen years of life, he had finally caught his first glimpse of royalty.

It had been hard to see much of the Count among the sheeting rain, but from what Dieter had seen he seemed every bit the powerful, imperious ruler he had been led to expect. The Count was a tall, thin man, but there was no hiding his strength – both in his limbs and in the cold fire of his eyes. He had appeared to be something of a haughty fellow, although in Dieter's experience most aristocrats were like that.

A hawk had sat perched on the Count's shoulder. It was a hunting bird, no doubt raised from the eggshell to obey its master. The Count had long been famous for his collection of hunting birds. Even more impressive was the weapon Dieter saw sheathed at the Count's left hip. Dieter had never seen it before, nor even hoped to, but there was no mistaking the identity of the Count's sword. It was a runefang, one of the twelve ancient magical blades which, according to legend, had been forged by the dwarf runesmith Alaric the Mad at the dawn of the Empire.

Seeing the Count's runefang, even with the blade sheathed, had been enough to make Dieter's breath catch in his throat. Its very presence seemed to promise victory.

In the cold light of morning, as Dieter waited with the rest of the army for battle to begin, he wondered whether the promise he had seen in the presence of the runefang was not just wishful thinking. They were facing so many greenskins it was hard to believe victory was possible.

Once, the fields below the rise Dieter was standing on had been meant for agriculture. Long before that, they had been forest. They had been cleared by weeks, months or even years of back-breaking labour. Now, it seemed likely they would be given over to more bloody labours.

There was movement in the greenskin lines. Dieter saw a large group of goblin wolf riders detach themselves from the main body of their fellows and start to make their way slowly up the rise. They were headed in the Scarlets' direction.

'Stand fast,' Captain Harkner called out in a warning tone. He stood with the men of one of the front-most ranks of the Scarlets' formation. 'Remember our orders. We're to hold this position. If enemy skirmishers come this way, we will drive them off if we can. But it's more important that we hold the position.'

The Scarlets were at the right edge of the Hochlanders' battle line, affording them an excellent view of the rest of their army. Given the elevated nature of the ridge, Dieter could see almost every unit and regiment in the army from where he was standing. He found it vaguely surprising that General von Grahl hadn't chosen the same spot for his headquarters, but he supposed it was too far away from the army's centre.

The majority of the army's small force of cannons were situated on a high ridge to the right of the Scarlets, affording them a clear field of fire to shoot at the greenskins as they advanced on the human positions. Dieter realised the Scarlets had been placed on the next ridge to the artillery, along with a regiment of spearmen and several militia free companies, in order to guard the approaches to the artillery's position and prevent the enemy's fast cavalry from attacking the gunners.

To the left of the Scarlets' position, the centre of the human line was made up of alternating units of halberds and spearmen, as well as the occasional mercenary unit of Tilean pikemen. Smaller detachments of swordsmen had been positioned immediately behind the main infantry line, alongside several more free companies. In a classic tactic beloved by Empire armies, the units of halberdiers and spearmen were meant to hold off the orcs, while the detachments behind them rushed out through the gaps to attack the enemy in the flanks.

Finally, General von Grahl had put the majority of his cavalry in a slightly withdrawn position to the left of the main body of his army. Compared to the infantry forces General von Grahl had at his disposal, his cavalry was relatively short on numbers. The army's heavy cavalry was made up of a small force of knights from the Order of the Blazing Sun, alongside a few local noblemen who had rallied to General von Grahl's banner once it became clear he intended to make a stand against the orcs. The general had positioned his knights behind a screen of pistoliers and outriders, perhaps hoping to hide the paucity of their numbers from the enemy.

Dieter was no great military mastermind, but even he could see that von Grahl had done everything in his power to make sure he could get the best from the forces at his disposal. The general had even held back a trump card.

Behind the Hochlander positions, a second army of several thousand bowmen had been held in reserve, out of sight of the greenskins. They were militia archers, mostly local peasant bowmen and huntsmen who had been press-ganged into service by General von Grahl as he passed from village to village on his long ride northwards. They had received no great training, but each man was at least a middling bowman, possessing enough skill to put an arrow in the air with some hope it would hit its target. The greenskins had no way of knowing it as yet, but an unpleasant surprise waited for them once their army advanced to attack.

In the meantime, however, it was important that the enemy did not become aware of the archers' presence. General von Grahl had issued strict instructions in that regard. No matter what the provocation, no archer was to notch an arrow – much less loose it – until von Grahl himself gave the order.

'Here they come,' Holst said. He was standing next to Dieter in the front rank of the Scarlets' formation, alongside Gerhardt and Rieger. 'Did I ever tell you the story of how I saved Count Aldebrand's life at the Battle of Tannesfeld?'

'Tell me later,' Dieter told him. 'After the battle.'

'A good idea,' Holst nodded. 'It will give you something to look forward to.'

Ahead of them, the wolf riders had almost completed climbing the rise. Raising their bows as they rode toward the Scarlets, the goblins prepared to fire.

'Shields high!' Captain Harkner shouted an order as the enemy loosed their arrows.

Acting as though with one mind, the Scarlets complied with the order. Each man raised his shield high, angling it to form a barrier against the incoming arrow storm as the enemy's shots arced their way towards them. As the arrows made impact, Dieter was reminded of the sound of hail stones striking a wood shingle roof. Being of poor quality goblin manufacture, most of the arrows shattered as they hit the Scarlets' shields, although Dieter heard several screams behind him as unlucky men were struck by arrows slipping past their shields.

Undeterred in their efforts, the wolf riders fired another volley of arrows, then another. Each time, the result was the same. The Scarlets lost a few men to each salvo, but the majority of the goblins' arrows failed to hit their marks.

At the same time, Dieter was struck by the cruel irony of the situation. Barely a stone's throw away, the Hochlanders had a supply of archers capable of vastly outshooting the wolf riders. Yet, for tactical reasons, the Scarlets had to stand and take the enemy's punishment so as to avoid interfering with their general's battle plans.

The stalemate continued for long minutes as the wolf riders sent in salvo after salvo of arrows. Eventually, a line of handgunners advanced from further along the centre of the Hochlanders' battle line and fired their own counter-salvo from their muskets. The wolf riders were quickly put to flight, while the men on the ridge cheered the sight of the enemy's retreat.

'Listen to that,' Holst said, referring to the cheers. 'You'd think we'd won the war from the sound of it. I hope those cheering idiots realise what's ahead of them. This battle is barely begun. Mark my words, there will be a lot more blood before the day is out.'

HOLST'S PREDICTION WAS swiftly proven right. Watching from his position on the ridge, Dieter saw the centre of the enemy battle line move sluggishly into action. Led by the orcs in the centre of the line, the greenskin horde started to pick up speed.

In contrast to the last battle between the two sides, Dieter noticed there were few boar riders in the enemy ranks. He hoped it was a sign the Scarlets and their comrades had slaughtered most of them at the first battle, but he could not be sure. In their place, the majority of the enemy army seemed to be made up of a mixed force of orcs and goblins on foot.

Despite the greenskins' best efforts to close with the Hochlanders quickly, they found it slow going as they crossed the open fields separating the two armies. Watching their progress, Dieter was suddenly struck by two factors which might not have been immediately apparent to the orc commander.

The slope that separated the orc and human armies was misleading to the eye: the incline was steeper than it looked, and the greenskins were headed *uphill*. Added to that, the heavy rain of the last day had turned the open fields into a quagmire of mud. Excitement building in his heart, Dieter realised the greenskins had been lured into a trap.

Abruptly, the true nature of General von Grahl's battle plan was revealed. As the orcs and goblins struggled to climb the muddy slopes towards the human positions, the order was given for von Grahl's small army of militia archers to start firing. A vast storm of arrows filled the air, followed swiftly by volley after volley of the same.

Meanwhile, the Hochlander cannons also started firing. Caught in no-man's-land, the orcs and goblins were subjected to a punishing barrage of missile fire. Watching from the ridge, Dieter saw scores of the enemy fall as the arrow storm hit them.

Soon, the number had grown to hundreds, even thousands. The advancing greenskins were devastated by the relentless rain of death. Amazingly, Dieter could even see that some of the orc units had started fighting amongst themselves, the creatures' natural animosity pushed to a level of senseless violence against their fellows by the frustrations of the situation they found themselves trapped in.

Yet still, despite their losses, the greenskins pushed on. As Dieter watched, he saw the foremost units of the enemy meet in combat with the halberd and spearmen regiments at the centre of the human line.

Dieter held his breath: if the Hochlanders' line broke now, the battle would be over. Incredibly, despite the appalling casualties they had sustained in crossing the muddy slope, the orcs seemed eager and ready for battle. For all that, though, the Hochlanders' missile fire had done the trick. Having lost great numbers of warriors to the arrow storm and the human artillery, the greenskins were unable to push the Hochlander infantry back. Instead, the Hochlanders held their position, slaughtering vast numbers of greenskins in the progress.

As yet, the Scarlets had not featured in the battle. Forced to watch from the sidelines as the great issues of the day were decided by others, a shiver of impatience passed through their ranks. Dieter felt it too. After suffering humiliation once at the hands of the combined orc and goblin army, he was eager to play his part in their defeat.

Even from his elevated vantage point above the main battle, it was difficult at times to preserve any clear picture of how the conflict was going. The advantage in the battle see-sawed from one side to the other: at one point it seemed the Hochlanders were on top, then the orcs, then the Hochlanders again. Isolated from the cut and thrust of the battle itself, Dieter saw acts of bravery play out that would live forever in the annals of Hochland.

At one stage, an attack by a group of orc shamans seemed about to swing the battle in the greenskins' favour. Calling on their dark magical powers, the shamans sent a series of flaring, unearthly missiles hurtling towards the human lines, leaving devastation in their wake.

Quickly, however, a human wizard stepped forward to oppose them. Clad in the blue robes of the Celestial Order, his cloak covered with the pattern of a plethora of stars, crescent moons and comets, the wizard spread his arms wide and called down the wrath of the heavens. For a split second, clouds formed in the sky above the shamans' position as dozens of lightning bolts rained down upon them. Then, just as swiftly, the clouds dispersed with unnatural haste, while the shamans had been left reduced to charred bodies by the wizard's power.

Elsewhere, Dieter saw doughty spearmen hold the line against vast numbers of orcs. He saw greatswords step bravely into the fray, cutting a swathe through the enemy. He saw pistoliers and outriders play a game of hit and run, charging forward to unload their weapons at the enemy, before disengaging to reload and begin the game again.

Bit by bit, it seemed as though the greenskins were being pushed back. Certainly, the enemy had suffered horrendous casualties. Dieter wasn't sure whether it was seemly to find anything to admire in an enemy – especially when the enemy in question was an orc. Whatever his misgivings, however, he was forced to admit the greenskins possessed at least one quality in ready abundance – tenacity. No other army could have taken the punishment the Hochlanders had meted out against the greenskins without crumbling. In that regard at least, the greenskins were formidable opponents.

Despite this, it seemed to Dieter that the Hochlanders were winning the battle. For all that, however, he realised the matter was finely balanced – still capable of tipping one way or another.

'When are they going to give us the order to advance?' he asked impatiently. 'The battle will be over by the time we get into it.'

'We'll be in it soon enough,' Gerhardt said. Staring down the slope with dark, shrewd eyes, he pointed to a group of approaching figures. 'Hnn, you should be careful what you wish for, Dieter. It looks like some goblins have broken off from the main force and are headed our way.'

Gazing in the direction Gerhardt was pointing, Dieter saw a large force of goblins advancing up the slope in the Scarlets' general direction. For an instant his heart stopped in his chest as he saw a monstrous figure walking in the midst of the goblin horde.

It was a troll. Dieter had no way to be sure, but looking at the creature's odd, rolling gait and its blue-grey, stone-like hide, he felt almost certain it was the same troll he had seen kill the Golden wizard at the battle of the encampment two months earlier. He remembered how unstoppable the creature had seemed on that day – like some malign, primeval force had been given physical form.

On the slope below, the goblin horde had begun to turn towards the Scarlets' right. Ignoring the swordsmen and other assorted regiments in front of them, they altered their course and started for the artillery emplacements on the next hill along.

'They're headed for our artillery,' Gerhardt said tersely.

'But that's good, isn't it?' Dieter asked. 'The way they are trying to bypass us, we'll be able to take them in the flanks. Hopefully, we'll roll right over them.'

'There's still the troll to deal with.' Gerhardt's expression was tense. 'It will take more than swords to stop that monster.'

'Maybe the artillery will be able to kill it,' Rieger said.

'It's too fast moving,' Holst said. 'They'll never manage to draw a bead on that thing. Ach, where's a wizard when you need one. Or, failing that, some divine intervention. Sigmar knows, I'm not fussy.'

'Sometimes, the gods help those who help themselves,' Gerhardt said, while to the side of him, Rieger shook his head at his comrades' impiety.

'I wonder…' Turning to look to the right of the Scarlets' position, Gerhardt's eyes seem to catch sight of something that interested him.

'Come on,' he said to the others. 'I have an idea.'

Following Gerhardt's lead, they slipped through the ranks of the men behind them until they found Captain Harkner. Consulting quickly with the captain out of earshot of the others, Gerhardt outlined his plan.

'Very well,' the captain nodded his agreement after a moment. 'It's a mad scheme, but it might work. I can't spare you any more than five men, however. Take Holst, Rieger, the new blood, Krug and Febel.'

Thanking the captain, Gerhardt quickly gathered the assigned men around him. Moving them to one side of the rest of the regiment, he swiftly set each man's duties. For once, even Krug listened in silence, not complaining. Given the gravity of the situation, it was clear it was a time for action.

In the meantime, the goblins having advanced until their flank was right in front of the Scarlets' position, Captain Harkner gave the order for his men to attack. With the spearmen regiment and the free companies to the sides of them, the Scarlets charged into the fray. Catching the enemy in the flank, they unleashed a deadly torrent of steel. Goblins fell in great numbers, but despite the Hochlanders' combined efforts, the goblin vanguard and their troll ally pushed on toward the artillery emplacements.

'Come on,' Gerhardt yelled. 'It's now or never.'

Following his lead, Dieter and the others raced after him as Gerhardt sprinted toward the artillery emplacements. Suddenly, having advanced ahead of the rest of the vanguard, a group of goblins appeared in front of them.

'Krug! Febel!' Gerhardt shouted orders. 'It's up to you to hold them back!'

Much to Dieter's surprise, Krug and his crony followed the command. Without flinching, they broke away from the small group of swordsmen and ran to head off the charging goblins. Even granting the goblins' lesser stature, Krug and Febel were outnumbered six to one.

Shocked, Dieter realised Gerhardt had just ordered the two men to their deaths. Even more extraordinarily, they had complied with his order without batting an eyelid. Krug and Febel were prepared to risk sacrificing themselves to ensure the success of Gerhardt's mission. Whatever Dieter had thought of the two men before, he was forced to reassess his opinion. Krug and Febel might be mean-spirited, cruel, even venal men. In the end, however, they were soldiers. They were Scarlets. They were prepared to put their lives on the line in the cause of achieving victory.

Charging to meet the goblins, Krug and Febel tore into the creatures like men possessed. Within seconds they were lost amid the green tide, but Dieter could not afford the time to stand watching and observe their fate. Instead, with Gerhardt and the others, he pushed on toward the emplacements.

'This way!' Gerhardt said. 'Now I just hope this wagon has what I think it does inside it.'

He led them toward a cart parked behind the artillery emplacements. Following Gerhardt's instructions, Rieger and Holst set about unhitching the dray team from the front of the cart, while Dieter joined Gerhardt in inspecting the wagon's contents.

'Will you look at that?' Gerhardt said, lifting the canvas cover that hid the supplies in the back of the cart. 'I'm no expert when it comes to black powder, but I think there's enough here to suit our purpose.'

The back of the cart was filled with black powder stored in wooden casks and waterproofed sacks, intended to supply the army's cannons and mortars. Dieter had no real knowledge of gunpowder, other than the fact it was dangerous stuff that only mad men were willing to deal with. In contrast, Gerhardt seemed to know what he was doing.

'See if you can find some lanterns,' Gerhardt said, pulling back the canvas. 'Make sure they are not lit, mind. It's the oil we want, not the lanterns themselves.'

Hurrying away to fulfil Gerhardt's instruction, Dieter was soon able to go one better. Noticing that another cart load of supplies had been parked near the first, he checked the back of it and found a barrel of lamp oil among the contents. It was a relatively small barrel, and with some effort Dieter was able to balance it on his shoulder. He raced back to the others with his prize.

'Found it in the back of another cart, you say?' Gerhardt lifted an eyebrow once Dieter explained his find. 'Again, I'm no expert, but that sounds like a recipe for disaster – storing lamp oil and black powder so close together. Still, in this case, you have to thank whatever mutton head made that mistake. Let's see if we can make the best of it.'

Gerhardt had already forced open some of the black powder casks. With Dieter's help, he balanced the barrel of oil at the back of the cart, gouging a hole in the barrel's side with his knife so a thin stream of oil flowed freely over the wagon's backboard and onto the ground.

'Get a torch,' he told Dieter. 'A lit one this time. But make sure you keep it away from the oil trail.'

By the time Dieter returned with a flaming torch, having persuaded a member of one of the gun crews to part with it, Gerhardt and the others had already begun to move the wagon. Alongside himself, Rieger and Holst, Gerhardt had commandeered several artillerymen to help them push the wagon.

'We only have to push it as far as the lip of the ridge,' Gerhardt said as the men strained to move the recalcitrant wagon. 'After that, the slope will do the work for us.'

'And what about the troll?' Holst asked. 'Are you expecting it to hold still long enough to be run over by this cart?'

'It won't need to. Once the oil trail is set alight, anything within thirty paces of this cart will be blown to pieces. And, besides, it's not as though we have much choice. I don't think we'll find someone willing to sit on the cart and steer it down the hillside. Not unless you're about to volunteer for the job.'

As the cart reached the edge of the ridge, the troll could be seen climbing eagerly up the slope at the head of a sizeable force of goblins. Further along the slope, the Scarlets were still engaged in close combat with the rest of the goblin horde, but to Gerhardt's eye the men of the regiment were far enough away that there was little danger of them being caught in the blast.

'All right,' he said, once they had lined the cart up as much as possible. 'Let 'er go!'

Once the cart's brake was released it began to roll down the slope, picking up speed. Gerhardt waved a signal to Dieter.

'Now! Set fire to the oil!'

Touching the torch to the oil trail, Dieter watched for a second as the oil took light. The flame sped on, following the cart over the brow of the slope. Dieter ran after it, hoping to see the cart hit. By the time he reached the place where the others were standing, it was clear their efforts had been more on target than anyone could have hoped. The hurtling cart was headed straight for the troll, the flaming oil trail racing to catch up behind it. Dieter saw the troll lift its head to look at the cart in dumb confusion. Then, he heard Gerhardt's voice.

'Get down!'

Even as Dieter dived for cover, he kept one eye on the unfolding drama further down the slope. Inspired perhaps by some misplaced predatory instinct, the troll actually moved *closer* to the rolling cart, spreading its monstrous arms wide to catch the cart and stop it. The flaming oil trail reached its destination a second later, resulting in an explosion that made the ground shake. The troll was blown to pieces, burning fragments of troll flesh falling in a broad radius like some form of grotesque rain.

The explosion caused similar havoc among the goblins. Beyond the casualties it created, it spread panic in its wake. Having received a fatal blow to their morale when the troll was killed, the remaining goblins on the slope fled.

'We'll have to put every piece of troll to the torch,' Gerhardt said, gazing at the bloody pieces of meat strewn about the slope. 'I hear trolls can heal almost any wound, even if they get chopped to pieces. But fire is supposed to work at killing them.'

Dieter was about to compliment Gerhardt on the success of his plan when his attention was distracted by something else. As he scanned the landscape around them, it became clear the entire greenskin army had been put to flight. Initially, Dieter wondered whether the defeat of the troll had caused a general panic that had spread throughout the enemy army, but a closer look at the battle unfolding in front of him soon disabused him of any such pigheaded notion.

General von Grahl had unleashed his cavalry, he could see that now. Gazing into the open fields below the slope, he saw the entire force of the Hochlanders' cavalry – knights, pistoliers and outriders – had been unleashed at the orc centre of the enemy line in one cataclysmic death-or-glory charge. Apparently, von Grahl had waited until the optimum moment to strike. It was equally apparent the tactic had worked.

Everywhere Dieter looked the greenskin army was in full retreat. The Hochlander pistoliers and outriders were giving chase to the enemy, but even without them Dieter doubted whether the greenskins would have rallied. The enemy appeared to be broken. And, with that thought came the dizzying realisation that they had won the battle.

Peering down to the foot of the slope, Dieter saw a thin powerful figure in full plate, riding a charger. As the knight pulled back his visor revealing a hawk-nosed profile, Dieter realised it was Count Aldebrand. The Elector Count was holding his runefang high in the air, calling out to the knights around him as they cheered and exulted, celebrating their victory over the orcs. Hochland had been saved.

It was entirely in keeping with his experience of war, Dieter decided, that he and his comrades had been so busy with their own small battles that they had completely missed the climax of the larger battle around them. In the end he supposed that was the nature of the foot soldier's lot. The knights claimed the glory, while the infantryman did the marching.

Listen to me, Dieter thought. Only a soldier for a few months, and already I'm turning into a bitter curmudgeon. I wonder what I'll be like after twenty years with the Scarlets.

He smiled to himself at the thought of it. Then, he went to join his comrades as they celebrated the victory. All along the hills and ridges, he heard the sound of cheering. It was good to be alive, he decided.

On days like these, it was good to be a soldier.

CHAPTER SEVENTEEN
AFTER THE BATTLE

'THEY LOOK SO young,' Dieter said.

It was later in the day, and he was sitting on a rock by the side of the trail, resting with his comrades as they recovered from the exertions of the battle and its aftermath. While the army's pistoliers, outriders and knights gave chase to the fleeing greenskins, the infantry had been assigned to a variety of less glamorous tasks, including mercy duty, acting as stretcher bearers and serving in burial parties to give a final resting place to the Hochlander dead. It had been hard, thankless work, but Dieter supposed these tasks were as much part of being a soldier as the cut and thrust of battle.

Ironically, with the battle over and the orcs defeated, fresh reinforcements arrived in the shape of several thousand of the newly-trained soldiers called up by the Count's muster. Dieter and his fellow

Scarlets had decided to watch the new men as they arrived. The reinforcements marched in double file along the trail, weapons and equipment slung over their shoulders.

'Young, you say?' Holst smiled at Dieter's remark. 'You should look at yourself in the mirror, young blood. You're the same age as most of these babes-in-arms.'

'I suppose you're right,' Dieter said. Looking back at the new recruits, however, he found it hard to credit that he was the same age as the boyish faces he saw before him. He had been a soldier barely a few months, but already he felt years older.

'You have to say they timed it perfectly,' Holst said, turning back to watch the steady files of recruits as they marched past. 'You ask me, there's no better time to join a war than when it's just about over.'

'Over?' Rieger raised an eyebrow. 'I never had you for an optimist.'

'Eh? What do you mean?' Holst looked at him warily. 'You're not about to launch into another sermon, are you? Something about how the war's never really over, Sigmar's enemies are all around us, and so on, and so on. Please, Rieger, we've just won a victory. Give the sermons a rest.'

'No sermon,' Rieger shook his head. 'Just an observation. We've won a battle, Holst. Nothing more. The greenskins may be fleeing now, but they'll be back. Remember, we may have beaten them here, but large parts of northern Hochland are still in their power. I suspect this might well turn out to be the beginning of a long campaign. The war will go on.'

'Rieger is right,' Gerhardt nodded. He looked wistfully at the fresh-faced ranks of new soldiers passing by them, as though the presence of the new recruits reminded him of something lost and long ago. 'I was just speaking to a sergeant from the Fourth Hergig Spears. He told me Count Aldebrand has appointed General von Grahl as commander of all his forces – not just his armies in the field, but all his armies including every garrison, every newly mustered regiment and even the new troops that haven't yet answered the muster. Von Grahl is a wartime general, he always was. If the Count has made him his foremost commander, it means they expect the war to last some time.'

There was a brief period of silence between the comrades as they digested the news. It was Rieger that broke the silence.

'I understand that isn't the only promotion in the army. Is it, *Sergeant* Gerhardt?'

'You heard then?' Gerhardt grimaced. 'I hadn't expected the news to spread so quickly, but I suppose that's the army for you – the only thing soldiers can't do is keep a secret. Yes, it's true. Sergeant Bohlen was wounded during the battle. They say he'll survive, but he'll be out of action for a while. Captain Harkner has appointed me as file sergeant in his absence.'

Overjoyed, the others huddled around him to shake his hand and offer congratulations. For the first time since Dieter had known him, Gerhardt seemed embarrassed.

* * *

IT WAS STRANGE when Dieter thought about it later, but in the aftermath of battle everything seemed different somehow. Certainly he felt different. After tasting defeat in his first battle as a Scarlet, it felt good that his second major battle had been such a resounding victory.

Dieter had been part of that victory, as had thousands of other men. Some had paid the ultimate price, sacrificing their lives for the sake of their province and its people. Others had survived, hopefully to grow wiser and become better soldiers.

Krug and Febel had been among those who were killed. Dieter had never liked either man, but in the wake of their deaths he realised the bonds between himself and the other men around him went beyond such questions. Whatever their faults – and of those there were many – Krug and Febel had been Scarlets. They had been soldiers, and they had died as soldiers, bravely facing the enemy. Tonight, when the Sigmarite priests gathered together the faithful to offer thanks that the enemy had been defeated, Dieter would make sure he would say a prayer for Krug and Febel.

There were others who would feature in his prayers: dead Scarlets like Breitmeyer and Rosen, his comrades like Gerhardt, Holst and Rieger, his leaders like Sergeant Bohlen and Captain Harkner. He would offer prayers for General von Grahl and Count Aldebrand. He would offer prayers toward the success of their efforts. He would pray they could keep Hochland safe, and that the greenskins could be driven back into the mountains never to return.

Dieter had survived a great battle. He had hoped he had learned something by it.

Either way, come tomorrow, the war would go on.

From
The Testimony of General Ludwig von Grahl
(unexpurgated text):

And so, in the end, despite months of careful planning and the efforts of thousands, the battle was won in a single moment.

Perhaps that may seem an exaggeration, but let me explain.

As any commander knows, a battle is a confusing, disorderly business. A thousand small details may play their part in its outcome, often unexpectedly. This is why it is always better to keep your battle plans as simple as possible.

In this case, it seemed as though my plans were working. From my position on the left flank, at the head of the army's contingent of knights, I could see the enemy was beginning to falter. Weakened by the relentless fire of our archers and artillery, the greenskin attack on the centre of our battle line had ground to a halt. With the enemy starting to fade, it was only a matter of time before the infantry pressed home their advantage and forced a rout among the greenskins.

I thought victory was in my grasp. Then, my opponent showed his cunning.

It seemed Morgoth Ironfang had not committed all his resources to the battle. Displaying a degree of forethought almost unheard of from an orc commander, he had held back a sizeable contingent of boar riders. Apparently intending to use them as a mobile reserve – in itself a novel concept among orc commanders – he had positioned them some distance behind the rest of his troops so they were kept out of sight of our scouts.

Signalling the boar riders forward once the battle began, Ironfang had held back committing them to action until the battle reached its tipping point. Realising that the orc forces in the centre of his battle line were about to crumble, Ironfang ordered a massed charge by his boar riders directly at the human infantry holding the Hochland centre.

Ironfang led the charge himself, seeking to rally as much of his army as possible and push through our lines.

Meanwhile, from my position on the left flank, it was clear the battle had reached a climax. Seeing Ironfang's charge, I committed my own cavalry to an immediate countercharge.

Realising its importance to the battle as a whole, I decided to lead the countercharge myself. Count Aldebrand rode beside me, alongside his bodyguard, at the head of a motley collection of knights, pistoliers, mercenary cavalry and outriders. I had gathered together every mounted warrior at my disposal, but still

our cavalry strength was far outnumbered by Ironfang's
boar riders – never mind the larger greenskin army.

Such is the way with all battles. We hope to achieve
supremacy over the enemy by subtle stratagems and
incisive manoeuvres, but all too often it comes down to
a test of will. In the end, the battle would be decided by
the elite of my army versus Ironfang's elite – brawn
against brawn, steel against steel, with no quarter
given.

Let me tell you, I have now ridden to battle beside our
Count, Aldebrand Ludenhof, on three separate occasions – enough to hail him as one of the great warriors
of our age. Whatever my private concerns at the
Count's haughtiness, his aloofness regarding his
province and its people, I recognise in him a kindred
soul when it comes to the call of arms.

Together, at the head of our cavalry, we smashed into
the enemy. The full story of that conflict is a tale that
will no doubt be told elsewhere in the annals of our
noble province, but it was as hard and brutal a fight as
any I have ever faced.

Sometimes, a cavalry charge will be met by a sudden
dispersal of the enemy – terrified at the prospect of facing cavalry an enemy's morale will often falter, leading
to a rout. In Ironfang and his boar riders, however, we
faced a more formidable foe.

Seeing us as we charged towards them, they did not
for a moment falter. The boar riders simply turned and
charged towards us, eager to meet our knights head-on
in battle.

Sigmar was with us, however. Although they fought
with tenacious strength, we managed to defeat the boar

riders. Adopting a wedge formation, we sliced through them like an arrow through flesh. Meanwhile, seeing the toll we had taken on the best of their warriors, the other orcs and goblins of Ironfang's army began to flee.

Earlier, I spoke of the battle being won in a single moment. Equally, in the moment in question, it could have been lost. I was driving through the enemy hordes, laying about me with the sword the Count had gifted me, when I saw a huge and battle-scarred orc riding on top of an equally impressive beast.

A pair of metal tusks jutted from the orc's lower jaw, apparently serving as over-sized replacements for two teeth that had been lost – though whether this oral disfigurement was as a result of some earlier wound sustained in battle, or some excess of orc dentistry, I could not comment.

Realising this could only be the much-famed orc general, Ironfang, I immediately spurred my horse towards him. Smiling in a way that was made more sinister by his iron teeth, the orc likewise spurred his boar and charged towards me.

We met with the ringing of clashing steel as we each struck at the other simultaneously. My sword tore through his armour and inflicted a grievous wound to his chest, while his axe struck my head.

The blow glanced off my helmet and smashed away my visor. For a moment, I was blinded as blood ran freely down from my scalp into my eyes. Ironfang could have finished me then, but Count Aldebrand had seen my distress. Sending his hunting hawk to harry and distract Ironfang, he charged forward with his bodyguard to save me.

By the time I cleaned the blood from my eyes, I was surrounded by friendly faces. Ironfang was gone, however – disappeared amid the shifting tides of battle.

As short as it was, that brief and bloody meeting between Ironfang and myself turned out to be the climactic moment of the battle. If Ironfang's axe had struck a finger's-width lower, it would have taken my head from my shoulders – perhaps dealing a deadly blow to the army's morale. As it was, I was fortunate – both in terms of the placement of Ironfang's blow and the Count's quick thinking. Otherwise, I would be in my grave.

Such, therefore, was the way by which the battle was decided. Wounded, Ironfang fled – though, sadly, I have to accept the wound he sustained is unlikely to prove fatal. In his absence, his army's morale collapsed. The enemy were routed.

For myself, I have a new scar to add to my collection. When I removed my helmet after the battle, we found that Ironfang's blow had added a thin new crease to my scalp. The surgeons tell me I am lucky. Head wounds are notoriously difficult to treat, but I have suffered no more adverse effect than a few headaches. And what are headaches when there is a war to fight!

Grateful for my service, the Count has made me commander of all his armies. I have been given carte blanche to take the war to the orcs and drive them from Hochland – perhaps to even follow them to their haunts in the Middle Mountains and remove their scourge from the face of the world forever. I warn the Count such lofty ambitions do not come to reality without paying a hard price in blood and sweat, not to mention gold, but he seems ready to meet the cost.

Tonight, there will be a celebration. The army will rejoice in its victory. The men will drink, and laugh, and jest, and dream of days of peace.

Come tomorrow, the war goes on.

ABOUT THE AUTHOR

Mitchel Scanlon is a full-time novelist and comics writer. His previous credits for the Black Library include the novel *Fifteen Hours*, the background book *The Loathsome Ratmen*, and the comics series *Tales of Hellbrandt Grimm*. He lives in Derbyshire, in the UK.

AN EMPIRE ARMY NOVEL

REIKSGUARD

Buy these
books or read
free extracts at
www.blacklibrary.com

RICHARD
WILLIAMS

WARHAMMER

UK ISBN 978-1-84416-726-5   US ISBN 978-1-84416-727-2

IRON COMPANY

CHRIS
WRAIGHT

UK ISBN 978-1-84416-778-4   US ISBN 978-1-84416-779-1

TIME OF LEGENDS

HELDENHAMMER
The Legend of Sigmar
GRAHAM McNEILL

ISBN 978-1-84416-538-4

NAGASH THE SORCERER
The undead will rise...
≺MIKE LEE≻

UK ISBN 978-1-84416-660-2 US ISBN 978-1-84416-556-8

MALEKITH
A Tale of the Sundering
GAV THORPE

UK ISBN 978-1-84416-673-2 US ISBN 978-1-84416-610-7

This all-new series explores the tales of the legendary heroes and monumental events that shaped the very fabric of the Warhammer World.